BEGINNING AGAIN
AT ZERO

A Novel

by

Jack A. Saarela

2016

*Dedicated to my parents, Elsa and Veikko Saarela,
and other Finns like them,
who took the leap of faith
to begin again at zero
in a new and strange land.*

When you emigrate, you lose the crutches that have been your support; **you must begin from zero,** *because the past is erased with a single stroke and no one cares where you're from or what you did before."*

— *Isabel Allende*

PROLOGUE:
January 9, 1940
Suomussalmi, Kainuu Province
Finland

The noon January sun that had peeked over the horizon barely an hour earlier watched hesitantly over the eastern Finnish lake and forest, as if it were warning in advance that it couldn't be depended on to be around for long. The frigid air cut to the bone like a sharpened knife. Just the day prior, the present wintry quiet of this place had been shattered by the ear-piercing staccato of machine guns and the blasting of grenades.

In their ragged coats and leaking boots, Russian soldiers had been retreating eastward from the ferocious counterattack by the Finnish forces on the ruins of the village of Suomussalmi. But now the landscape was silent and serene, the lake blanketed by snow brilliant and blinding even in the muted sunshine of January. It was littered like a cluttered junkyard with abandoned Russian heavy artillery and an occasional brown clump of a Russian corpse, frozen within minutes of the moment a man's wounded torso hit the snow.

Aulis Riihimäki skied silently and cautiously from the shelter of the forest out onto the frozen surface of Lake Vuokkijärvi, a solitary figure barely indistinguishable from the snow in his white snowsuit and helmet painted white to match. In the freezing white hell of January 8, Riihimäki had been separated from his company as it was advancing to the Raate road, relentlessly pushing the enemy back eastward from whence they had come on November 30. These were the lakes and forests of the Finnish people upon which Stalin's men had encroached uninvited. The men of the Finnish army defended the land as though each one – the one from the capital or from Turku, one from a farm in Tavastia or Ostrobothnia, another from a village on the western coast - had a proprietor's stake in it. Their determined defense of it was their nation's only hope.

4

The Russians had taken Suomussalmi a month earlier in the opening days of the war with little resistance from the tiny Finnish contingent defending it. Stalin's strategy was to sever Finland in half like a piece of hardtack from east to west by taking Suomussalmi and any other villages in his way, and advance relentlessly westward towards Oulu on the Gulf of Bothnia. The Finns would then have to face the enemy on two fronts: the north, and on the Karelian Isthmus in the south.

The day after taking the village, the Russians had tried to advance across the frozen lakes to the west, but the 16th detached battalion that had just arrived as reinforcements shot the advancing Russian soldiers from the protection of the birches and pines as though the battle were a duck shoot at a carnival, the dark figures of the Soviets standing out fatally against the snow on the lake. By the next day, General Hjalmar Siilasvuo had arrived with his 27th regiment. A native of Oulu himself, he was damned if he was going to allow Stalin to a single step towards Oulu. He knew that the splitting of the much-outnumbered Finnish forces into defenders of two fronts would be grave.

Two days after Christmas, Siilasvuo directed a ferocious counterattack. The Finns had advanced stealthily towards the village under the cover of the long and dark January night and morning. The Russians had relaxed their security detail and most ruinously, their discipline. Many of those assigned to sentry duty were still sleeping off their Christmas drunk. When the first of the Finnish platoons had come over the horizon within shooting range of the Russians, the Russians were as surprised as a swarm of ants exposed to light and air when a rotting log is turned over on the forest floor. Russian soldiers had scampered in a frenzied panic as the Finnish gunfire exploded. Many of them fell lifeless to the ground. The rest bolted from the village without weapons into the surrounding forest with only the clothes on their backs, the Finns in heady, triumphant, thrilling pursuit.

On the second day of the final and decisive counterattack, Aulis Riihimäki had been skiing, just as he was today, only as part of a whole platoon advancing on the occupied Suomussalmi. A young private near him was hit by a Russian bullet from the direction of the village, and collapsed in front

5

of him, injured and bleeding, but still alive. Aulis grabbed the man instinctively, and stuffed himself and the victim into a tiny space between a forsaken shell of a Soviet tank and field kitchen cauldron to avoid the whizzing bullets. Meanwhile, his battalion proceed inexorably towards the Raate road.

Riihimäki dug into his syrette bag for morphine, sulfa, and bandage to apply to the man's wound in his chest. That he might need the medical supplies himself later didn't enter his mind. His nerve endings didn't register the biting cold either, his brain oblivious to everything but trying desperately to save the man, seemingly no older than 19 or 20 at most, until medics would come by.

The bandage was virtually useless against the unyielding outpouring of blood from the kid's wound. Riihimäki took the wounded man into both arms as if he were embracing the woman he had just married before war broke out. The body he enfolded so desperately provided welcome warmth for Riihimäki in the frigid makeshift bunker between the tank and the cooking cauldron.

Already the sun had set and the premature winter night was fast approaching. He'd have to wait it out in the cold and dark until the sun rose again the next morning to make its brief appearance.

BOOK ONE:

BEGINNING

"Not I, nor anyone else can travel that road for you.
You must travel it by yourself.
It is not far. It is within reach.
Perhaps you have been on it since you were born, and
did not know."

\-   *Walt Whitman*

Chapter One:
Peurajoki, Northern Oulu Province, Finland
December 24, 1928

Kuokkala was an unassuming farmstead not unlike others in the flat countryside surrounding the village of Peurajoki. Kuokkala consisted of a log farmhouse with four rooms, grey from weather and age; a concrete barn with a stucco covering, also grey, for a few milk cows; a small shed to store hay for the cows and the one workhorse; a sauna for the weekly Saturday evening family cleansing ritual; and, of course, a privy.

In its seventy or so years before 1928, Kuokkala had rejoiced in births, including Onni Syrjälä's in 1922; grieved deaths; undergone several renovations; and endured the modest joys and mundane travails of its peasant occupants.

It would brave yet more tragedy in years to come. Again, in that regard too, it was not unlike others in the north of Finland.

The three women, Tyyne, and her daughters Hilja and Alma, proceeded from the mud room into the Kuokkala *tupa* soberly, given the purpose of the mission from which they were returning. They were coming from the church cemetery where they had followed the age-old Finnish custom of lighting memorial candles on Christmas Eve on the graves of loved ones. They had done so at the graves of Tyyne's parents Aatu and Fredriikka, and her brother Tauno, who had fallen in the civil war of 1917 – 1920.

The moment they stepped into the house, they were greeted by the familiar pleasant yuletide aroma of the freshly cut six-foot spruce which in the women's absence, the menfolk had erected in the corner of the room.

Tyyne went directly to a lower cupboard and took out a black cast-iron pot. The thigh of the pig she had placed in the oven before they left for the cemetery, with instructions for Martti to make sure not to let the fire go out. She filled the pot with water and the potatoes the girls had peeled earlier. She sent Hilja to the root cellar to retrieve the beet-based vegetable salad, *rosoli,* the three of them had prepared together earlier in the week.

Meanwhile, Alma went to another cupboard and took out small white candles and a box of clip-on candleholders and gave them to Martti. Martti summoned Väinö and gave him a dozen or so of each.

Looking towards Väinö's younger brother, he said, "I wonder, Onni, if you are old enough this Christmas to put some of the candles on the tree with us?" he said with a smile. Onni knew it must be Christmas because his father didn't usually smile like that very often in the course of ordinary run-of-the-mill days. He had also seen his father take a few swigs from a bottle when they were in the barn, in spite of the prohibition law.

The blond pine dining table was set with a festive embroidered tablecloth as the boys stepped into the *tupa.* The tree had been decorated with small hanging figures of billy-

10

goats and angels made of straw which Tyyne and Martti had received as a gift from the Lindholms a few years back, as had all of Lindholm's former tenant farming families. The tree was topped by a large star also made of straw. The candles were still unlit, but Onni knew, in this his seventh Christmas celebration, that the time for lighting them would be later.

The festive but modest feast was particularly delicious. Onni was able to be more mindful of the taste of the potatoes, turnip, *rosoli* and the ham than in previous years. A six-year old, though still impatient and anxious with the painstakingly deliberate pace of the evening, knows something instinctively about the thrill of anticipation. He'd learned that from the adventure books that Hilja or Alma would read to him in the long winter nights. Even in a story he had heard dozens of times before, he could sense himself sitting up in the tension and suspense as the story proceeded to its inevitable climax. The climax wasn't a surprise for him any longer, but the sweet anticipation for it, the thrill of expectancy, was just as satisfying and rewarding as the climax itself. That's what this Christmas Eve ritual was beginning to feel like for him now.

There was to be more suspense and ritualistic delay as the evening progressed. Martti took the boys outside into the crisp frigid air and gave each of them a sparkler and lit them. The boys ran around in the ankle-deep snow holding the sparkler in their hand up high and emitted shouts of joy and freedom, mingled, at least in Onni's case at least, with slight apprehension of a spark's striking him on the eye.

There was rice pudding and the freshly-baked *pulla* for the family enjoyed together after dinner. Onni couldn't help glancing at the tree and seeing the gifts at the foot of it wrapped in plain brown paper and tied with red string. These had been placed under the tree by *joulupukki*, probably when the men had been outside in the yard with the sparklers and the women occupied with the dishes, Onni reasoned. Undoubtedly the Christmas caller made his stealthy visit and left by the back door before anyone even knew he had been there. *Joulupukki* had ignited the candles on the tree, too, which were now glowing softly. Onni was the first to finish his rice

11

pudding and ran to take a seat cross-legged on the floor by the tree.

As the youngest in the family, it was Onni's job of handing out to the gifts. He was able to read some elementary books by himself now, a skill that he utilized more and more every day. But for several Christmases now, even before he could read, he had learned the shape and length of the printed name of each member of the family on the tags attached to the gifts. He handed a small wrapped package to each of the girls first, then one to Tyyne. This caused her to raise her eyes slightly in Martti's direction with a silent reproof that Martti had spent precious money in this profligate way. But there was a package for his father under the tree, too, and Onni presented him with it.

Onni pretended at first not to see a gift under the tree for Väinö, and even extended the period of his not appearing to see so that Väinö would have to pay the price for being older and bigger and feeling superior now that the childish task of handing out the gifts was no longer his.

"Oh, I guess this very little one must be for you, Väinö," Onni finally said, bringing a look of annoyance mixed with relief to the face of his older brother, and knowing smiles to the faces of the others, impressed that the little man could now be the initiator of pranks and jokes, not just the subject and victim of them.

"Where's the one for you, Onni? Maybe *joulupukki* didn't leave anything for you," Martti joked, although Onni didn't see it as a joke at all.

Defiantly, a stung Onni shouted, "He did so! It's this one, the biggest of all of them!"

He took eagerly into his hands a package roughly in the shape of an oval forty or so centimeters tall. He felt that the bottom was solid even though the paper on the sides collapsed slightly when he held the package there. Onni recognized the wrapping paper as exactly the kind that Mr. Manninen at the co-op store uses behind the counter to wrap items that his mother or father bought from him there. He began to tear at the paper which took all his might because it was strong and unyielding.

Finally, Onni succeeded in uncovering the object of its paper wrappings. It was a round sphere connected by a piece of metal to the base. The sphere could be spun like a ball. The surface of the sphere was covered with large areas painted a pale blue, and other blotches of varying colors. There were many areas of a light pink color. Onni had seen a similar sphere, though a larger one, in the small village library, so he knew what it was. It had fascinated him. He had asked his mother what it was. Upon being told that it was a globe that depicted the world, he begged her to point out where on the sphere they lived. A look of recognition and unbridled pleasure washed across Onni's face now as he held a sphere of his own aloft and admired it.

"What did you get?" Väinö asked.

"It's a globe, you dummy. Don't you even know what the world looks like?" Onni said in a mocking, somewhat defensive tone of voice.

Väinö shrugged indifferently and overlooked his little brother's attempt at an insult. He dug his teeth into the gingerbread cookies and orange that had been in his Christmas package. Onni meanwhile spun the globe several times, then stopped its spinning. He studied it diligently, and then put his index finger on one of the pink areas.

He stood up with his finger riveted to the spot and approached his mother. "Look, mother, I can find where your father went before you were born."

His finger was pointing to one of the pink areas on the globe, the one labeled Canada, to a spot near the dotted line on the globe that separated Canada's Ontario province from the province of Quebec.

13

Chapter Two:
Peurajoki
April, 1931

Onni was making his way through the spring mud from the cow barn to the house with his father. It was an uncharacteristically bright day for the usually grey month of April, the sun higher in the sky now. The air was still chilled, but held the promise of warmer, even brighter days to come in the weeks and months ahead.

The stillness was punctured suddenly by a resonate and low-pitch *kaw-kaw-kawing* from high above. A flock of eight or nine birds were passing over Kuokkala in a northerly direction. Onni could tell by the slower, more deliberate speed with which the birds were flapping their wings that these were not the small greenfinches whose arrival in the Peurajoki skies heralds the promise of spring. The birds flapped their wings and bobbed their heads at the end of their necks in unison, giving the impression that they had rehearsed an intricate aerial dance to perform for the entertainment of any humans below who might be watching. Though the flock seemed to be flying at a significant height above them, the wings of these birds seemed massive from even that distance. The span between the end of one wing to the end of the other appeared enormous.

"Are those geese, father?"

"Close," his father informed him. "I'm pretty sure these are the whooper swans returning back from the south. It's about the right time of year. The ice in the Gulf and on the rivers has cracked and broken up to welcome them back. Do you still remember how you enjoyed feeding them grain from your hand when they swam in our direction down at the riverbank?

"You mean they are flying from Helsinki?"

"Oh, they're coming back from farther south than that. They usually spend the winters in the Adriatic and Mediterranean seas."

14

Onni recognized the names of the seas from his almost daily study of his globe.

"That far!? That's a very long distance to fly."

"Yes, that's probably . . . what? Some 3,000 kilometers away. They fly down from here when the first frost comes in the fall, and then back again like this in April or so."

Onni knew that it was sixty or so kilometers to Oulu and a few more than that to Kemi. So he wondered as they walked what 3,000 kilometers would feel like.

"How are the swans able to fly that far?"

"Oh, I reckon that their wings are very strong, stronger than any muscle you or I have. But you know, they can fly through even the more turbulent storm and into the fiercest wind on their journey. Do you know how?"

Martti looked down at Onni. Onni didn't answer, but Martti could see from the puzzled but interested look on his face that Onni was eager to hear the answer.

"When the flight gets rough, they actually stop flapping their wings. They spread out those big wings of theirs and let the air hold them up and carry them."

That seemed to surprise Onni even more. *They stop flapping their wings when the winds get rough? I think if I were the swan, I'd flap my wings harder against the wind. How could air hold these huge birds in the air and actually carry them forward? Something I'll look up in a book at the school library.*

"But you know, Onni, the distance those swans fly back to Finland every spring is very short compared to what the arctic terns have to deal with."

The terns we can see sometimes up at Lake Närrä?"

"Those are the ones. We'll have to keep our eyes peeled to the sky when they fly back in May. They'll be coming back all the way from Antarctica where they flew in August from Närrä and Lake Inari, and even the Arctic Ocean."

When they entered the house, Onni threw off his boots and ran straight into the bedroom. He took the globe in his hands. Placing his right thumb over the area northeast of Oulu, he spread and twisted the palm of his hand and placed the little finger on the Adriatic Sea. He marveled at how far that distance was. Then he did the same with his left thumb, and tried to see how far he could spread his palm and place his little finger on the globe. He repeated the process, and discovered that the arctic terns flew more than five times the distance back to Finland than the whooper swans.

Just for the heck of it, he spread his palm between the approximate location of Peurajoki on the globe and northern Ontario in Canada. It took only two spans between his thumb and little finger.

Chapter Three:
Peurajoki Village School
October, 1932

Like many Finnish farmsteads, Kuokkala took its name from the family that lived there. Aatu and Fredriikka Kuokkanen had managed to buy the buildings and the surrounding twenty hectares in 1920 from the lord of the manor, Birger Lindholm. That year, the new Finnish government passed land reform legislation and provided cheap loans to peasants like Aatu to purchase the land on which they had toiled as tenant farmers.

Sadly, Aatu died in early 1920 before he could see the day when Kuokkala was liberated from its tenancy. The fiercely independent Fredriikka had to concede that she could not manage Kuokkala on her own. She made room at Kuokkala for Tyyne and her landless husband Martti, and their three children: their early adolescent daughters Hilja and Alma, and their then-infant son Väinö.

Two years later, a new arrival, Onni's, colicky crying started to fill the crowded household. Not long afterward, Fredriikka died in her sixty-fifth year.

Onni's third grade assignment:

"The person I have chosen to write about for this assignment is my grandfather, Aatu Anselmi Kuokkanen. I never met my grandfather, who is my mother's father, because he died two years before I was born. He died in the barn on his farm. Actually, it was not really his farm because it was a part of the estate of the landlord, Mr. Lindholm.

"I have chosen him as a person who is like a hero to me because he was adventurous and brave. I have heard about my grandfather a little from my mother, his daughter, and my father, but mostly from my grandfather's brother Eemil, who is dead now. I guess he would be my grand-uncle? Anyways, he told me how my grandfather left our village

17

when he was a young man because his mother and father had too many children to feed on the farm. They were their children, but they had grown up to become grown-ups. Two of my grandfather's brothers had already left my grandfather's farm and moved to the city. One went to Oulu and got a job inside the mill where they make paper, and the other went to Kemi, which is a little farther from our village, and his job was to organize the logs floating on the river so that another man (many men, I think) could tie them together and pull the logs up the hill to another paper mill. Actually, I think the men led a horse that did the pulling. The logs are too heavy for a man.

My mother says that when my grandfather turned 19 in 1880, the paper mills had enough workers already and so he would have to try to stay on the farm and help his father. But another man from our village had gone on a boat to Canada across the ocean I think five years earlier. Maybe it was six or seven, I'm not sure. But anyways, this man in Canada wrote to my grandfather and said that the leader of his new country had made a rule that said a railway for trains needed to be built so that people and things could travel on the train from the ocean on one side of the country to the big ocean on the other side of the country. My mother says that Canada is a much bigger country than Finland, almost as big as Russia, which is bigger now because it is called the Soviet Union. Anyways, this other man in Canada told my grandfather in a letter that they don't have enough men in Canada to build the railway and they needed more men to work there. He said my grandfather could get a job on the railway just like him.

"So my grandfather borrowed some money from his father and mother and brothers and sisters and then went to Oulu to get a ticket for a train ride to Hanko where the boats leave from to go to Canada. The boats don't go right away to Canada, but stop in Denmark and England first, so it takes a very long time to get to Canada on the boat. But my grandfather seems like a hero to me because he was brave enough to get on a boat that could sink in the ocean when there is a storm, and he was only 19 years old.

"When he got to Canada in a place called Montreal, a man helped him find a train that would take him to the end

18

of the railway that had been built so far. Later, my grandfather had sent a letter to his girlfriend Fredriikka, who later became my grandmother, and said that the ride on the train seemed almost as long as the ride on the ship.

"He finally got to a little village that was smaller even than Peurajoki. It was called Bonfield, Ontario. Ontario is a province like our Oulu Province but it's I much bigger. My father says that you could fit four or five Finlands just into that one province, and in 1880 there were six other provinces and big parts of the country that weren't called provinces yet.

"My grandfather became part of a company that started to build the train tracks in Bonfield and headed west. He didn't have his own house there, but slept and ate with the other men in buildings in a camp. There were other young men from our country working with that company, but there were also men from many different other countries in Europe. My grandfather's brother says that there were a lot of men from China who helped build the railway, but they were mainly far away in a province named British Columbia.

"One time my grandfather was injured really bad when another man's hammer hit him in the foot. It hurt so bad that he couldn't keep working for a long time, and had to stay in a hospital in a bigger city called Sudbury. There were a lot of Finnish people in Sudbury, and the pastor of the church came to visit him in the hospital. But my grandfather had to pay with his own money to stay in the hospital and because he wasn't working, the railway company did not pay him any money. My mother says that there was an organization of Finnish people in Sudbury who helped pay for my father to be able to stay in the hospital.

After he got out of the hospital, my grandfather missed his girlfriend Fredriikka back in Peurajoki who had begged him to come back so they could get married. My grandfather had saved a lot of his pay because he didn't drink whiskey all the time and play cards like so many of the other men. He kept his extra money in the bank for workers that the railway company had started. He told his boss one day that he was going back to Finland. He took his money out of the bank, and got a free ride on the train back to that place called Montreal because that railway was now a part of the company my grandfather worked for two years, the Canadian Pacific Railway. He bought a ticket on a ship and got to Hanko in about three weeks. From there he took the train to Oulu and one of his brothers came to pick him up in a wagon and bring him back to Peurajoki. Not much later – I am sorry that I don't remember exactly how long it was – he married his girlfriend Fredriikka and they moved into his father's and mother's house, Kuokkala, and helped his father with the farm work.

"Some day in the future when I am grown up, even though I know it is far away, I hope to go to Canada to see where my grandfather lived and worked. I don't think I am strong enough like him to work on the railway. Anyways, I hope to be brave like him to go to a new place that he didn't know. I also want to be brave like him and learn new things and meet new people."

-- Onni Syrjälä, third grade class

Chapter Four:
Peurajoki,
February - October, 1936

The days were beginning to lengthen ever so slightly since it was February. On this particular day, the sun reflected off the snow as to almost blind one. But this day was an exception in Peurajoki that winter. In fact, existence itself in this decade had become cloudy grey to match the winter sky. The few shops that there were in the church village were suffering from a dearth of customers to purchase their wares because the customers lacked the money with which to make a purchase. They lacked the money because the return on their crops had come falling down in a crash. Kuokkala's two cows weren't aware in the least that there was a global depression and continued to produce milk just as before. Martti continued to load the steel cans containing raw milk on the dock by the side of the road to be picked up by Jaakko Taipale on his flatbed truck – the only truck in the area - and delivered to the co-op dairy to be pasteurized. But at the end of the month, the check that he received in the mail from the co-op was a fraction of what it had been just six years earlier.

"Martti, there were vegetables from the garden preserved in the root cellar for the winter, and potatoes from the fields, and unpasteurized milk from the cows for the family to drink. Some people don't have that much." Tyyne never tired of saying this when she saw Martti's downcast visage after opening the envelope with the cheque from the dairy.

"Yes," Martti retorted in his customary glass-half-empty kind of way. "But last time I checked, the bank won't accept eggs and potatoes as repayment for the loan for that new cow barn."

"Yesterday, two Gypsy kids came to the door to ask for bread," Tyyne confessed, even though she knew Martti would be annoyed. "Martti, their faces were as dirty as a barn floor in mud season, and they looked so miserable that I couldn't help but feel sorry for them. I put a few pieces of bread in their cupped hands. But I warned them that I wouldn't do so again if they came back to our door."

"Damn! Now they've found you! They can smell a soft-touch ten kilometers away. Count on them being back. As if we have bread to spare . . ." Martti muttered.

Martti had intended to paint Kuokkala when it passed from Fredriikka to the Syrjälas'. But there was never enough money, so it remained in its original unpainted state, the naked wood turned a tired grey years ago. It seemed as though the only house with paint was the Lindholms' manor in its mustard yellow, and the homes of the other former lords of the manors. To drive your wagon through the village and its environs was to tour a world of various shades of grey.

The nation's political situation did nothing to brighten the lives of Finns, either. Peurajoki was far off the beaten track, to be sure; but events and developments in far-away Helsinki and other places in the south still cast a shadow nonetheless over the distant skies of the parish. The peace that the people expected after the end of the civil war never really got traction. The tensions between the victorious Whites and the defeated Reds, or even the next generation of their descendants, hadn't abated much in almost two decades. The threat of the resumption of violence always festered not far beneath the surface. The Reds continued to press for opportunity to Bolshevize the nation, while some of the more nationalistic and fanatical Whites looked enviously to the continent where one Adolf Hitler was consolidating his fascist hold on Germany and forcing the communists and socialists to the periphery when not imprisoning them.

Furthermore, independence from Russia did not guarantee that the Finns could become complacent about their big neighbor to the east. The Finns had escaped the brutal bear's clutches in 1917 while the bear had been distracted by an uprising in its own belly. But not a single development in Finland went unnoticed in Moscow. Stalin was waiting like a bird of prey for the chance to pounce on its diminutive neighbor and restore to the Soviet Union the nation that had been part of the Russian Empire since 1809.

But an adolescent boy's heart is not darkened by political movements or economic downturns. For one thing, Onni had the books he borrowed from the school library.

Most evenings he sat up in his bed and read by the light of a kerosene lamp. Reading had been made easier, however, when Kuokkala was put on the county electric grid in 1931.

A particular source of brightness for Onni was Anna-Liisa Huhtamäki.

Onni had had "girlfriends" before, but they had been literally friends who happened to be girls. Growing up on a farm on the outskirts of a small village meant you didn't have a lot options for playmates. Väinö had become bored several years ago playing with his younger brother because Onni had been too small to climb trees in the woods or pick up larger rocks from the banks of the creek to build a dam, which is what Väinö liked to do. But Salme Vuotila lived on the neighboring farmstead, and was almost the exact same age as Onni. While Onni was still a preschooler, after Väinö and Salme's older sister Toini had left for school in the morning, Onni would head towards Toivola and find Salme crouching on her haunches in the yard piling small chunks of ice to dam the rivulets of water flowing from the puddles left by the morning's thaw. Onni would join the engineering project, often without saying a word, and Salme would look up and not utter a word either, and the two would complete that project until one or the other came up with suggestion for an alternative activity. Onni and Salme were boyfriend and girlfriend, and Salme had even told her mother that she would marry Onni someday.

But now, at age 14, without any intention on his own part, Onni had begun to evolve into wanting something approximating a *real* girlfriend for the first time. Anna-Liisa was just as shy and reserved as he was, and neither could claim that he or she had ever said more than two or three words to the other. But she caught his eye as she arrived in the classroom at the village school one morning. Onni noticed her as if for the very first time ever, and marveled at her striking face that in its own way was still childlike, but simultaneously very grown-up as well. She had a finely-sculpted visage. She was wearing her light brown hair in a single long braid that seemed to flow smoothly down the length of her back. He made note, too, that she had glanced at him a little longer than usual, just long enough for him to detect the glance, but not long enough as to be obvious to any classmate except the most perceptive or undistracted. Then suddenly she looked away self-consciously as if, on the one hand, she enjoyed his attention, but then again, wasn't sure she wanted *him* to notice that *she* had noticed him. But she couldn't conceal from Onni that her cheeks had turned a tender red.

On Saturday mornings, Onni often accompanied his father on errands to the church village. One fall Saturday, as their wagon was passing the village church, he noticed a group of girls walking up the steps that led to the huge wooden front door into the parish hall. He recognized most of the girls from school. They were school classmates of his, in fact. His heart hoped that Anna-Liisa would be among them.

His heartbeat quickened when, indeed, he spotted her in the group, chatting and laughing with the others.

"What's going on in the church on a Saturday, father?" Onni enquired.

"I think it must be the confirmation school."

Onni had heard about confirmation school, of course. His school pals Ahvo Launikari and Lasse Asikainen attended the classes, too, they had told him, with envy in their voices that he didn't.

"How do you manage to get out of having to go?" they asked.

It's not that Onni had somehow engineered a scheme to get out of spending Saturday mornings in a class led by the village rector, Veikko Sillanpää. The possibility had simply not been brought up to him.

His older sisters Alma and Hilja had been confirmed so that they could marry their husbands in the church. Väinö completed the process because he wouldn't be able to serve in the Finnish military when the time came as he wanted un-

24

less he were confirmed. By the time Onni had grown to confirmation age, his parents had seemingly been distracted by other things and never mentioned confirmation.

So Onni brought up the subject himself. When   he told Martti about his desire one day in the cow barn as he was helping his father clean the milk cans, all Martti said was,

"This is what you want to do, is it?"

When Onni replied that yes it was, Martti added,

"Well, you're almost a man now, so you can do as you please. I'll go talk to the rector on my next trip to the church village."

"Father, that's alright. I think I should talk to the rector myself."

Martti looked up at his son and paused, and then said, "As I say, you're almost a man now. I suppose you can do your own talking for yourself."

And that Onni did do. He drove himself in the wagon to the parsonage in the church village. He was as direct as his father might have been in requesting the rector's permission to come to the class.

The rector didn't know whether to be grateful that a young person in the parish was actually petitioning to come voluntarily to confirmation classes when it was clear that most of the others in the class, especially the boys, sat like bumps on a log because their parents had insisted that they be there. He also didn't know whether he ought to be suspicious of the boy for some reason. But the boy seemed earnest enough, thought the answers he gave seemed a make rehearsed. Nonetheless, the rector thought, Onni Syrjälä had always struck him, in the rare and brief moments that he'd been anywhere near him, as a bright and curious boy.

Chapter Five:
Peurajoki
May 1937

Pertti Laakso arrived at Kuokkala every Monday and Thursday. Pertti was the assistant to the postmaster Sven Lagerquist, whom the farmers in the parish seldom saw because it was Pertti who delivered the mail. In the summer, he arrived on his well-traveled bicycle, carrying a dirty canvas bag over this left shoulder containing the mail. In the winter, he'd make his rounds on skis. He was a very gregarious sort, almost always taking time to chat if he found you in the yard or out by the barn. That made him so unlike most of the men in Peurajoki.

The Syrjäläs seldom received letters in the mail. Occasionally Hilja would send a letter from Oulu, and sometimes enclosed a black and white photo of their house that her photographer husband had taken and developed at his shop. Of course, the province and county would send their annual tax bill, but that was the extent of it.

It was the *Kaleva* newspaper that Martti and Onni looked forward to. The newspaper was published three times a week in Oulu, and covered happenings all over Ostrobothnia. But since there was mail delivery just twice a week, in the Monday delivery there were often two newspapers, the Saturday and Monday editions.

The most recent issue of the *Kaleva* would be waiting for Martti on the short table beside the reading lamp when he came in from the barn for his morning coffee. No one would describe him as a political man. The goings-back-and-forth between the socialist Reds and the Whites that lingered even some sixteen years after the civil war made him irritable. But he did scan the political headlines in the newspaper, seldom taking the time or investing the interest in reading the story. When a story appeared reporting a farm accident somewhere, or a house or building fire, Martti would read that with rapt focus, making the occasional comment to Tyyne or anyone who might be within earshot. He also turned to the sports section to see how the Oulu or Kemi bandy teams were faring on the ice. The *Kaleva* had extra pages of coverage whenever a Finnish national all-star bandy team played a friendly against Sweden or Estonia.

Then he'd fold and put the paper back on the table and go out to resume his project in the barn or yard.

Then Onni would eagerly pick up the paper and launch into it. What first attracted Onni to the newspaper were the *Pekka Puupää* and *Mister Pulliainen* comic strips when he'd learned to read in grade school. But he began to skim pages beyond the comics when he was about 9 or 10. Getting the latest bandy and track and field results from the sports pages gave him something to talk about with his father, although Martti would often cut the conversation short, citing the need to get back to work as the reason.

Onni didn't understand the articles detailing the complex political happenings in his own nation's capital, but he did think it important to know who the current president and prime minister of Parliament were. Most of his classmates marveled at why any farm boy would even care who was president, but teachers were impressed and encouraged him.

When Onni saw a dateline from a foreign capital, however, he would read the article in depth, often comprehending only a small portion of the information in the article because of the dense political terminology. But he was able to grasp the gist of what was being reported. He knew, for example, that a man named Roosevelt had become President of the United States in 1932, and that Adolf Hitler and his Nazi party had gained the plurality in the German Reichstag in the following year. More ominously, he learned that Josef Stalin was imposing famine and terror on the Ukraine.

But almost never did he see an article about the Canadian prime minister, or any significant events in Canada. He did read, however, that in 1932, pilot Amelia Earhart took off from an airport in the neighboring colony named Newfoundland to be the first woman to fly solo across the Atlantic to Northern Ireland.

One day, Onni was helping his father plant the rye crop. Marti handed him a cloth bag, which Onni hung over his left shoulder. With his right hand, he scooped up a handful of rye seeds and scattered them in the furrows in the ground that Martti had carved with the plow. Onni started at one corner of the field, while Martti started at the other.

After an hour of such sowing, Onni's mind began ruminating. It stuck him as he spread the rye seeds, that throughout his fifteen years, the seed of an aspiration and dream had been sowed in the fertile furrows of his imagination. Like the rye seed, the seed had been dormant and unseen. But year by year, it had been taking root.

Onni became conscious of the dream whenever he felt a restless excitement. He had felt eagerness and expectancy before when he was younger, but it always passed like the morning mist in the autumn when his attention was caught by some other attraction or idea. This sensation was new, however. It felt deeper and more enduring somehow. It came upon him like an astonishing shaft of light at midnight. The world was much bigger than Peurajoki, or even Ostrobothnia, he began to see. It was what he began to sense years ago when he had first heard about his grandfather Aatu's venturing to Canada as a nineteen-year-old.

His sensation was of a new undiscovered world opening up to him, with infinite possibilities, beckoning him somehow, but not requiring him, at least not yet anyway, to leave the hearth of his old familiar, familial world. He became conscious of the potential for making choices for his life, choices that his parents were not offered when they were young, choices that even Hilja and Alma had not been aware existed.

As he read the newspaper, Onni began to envision himself in Berlin, or Moscow, or Paris and London, New York or perhaps a city in Canada, in any of those black dots or encircled stars on his globe. His heart beat with elation as he imagined himself filing reports with the *Kaleva,* or even the *Helsingin Sanomat,* from those foreign capitals and seeing his name in the byline the next morning.

~~~~~~~~~~~~~~~~~~~~~~~~~~~~~~~

Easter morning at Kuokkala was spattered with light. The sun shone more brightly, it seemed, than on any other day that spring that the Syrjäläs could remember. The snowdrops had begun their brilliant blooming, poking their heads through the crust of the few patches of snow still stubbornly littering the shaded parts of the yard, although the other trees were still brown and without leaves. Not completely brown, however, because the observant eye could detect a subtle shade of mossy green on the tips of the branches where leaves tightly enveloped within buds all winter and early spring were whispering their impatience and urgency to erupt. The puddles on the path to the privy had mainly dried, and the sun had warned the ground sufficiently that Onni could make his way to the privy in his bare feet that had been covered by two layers of socks just a few weeks prior.

You could hear the kaw-kawing of crows in the woods all winter long, as though the crows were too lazy to make the trip south to Italy or Portugal or the Azores like other species. But on this Easter morning, Onni could hear the greenfinches in the birch trees behind the house, and noticed a couple of robins and redwings making a survey of the yard in search of worms that might have been aroused by the warmer weather and longer days. Winter was easing its tight grip finally on Peurajoki for another four or five months.

The Syrjäläs were going to join their neighbors and the villagers at Easter service. The family climbed onto the wagon they reserved for more formal trips to the village, such as this one to the stately village church. It had carried them to the church when Hilja and Alma were finally confirmed, and three years ago when it was Väinö's turn. And in another month, Onni would partake of the bread and wine for the very first time, too

As the family filed into a pew near the rear of the unusually filled church, Onni spied the back of the Huhtamäkis' heads about four or five pews in front of them. Someone in the pew behind the Huhtamäkis must have said something funny because suddenly Anna-Liisa turned her head back to see the originator of the joke and join in the tittering.

29

Anna-Liisa looked so thrillingly regal in her new white Easter dress. It made Onni feel even more awkward in Väinö's hand-me-down suit that he was wearing. She looked so much like a woman, not an adolescent girl as she usually did at school and in confirmation class. The shape of her waist and hips were highlighted by the dress, and the top of the dress was filling out. Her hair was parted off to the right side and the locks rolled elegantly into waves as though she were a movie actress.

As she turned to face the girl behind her, Anna-Liisa's eye caught Onni's observing her. She didn't look away immediately this time as she usually did in confirmation class when she caught him looking at her, as if to deny that she had noticed him at all. Onni had done the same when he saw her looking in his direction. This time she flared a shy smile his way, and Onni smiled and nodded his head slowly and nobly in her direction to indicate that he acknowledged her attentiveness, however brief and hurried, and that he liked it. He felt his face turning red after she had turned to face the front once again. He hoped that none of the members of his family, especially Väinö, noticed the silent exchange.

It occurred to him that this was the very first time that he and Anna-Liisa really acknowledged each other. Onni had looked down at the floor or ground whenever he passed her coming in or going out of the confirmation class, and because he didn't look at her directly, he couldn't tell if she did the same. He didn't know how he would have responded if his eyes ever met hers. He feared he might become paralyzed with anxiety, with the fear of having to respond to her greeting him, with terrible trepidation about what to say that wouldn't betray his excitement. Yet what he feared even more was if she simply passed him indifferently without noticing him at all.

Onni felt there was no one he could consult about the matter of strong attraction to a girl. He knew that Väinö had more experience in this department. Väinö was often surrounded by girls after a track meet or cross-country skiing race at the field behind the village school. But Onni was certain that he could not confide in him about something so personal. It would mean admitting to him his ignorance about girls.

As he grew older, neither could Onni even consider the possibility of confiding the matter to Martti. The two had been close through the years, and but their conversation never strayed beyond matters related to the farm, the hay crop, the care of the cows, the yield price for potatoes in a particular summer, or Martti's hopes to begin harvesting timber from the patch of woods between Kuokkala and the Vuotilas' property. He had never seen any physical display of affection between his parents, though he knew from their supper table banter that they enjoyed a kind of almost fraternal bond of closeness. Anything Onni knew about the birds and the bees he learned in secret from books in the school library. Martti had never broached the subject. To bring up the subject of Anna-Liisa, or to ask for any advice on such a matter, would not only cause Onni to feel very awkward. He feared that it would be devastatingly embarrassing for Martti, and he didn't want to put his father in such a position.

And he knew he certainly dare not divulge any hint of an attraction to Anna-Liisa to his school buddies Asikainen or Launikari. Those self-styled ladies' men talked a good game, but Onni knew they were as inexperienced with girls as he. They would have laughed at him, for sure. Or else offered to steal a condom for him from their older brothers' secret stash. Though Onni felt a current akin to electricity rush through his whole body as soon as he even thought of Anna-Liisa, he did not think of her in the same coarse and common way that he was sure Asikainen and Launikari would.

Onni was so exhilarated as the opening hymn began that he no longer had doubts that Anna-Liisa at the very least took notice of him, that her opinion of him was favorable, elated by the possibility that she might have experienced some of the same feelings towards him that he did towards her.

Onni opened the hymnal on his pew, but like all the other males in church that day, merely pretended to follow

31

the text of the hymn but didn't sing a note until the final "Amen".

As they sat down, Anna-Liisa stole a glance his way and once again, her beautiful mouth was shaped into a timid smile. Onni's nod of acknowledgement was brief and hurried this time, lest his family him notice.

The rector rose up the spiral steps into the ornate stylized pulpit against the wall to the left of the congregation. He paused and looked at the congregation below him for what seemed to Onni an uncomfortably long time. Then he launched into his sermon.

"We heard once again, dear congregants, the old familiar and precious account of the glorious and miraculous events of the first Easter; the miracle of the empty tomb, the irony of Mary's mistaking the risen Lord for the gardener, and the fearful disciples huddling in the upper room disbelieving her report that she had seen the Lord risen from the tomb as an 'idle tale'."

Onni's mind often wandered during his sermon on the routine Sundays, but on this day, the rector seemed to be so very earnest, his words so sincere and heartfelt. Though the rector had just started his sermon, Onni sensed that the rector wasn't going to run through the usual litany of the temptations of the feeble flesh as he usually did, the predictable appeal to the Ten Commandments as the means to a holy life. Onni intuited that the rector's sermon for this special day would have an import all its own, and so gave the rector his full attention.

"You undoubtedly walked past the old rusted metal gravestones in the original cemetery just outside the front door of the church. You entered our church with the reminder of the mortal nature of our human existence. If you allowed your mind to wander there, you will have thought about your own mortality, imagined in your mind your own gravestone."

The rector spoke as if he could read Onni's thoughts. For, on many occasions, when rising up out of the ancient cemetery on the stone steps leading to the imposing wooden door into the church, Onni had entertained such fantasies, imagining his own funeral by one of the gravesites. It was almost the only time that Onni thought about his own inevitable death. He had always considered it a strange, if not morbid feeling to have while entering the house of God.

"You have come hoping to hear a word of comfort from God this Easter morning that the parents or grandparents you have accompanied to the open mouth of the grave in our cemetery are assured eternal life in heaven. You are seeking, too, I'm sure, assurance that the grave will not be the end for yourself either. We want God's warrant that Einari Kukkohovi, to whom we said our farewells and buried this past week, will not be forgotten or abandoned to his dark grave, but that he has been raised.

Onni had given his intellectual assent to this seemingly unlikely idea, which he had heard before from this pulpit. He remained very unsure, however, about how it could be possible that his grandparents Aatu and Fredriikka, dead so many years, would one day be resurrected to a new kind of life, just as Jesus was so long ago. He wondered about the mechanics of resurrection.

Onni had been paying attention to a point, to the level of concentration commensurate to the ability a young man sitting just four or five pews behind the girl he considered the most beautiful in all of Peurajoki. But a seemingly abrupt and unfamiliar change in direction by the rector brought his focus back from his own mental meanderings to the rector's sermon.

"During the civil war in America in the middle of the last century, the funeral of one of the Union generals took place in one of the grand churches in New York. As the service was coming to a close, from the western end of the nave, a solitary young bugle boy played 'Taps', the poignant, melancholy tune that on the battlefield signaled dusk and the close of the day. But after a moment of stillness that followed the last plaintive note of that song, another bugler stood at the east end of the nave, the end that faced the rising sun, and played 'Reveille', the spirited, energetic song of the morning and the call to a new day.

"Friends, our God is a God of new beginnings and never-ending possibility. 'Taps' is followed by 'Reveille'. The dawn follows night. Darkness gives way to light. Life emerges out of death. Despair yields to hope. Oh friends, what joy!"

The organist didn't launch into his introduction to the next hymn right away as he customarily did. The congregation was strangely quiet. Onni couldn't hear any of the women's usual coughing, or the restless children's whining, or the impatient men's shuffling to the exit door to have smoke. It was as though the organist wanted to join the congregation in honoring the rector's words with silence.

In the ensuing years, Onni would recall the rector's words many times. They would seem so prescient then. Times had been hard in 1937, but in just a matter of two years, the Finnish people would be plunged into the darkness of war. At times, they would fall into despair and hopelessness as the independence of their nation, won in 1917, seemed to be slipping away. From afar in 1939, Onni would wonder if the rector had had some strong notion two years earlier of the troubles and the grounds for despair to come. Had the rector been offering this promise of hope to his people in advance?

As she rose to join in the triumphant Easter hymn that followed, Anna-Liisa turned her head slightly to look at Onni. The youthful and festive reflection in her joyful face which she was there before the service had receded slightly, and made room for a more pensive and almost profound look. It seemed to match the mood within him now.

The worshipers filed out of the church after the closing hymn. Families were leaving the church grounds now to go home to family celebrations. The Syrjälas were heading towards their various wagons or carriages when Onni saw Anna-Liisa on the Huhtamäkis' wagon which had already begun its journey home. Watching her shape slowly receding and getting smaller as the wagon proceeded farther from the church was extremely exciting to Onni, but incomparably and overwhelmingly sad as well.

Chapter Six:
Peurajoki
November 1937

Tyyne had just finished her cup of coffee that she looked forward to each afternoon as a welcome quarter-hour respite from housecleaning, laundry and chores in the barn. She was in the mud room putting on her boots and light coat when she looked out the small, smudged window and saw a figure coming through the gate to the Kuokkala property without stopping to close the gate behind him. He turned and faced the house and began a clumsy, inelegant walk toward the house, a lit cigarette dangling from his lips. He was walking very unsteadily, staggering actually. Tyyne feared that he might trip and fall onto the ground still wet from the melting of an early November snowfall a few days prior.

The figure noticed Onni coming out of the cow barn.

"Is that you, Onni my boy? Hell, you're getting so big your uncle doesn't recognize you anymore. I'm sorry that I wasn't feeling very well at all on the morning of your confirmation and wasn't able to come. You forgive me, don't you, Onni?"

Yes, I bet you weren't feeling well that Sunday morning. You were sleeping off another Saturday night at the Tuulan Talli tavern, I'm sure.

Onni recognized the voice and the familiar slurred words in his sentences. This was his uncle Heikki, his father's brother. Though Heikki was younger than Martti by a few years, the tired-looking eyes, the grisly two-day old beard, bushy unkempt mustache that had started to turn a snowy gray made him look ten years older. His cheeks seemed to be permanently flushed and bore a roadmap of red veins. Uncle Heikki was a friendly and cheerful enough fellow, but Onni knew that when Heikki had been drinking, conversation with him wouldn't be short, nor would it be particularly rational or productive.

Before Onni could answer, Martti emerged from the cow barn holding a pitchfork.

"What the hell are you doing back here?" Martti shouted angrily. "I thought I'd told you not to come back when we're trying to work. Not that you would understand what work is."

Onni seized the opportunity to shuffle off quietly towards the house. He'd been a witness to these angry fraternal interchanges before, and he wasn't in the mood to be a spectator at another one. As he pulled open the door to the mudroom, he was startled by Tyyne's being there looking out the window when he hadn't been expecting anyone to be there.

"That's not whom I think it is, is it, Onni?" she asked, obviously hoping for "No" as an answer.

"Yes, I'm afraid so." Onni sighed, "It's Uncle Heikki."

Tyyne was disappointed with the answer. Things in Heikki's existence were never good whenever he risked coming to the home of his older brother. Things at Kuokkala were seldom good when Heikki did come by. For a dozen years after the civil war, the sale of liquor had been prohibited in Finland, but still somehow Heikki had found a way to get some. Probably from Eetu Kojala's still in the old croft at the rear of his property, everyone figured. And when the people voted to end prohibition in 1931, and the state-run ALKO store opened in the village, Heikki had been practically the first customer, and a regular from then on.

"Now, now, Martti," Heikki pleaded. "Is that how mother and father taught us to greet visitors. I come in peace."

"And asking for something, no doubt, Goddammit!"

"Why do you always suspect me of the worst?" Heikki asked, steadying himself against the wall of the barn.

"Because that's what always happens. You need money to pay off this or that debt. Or to pay your rent. Or to buy your booze. It's always something!"

Tyyne could see out the window that Martti was getting red with anger. Her instinct was to go outside and intervene somehow, to prevent things from escalating as they had sometimes in the past. They had come to physical blows more than once, with Martti's sending Heikki to the ground with his fists. But she wasn't up to dealing with Heikki herself, didn't want his drunken sweet-talking to her, his patting her behind when he thought Martti wasn't looking. She took off her coat and boots and went back into the *tupa*.

Martti slammed the door behind him as he came storming in a quarter-hour or so later. He gave Tyyne the look that she recognized as his signaling to her to back off and not ask questions. So she didn't.

Until later that night as she and Martti were undressing for bed.

"What happened with Heikki today?"

"Oh, I gave him hell and held up the pitchfork, and he hightailed it out of here."

"What was his problem this time?

"Aino has had enough and locked him out of the house."

"Where's he been sleeping? The nights are cold in November."

"I don't know. And I don't want to know. I didn't ask him. With one of his drinking buddies or hussies, I'd bet."

With that, the lamp was turned off. But Tyyne couldn't sleep. Heikki was a definite pain in the backside when he was drunk. But he is family, she thought. He's Martti's flesh and blood. Heikki had always been respectful of her – when he was sober. He was the first one – the only one

37

– in Martti's family to welcome her into the family. Martti's parents had had their fill of him and he wasn't welcome at the homestead. Tyyne couldn't shake the image from her mind of Heikki lying in the wintry cold some place, or trying to break into a cow barn on someone's property. It was a fitful night for Tyyne.

At breakfast in the morning, Tyyne broached the subject of Heikki again with her husband. Onni was at the table with them.

"Martti, we can't let Heikki sleep out in the cold, or in someone's shitty cow barn. Just think: he could freeze to death some night. Then how would our consciences feel?"

"Mine would say that he brought it on himself. I'm not the one who bought the booze for him."

"But my conscience would be saying something else to me: 'Heikki died because your door was closed to him.'"

Onni could see where this conversation was headed. It was Martti's reasoned and practical approach contending with Tyyne's empathy and desire to help, as always.

"You aren't suggesting that we take him in, for God's sake?" Martti asked, flabbergasted.

"Maybe it will be different somehow this time. Maybe he'd be so grateful that he'd behave differently."

"He's damned incapable of behaving differently. It's always the same shit!"

"Martti, he's your only brother."

As much as he was made uneasy by the prospect of having Heikki in the house for any length of time, by now Onni was persuaded that Tyyne might be right.

Martti got up from the table with a sigh and angrily announced that he had work to do. Tyyne was downcast, but got up to begin her daily round of duties as well. Onni got ready to walk to school.

Nothing else was said about Heikki that day. Very few words were spoken between Martti and Tyyne.

Finally, the next day, Martti's voice sounded softer, as though he were seeking reconciliation.

"Where the hell would he sleep if he came here?"

"We'd have to move Väinö out of the girls' room into Onni's and they could share the bed."

"Do you really think the boys would agree to that? Not likely!"

"I think they realize this is their uncle, their family, who's in need of his family's support right now."

Later in the day, when Martti came in for the noon-time meal, he said,

"Alright, he can come here. But only for a trial period, is that understood? He's not to bring his booze into this house where we have two underage sons. He's not to bring his drinking buddies or his hussies into this house. He can't drink one single milliliter here. Any misbehavior, and his ass is out of here, I swear!"

And so, later that day, an overly contrite, pathetically apologetic, excessively humbled and polite, and surprisingly sober Heikki took his bedraggled duffle bag of belongings, smelling of stale cigarette smoke, into the bedroom Hilja and Alma had shared years ago, dropped it on the floor, and flopped down on the bed.

Chapter
Seven:
Peurajoki
February 1938.

When Pertti Laakso dropped off the mail at Kuokkala one Monday, there was more than the most recent issue of the *Kaleva* newspaper. There was also a light brown envelope addressed to Väinö from the Finnish Defense Forces. When Tyyne saw the envelope, she knew exactly what it was about. Her heart was aroused by pride, but plummeted simultaneously with dread.

She called Väinö and told him that he had mailing waiting for him on the dining table in the *tupa*.

Väinö emerged from the bedroom he shared with Onni and walked towards the dining table with a sense of excitement and anticipation in his step. He picked up the envelope and took it into the bedroom.

When Martti came in from the shed for his morning coffee, Tyyne said, "I think Väinö got his summons in the mail today. He's in the bedroom reading it right now."

Väinö came back out of the bedroom holding the folded letter. He looked up at Martti who gave him a knowing glance in return. Väinö couldn't bear to look at Tyyne at all. Onni was simply a silent observer of this ritual that was being repeated in thousands of homes across Finland. It would probably be played out again in two years with Onni as the principal character.

"Well?" Tyyne asked, somewhat impatient to know what she already knew, but wanting to get the inevitable over with.

"I am told that I need to report to Dr. Jokinen to get a physical examination. Then I'm to report to the armory in Oulu within 60 days, and be assigned to a unit for my service in the army."

Onni had seldom seen his brother standing taller and more erect as when he reported the contents of the letter.

The *tupa* fell silent. Every Finnish parent knows that this day is coming once a son is about to turn 19. Yes, when the news arrives, it's as though they'd never had advanced warning of the sudden sense of panic a mother feels in the pit of her stomach. Her son will be away from home for the very first time.

In 1938, the dread was amplified by snatches of news reports from the rest of Europe. Both Stalin and Hitler were growing increasingly mentally unstable, it seemed. How else to explain their insane determination to bring the chaos of war upon the continent *again?* In spite of supposedly strict limitations imposed by Britain, France, Russia and the United States upon Germany in the Treaty of Versailles after the Great War, it was public knowledge to anyone in Europe who read a newspaper that Hitler had been increasing the number of men in the armed forces exponentially, and converting peacetime factories into workshops for manufacturing tanks, armored vehicles, planes for the *Luftwaffe* and *Stargazer* assault rifles by the tens of thousands.

Stalin was purging his officers' corps and inserting new generals who shared his wild, uncontrolled bloodlust. He was hinting that he was about to ask the Finnish government to alter the boundaries the two nations had agreed to in the early 1920s and hand over more territory to the Russians.

The rancid smell of smoke hung in the air, and signs of a dark cloud in the firmament. There was the pounding of distant drums.

"When do you have to go to Doctor Jokinen to get your physical exam," Tyyne asked, trying to control her voice because she was on the verge of tears.

"As I said, I have to be at the barracks in Oulu within 60 days. I'll go to the church village tomorrow and ask at the doctor's house about a physical."

"Tomorrow, already?" Tyyne asked.

"Well, there's no sense delaying. I'm ready to go."

Onni sensed that what Väinö meant but didn't want to say so as not to hurt his mother was that he was rather *eager* to go. He'd been waiting for this day for some time now. He wanted to be prepared to defend his country if and when it became necessary.

Onni's heart was divided. On the one hand, even though Väinö and he seemed to be reared from different breeds and sown with different fabric, Väinö was a constant, a fixture in his life, a reference point, and at times, even a friend. He would miss him for these nine to twelve months. On the other hand, Onni's own primary and secondary education was nearing its end. He had notions of talking to his parents about moving to Oulu and working towards a diploma in journalism and eventually becoming a reporter on the *Kaleva.*

With Väinö not around the next year or so, I'm going to have to put these notions aside for at least a year and stay on the farm to lend father a hand. For the time being at least, I'll have to put my plans for journalism school aside.

Martti looked at his older son and saw a man on the cusp of assuming the responsibilities of adulthood. Tyyne looked at Väinö and all she could see was the babe in her arms and the toddler at her feet of 19 years ago.

Chapter Eight:
Peurajoki
April 1938.

Onni took off his muddy boots in the appropriately named mudroom and carried his rucksack full of schoolbooks into the *tupa*. He was met by Heikki sitting at the table with a cup of coffee in front of him, a lit cigarette between two fingers in his left hand. Heikki looked as scruffy and unkempt as usual, but he appeared to be sober for the time being.

"Another day of lessons done, eh, Onni?"

Onni knew it wasn't a question seeking information; rather, a way of breaking the ice.

"Yes, Uncle Heikki."

"What are they teaching down there at the school these days?" Heikki asked, again, not so much a question in search of an informative answer, but more like a preface to an editorial comment, Onni knew. That put Onni slightly on the defensive, anticipating a string of remarks from Heikki about how inadequate the education of the nation's children and youth is compared to what was offered twenty years' prior – which, of course, was when Heikki sat at desk in a classroom. He'd heard Heikki pontificate like that several times before, although at those times he had been noticeably intoxicated. Onni had never dared ask his uncle how the schools could possibly have been better when the rest of Finnish civilization had been in ruins as the civil war was raging in 1918 and the Reds and Whites warring over whose curriculum should be taught.

Onni took his time answering his uncle's provoking question. So Heikki filled the silence with a follow-up question.

"Any of what you learned useful? Or true?"

"Well, yes," Onni defended. "A person has to know how to read and write. We have to know our history. We have to know how to count."

"It hasn't exactly done me much good," Heikki said resignedly.

Onni recognized that this conversation had the potential to be more meaningful, perhaps even more enlightening, than their usual brief superficial exchanges.

"What do you mean, Uncle Heikki?"

"Son, you sure do have that journalist's ability to delve into things. Good for you. But it's not me I want to talk about today. It's *you*."

"Me? There's not much to talk about."

Onni hoped that he had telegraphed his reluctance to go on any further if things were morphing into an interview of him.

"You like hunting, boy? Or fishing?"

"Not really."

"What about skiing? Or dancing? You know, manly things?"

"I do like to go one long cross-country jaunts on my skis. Or hikes in the summer time."

"That's good, boy. But I detect just one issue with that."

Onni waited.

"I know you aren't interested in the idle gabbing of a drunken uncle after a whole day of listening to a teacher spewing out useless information. But let me tell you, Onni, I've got something important to say. Sometimes we drunks see the truth of things better than those who are completely sober."

Onni thought this conversation was patently unusual. But he had heard Heikki make some surprisingly discerning remarks to the family at the dinner table. He had noticed that whenever Heikki opened his mouth to speak, Martti would hang his head just the slightest and emit a muffled sigh. Tyyne had at least made the effort to look interested in what Heikki had to say, but she often tried to change the subject after Heikki had spoken, to appease Martti, Onni figured. But Onni judged that occasionally, if you really paid attention, Heikki came close to hitting the nail of some matter or other on the head.

So, Onni took the risk that Heikki was being earnest now instead of his taking his customary stab at irrelevant and sometimes irreverent humor.

"What is the one issue you detect, Uncle Heikki?" Onni ventured, knowing that this could backfire very easily. He could tell by the silence from the rest of the house that Martti and Tyyne were out in the barn or in the field behind the barn, so there was no danger of their overhearing this conversation.

"The issue is, every time I see you go out on your skis, you're alone. Same thing when you set out on a hike in the woods."

"I like doing things by myself."

"That can get lonely, can't it?"

"No, not usually. I like the silence, the solitude. Väinö always says there's something wrong with me, that I don't have friends."

"Do you?"

"There's Ahvo Asikainen and Lasse Launikari. They're good for a few laughs. But if I ski or hike with them, they won't shut up. They just prattle on about such trivial things.

45

I just want the silence, just me and the woods and the sound of the birds. You understand?"

Onni was surprised how desperately he wanted his uncle to understand his desire for solitude. Why? It's just his uncle.

"Oh, I understand alright. I like to enjoy my booze alone, too, without some loud mouths polluting the whiskey with their bullshit." Heikki let out a quiet laugh, looking to see how the boy was dealing with his profanity.

Onni felt sad imagining the image of his uncle sitting in his room alone with his whiskey. But he was gladdened in a way that his prodigal uncle, the black sheep, seemed to understand him at the moment. The two of them even shared a common trait, the same hunger for solitude, making Onni feel less odd.

"You know what I like best about being alone, Onni?"

Onni waited again for Heikki to say more.

"That you don't have to have anyone talk back to you. Nobody to contradict you, like my wife, or question you, or tell you you're wrong for thinking something."

Onni nodded. *No one to pour cold water on your dreams, or puncture your fantasy.*

"But you know, Onni, as much as I dislike those things, I've learned there's a problem feeling that way. Know what it is?"

Onni knew that Heikki wasn't expecting him to answer, but that he was enjoying providing his own answer.

"You're in danger of missing a chance to learn something, that's what."

Heikki looked at Onni for any reaction. He noted that Onni had that familiar look on his face whenever he was weighing the rightness or wrongness of an idea.

46

"I hate to admit it, but for all her bullshit, Aino knows me better that I know myself sometimes. Sometimes after I've said something to her, she just looks at me in a way that says what I've said is the real bullshit. That makes me angrier than hell. But you know, once I'm alone again and able to think about it, by God, I see that she's right. Not always, but often enough. And that makes me angry, too. But you know, Onni, I learn then to eliminate one more bullshit notion from my repertoire. One less bullshit idea from me that others have to listen to."

Onni doubted that Asikainen or Launikari could do the same for him. But he'd felt that way at times in conversations with Väinö. If he looked past the implicit judgment of him often implied in his older brother's remarks, if he overlooked the braggadocio to which Väinö was subject every now and then, once in a while a negative comment from Väinö bore some truth. It was difficult to hear, but immediately Onni knew the criticism was accurate. He understood what Heikki meant by eliminating something from his behavioral repertoire. Not that he'd admit it to Väinö.

"From what I see, Onni, your only friends are your books."

Onni felt judged. But he knew his uncle was right. Unlike human friends, you could pick up a book only when you felt like it and were in the mood for it. If a book was irritating, you could put it down and stop reading it. *Why wouldn't you want a book for a friend?*

"Yes, I like reading. I learn a lot from books."

"I suppose you do, I wouldn't know. But can I tell you what I've observed over the years about some people who are in love with books?"

Onni knew that Heikki wouldn't wait for his permission. He was about to tell him anyway.

"They observe the world in books; they don't live in the real world."

"You can learn a lot about the world in books. That's where wise people have recorded and preserved knowledge about the world."

"It's good to know *about* the world from a book. But goddamit, that's not really knowing the world through first-hand experience. It's knowing it through somebody else's experience."

Onni remained silent and rolled what Heikki had to say around in his mind.

"I know you've got to get on with your homework and your books, boy. But just one more thing before you go. Let your no-good uncle say to you as honestly and directly as I know how: don't settle for knowing about life from a book. Get out there and experience it first-hand. For God's sake, don't just look at all those dots on your beloved globe. Go and see them for yourself, boy."

Chapter Nine:
Peurajoki
April 1938

Onni wasn't able to see Anna-Liisa regularly for almost a year because her parents had enrolled her in the Christian Peoples' Academy in Pudasjärvi, some sixty kilometers away.

I wonder if she's thought about me at all in Pudasjärvi?

Onni inquired shyly of some of her former school mates at the village school whether they knew when she would be back home for the Easter break, trying to appear nonchalant and not too interested, lest they giggle behind his back once he departed from them.

Even though Anna-Liisa had been out of sight in Pudasjärvi, she had by no means been out of mind. Ever since last Easter, and the delicious furtive exchanges of smiles and nods between him and her at the service that day, Anna-Liisa had been very much in Onni's thoughts, in fact.

Strange, how is it that the less I see her, the more I think of her. The more obsessive I get about her, it seems.

Anna-Liisa would still be at home on the Sunday after Easter. Onni made plans with Tyyne to be in church then in the hopes that she and her family might be there, too. The sparser Low Sunday attendance would allow him to make contact with her, if only with his eyes. It turns out he got more than that.

After the worship service, at the bottom of the stone steps leading outside, Tyyne nodded in the direction of Mrs. Huhtamäki and approached her. Onni panicked for a second, while at the same time delighting. The two women exchanged greetings and pleasantries. Onni wasn't aware that Tyyne knew Anna-Liisa's mother very well, but the convivial chatting between them seemed to indicate that this wasn't the first time they had done so. Onni was surprised that his mother seemed so cheerful. It dawned on him as if for the very first time that Tyyne lived the very insulated and isolated life of a farm wife, as did Mrs. Huhtamäki. They were speaking to each other as adults who otherwise only had their taciturn farmer husbands, and perhaps in-laws, with whom to speak as adults.

The mothers greeted the other's son or daughter cordially.

"Anna-Liisa, you're such a young lady now. How are your studies at school in Pudasjärvi progressing?" Tyyne inquired.

"Thank you, Mrs. Syrjälä, they are going fine, but of course I miss my family and my friends here."

Onni wondered to himself, *Does that include me?*

"We miss her when she's away, too, but we look forward to the breaks when she comes home." Mrs. Huhtamäki added, and with that, the two women launched into small talk about the spring weather and the prospects for a good spring for planting flowers.

Anna-Liisa and Onni stood awkwardly in front of each other. Onni felt as though his tongue were glued to the roof of his mouth. Anna-Liisa waited for him to begin a conversation, but then took the first step herself.

"How was your winter? What news from Kuokkala?"

"The winter seemed long and cold." That took a lot of effort to get out.

"My brother Väinö has left for the army. He's stationed in Joensuu," he added quickly, realizing that his first remark seemed so pedestrian and mundane after such a long wait to see her.

The two mothers were bidding farewell and

50

adding their hearty see-you-laters. Anna-Liisa smiled once more, and then followed her mother to their wagon.

When they got to their waiting wagon, Tyyne turned to Onni and said,

"Onni, would you want me to drive the wagon home by myself while you and Anna-Liisa can perhaps take in some of the nice spring weather and walk her home to Huhtala?"

Onni was stunned by the offer. He was speechless.

How does she know? I've never mentioned Anna-Liisa to her. Am I doing such a poor job of disguising my feelings?

"If you think you are ok with the wagon alone, then, yes, I'll see if Anna-Liisa would like to do that."

The prospect of a half-hour walk and all the potential for nothing but painfully self-conscious silence between him and Anna-Liisa felt absolutely terrifying for Onni. But then again, he felt encouraged by his mother's unexpected offer. It said, *Don't let an opportunity like this pass you by.*

Onni surprised himself and called after Anna-Liisa as she was nearing her family's wagon. She turned around immediately with a hopeful look on her face as though she had been waiting for Onni to call her name and make the moment last.

Mrs. Huhtamäki exhibited a knowing smile and told Anna-Liisa that she was fine driving the wagon to Huhtala on her own. It would be nice, she said, if Anna-Liisa and Onni had a chance to get caught up on their lives since they hadn't seen each other since last summer.

Does Mrs. Huhtamäki have some inkling, too? What? Does she and my mother have some kind of secret pact to conspire like this? How do these women know?

There was a self-conscious silence at first when Onni and Anna-Liisa started walking along the church road towards the road that led to Huhtala. Onni's heart was beating nearly out of his chest and his mind was racing.

What to say? I must say something! I can't just be mute!

Onni began by asking Anna-Liisa how she liked the school in Pudasjärvi. She said she liked it just fine, that she had made some friends and that when she graduates she hopes they can maintain that friendship over the kilometers.

I wonder if she likes any of the boys?

Then Onni remembered that the boys were pretty well segregated from the girls at that school run by the pious Awakened Movement, and so the chances of her having much significant contact with a boy were slim.

Thankfully.

Anna-Liisa asked Onni if he was still friends with Asikainen and Launikari, to which Onni replied, yes, to a point, but they seem interested in other things. Spontaneously, both Anna-Liisa and Onni broke into conspiratorial laughter. He suspected she knew exactly what he meant, and they laughed again.

They both felt freer now, as if the ice had been broken and a load taken off their shoulders. They were more animated now, their stiff conversation more enlivened. They felt more natural talking about her favorite subjects at school (mathematics), and his ambition to write for the *Kaleva* someday Onni was pleased that the way she listened didn't make the ambition seem so juvenile. They went back and forth about things they had heard and read about happenings in the Soviet Union next door, how Stalin had been growing more paranoid of any opposition, and how those Jews who had the means and connections were rumored to have been fleeing Germany and Poland to England and Canada and the

United States, even to Argentina and Brazil. Anna-Liisa related a joke about Hitler that she had heard at her school, and again they laughed as they walked.

Though Kuokkala was on a different road, Onni was familiar with this road from his solitary Sunday afternoon explorations in the horse-drawn wagon. They were on a stretch of road passing through a spruce forest. But Onni knew that it was the last such stretch before Huhtala came into view, and therefore, he and Anna-Liisa came into view as well, should anyone be looking out the window of the house. Anna-Liisa knew that as well, of course. They both stopped in the middle of the road without having told the other, as if each knew that the hoped-for moment had arrived, that it was now or never, that she would be leaving for Pudasjärvi in the next few days, and that if he wanted to give her something by which to remember him up in Pudasjärvi, he had better take the risk and act now.

He turned and faced her, and she did likewise, again as though they were communicating their thoughts without uttering a word, and that their thoughts were identical. He looked into her face, and she into his. She had a shy, nervous smile on her face, but one that said she was nonetheless comfortable with this, with what she intuited was about to occur. He brought his face closer to hers and then leaned in to kiss her very hurriedly on the lips. His heart was in his throat. He felt his penis begin to swell and harden pleasantly the way it did sometimes when he thought of her as he was falling asleep on his bed at night and imagining her without her clothes on.

Her face was a blend of pleasure, relief, and disappointment that there wasn't more. He sensed it, too, and so he reached out and took her face tenderly into his hands and kissed her again, this time for a longer time before finally lowering his hands again.

They stood facing each other for a brief while and said nothing. Onni was sure that nothing needed to be said. Or, if she were to speak and he needed to answer, he didn't know what he would say.

Finally, she broke the silence. "I'm leaving for Pudas-järvi again on Tuesday. I'm glad we had this time together today."

"Honestly, I wish you didn't have to go. I will miss you - more than I know how to say."

At that, he took her right hand into his left and squeezed it gently.

As they arrived at the path leading to Huhtala from the road, she turned and faced him once more.

"Goodbye, Onni. Thank you for walking me home. I hope we can see each other this summer when I come back home. Until then . . ."

To Onni, even though the summer was only a few months away, the time between now and then was bound to pass slowly.

"Goodbye, Anna-Liisa. Have a safe trip to school, and good luck with your studies."

At that, Onni tipped his cap to her and turned back towards the church village and the long walk home. He didn't want to watch her walk down the lane to the house because he feared that he would run and take hold of her one more time to relive the thrill of the kiss.

The walk to Kuokkala didn't feel so long, however. He had a vivacious spring in his stride and he felt that today he could walk all the way to Oulu and back. He hummed a Georg Malmstén tune he had heard on the radio playing at Man-ninen's co-op store, and strangely he didn't care if anyone heard him. He felt as light as air and his spirit as giddy as though intoxicated with some special wine. That one moment seemed to encase an eternity. There was nowhere else he wanted to be at that moment, no one else he wanted to be.

BOOK TWO:

AT ZERO

"Ends are not bad things; they just mean that some-thing else is about to begin. And there are many things that don't really end, anyway, they just begin again in a new way. Ends are not bad and many ends aren't really an ending; some things are never-ending."
— *C. Joy Bell C.*

Interlude
Suomussalmi, Finland
January 10, 1940

In the morning, Riihimäki awoke between the abandoned tank and field kitchen cauldron with the body of the wounded soldier on top of him. The body did not move, nor did it give off the warmth that it had the night before. Riihimäki gently pushed the body off his own and laid it supine on the frozen snow.

The soldier's face had lost its peaches-and-cream color overnight and taken on a greyish-blue hue. The man's chest did not heave up and down, or in and out, in the slightest. Riihimäki knew that the unfortunate brother-in-arms had given up the spirit. Riihimäki pulled out the unused white handkerchief the army had provided in his syrette bag, opened and laid it respectfully, almost reverently, over the expressionless face of the young soldier. He said a short silent prayer, and then left the corpse in the hands of his Creator.

Riihimäki climbed out of the frigid womb of his impromptu shelter. His eyes adjusted to the sun rising over the frozen lake. There was no sight of his platoon, or any other.

He relied on his memory of maps of the region to proceed in the direction of the Raate road where his platoon had been headed before he had been separated from it the day before. Which is how he found himself alone now at the frozen western shoreline of Lake Vuokkijärvi.

Silently, he glided towards the forest over on the lake's eastern side. He paused at the edge of the lake and caught his breath, almost ceasing to breathe entirely in order to listen for sounds that would betray the presence of any remnant of the enemy. The woods greeted him with silence. He found space between some trees and slithered on skis into the forest, his eyes scanning his surroundings alertly and warily.

His heart came to sudden attention as he spied a shape in drab olive less than twenty meters in front of him, then another one, then yet another, discernible but as motionless as granite statues.

Without making a sound, he leaned his ski poles carefully against a tree and maneuvered the strap of his rifle over his head, took it into his hands and pointed it straight ahead in the direction of the figures in olive. Tentatively he slid forward on his skis, careful to avoid rubbing any part of his body against the branches of the spruce trees, lest he inadvertently break one and give his location away. Then another stride, and another, but still the statues did not move. All Riihimäki could hear was the thunderous beating of his own heart amplified by the furious rush of adrenaline in his veins and arteries.

What were these eerie, mysterious statues in the middle of a silent forest?

Chapter Ten:
Peurajoki
May 1938

The sun was approaching the Tropic of Cancer. The days were lengthening again. This made it easier and more pleasant for Onni to be reading.

His back was propped up against his pillow, which leaned against the wall behind his bed. He was preparing for one of his last final examinations at the Peurajoki village school, this one on European literature. His eyes were beginning to tire as he plowed through Book VI of Homer's *Iliad.*

Onni surrendered to his body's longing for sleep. He lay the book down on the plain pine nightstand beside the lower bunk of his bed. As he did so, his nostrils caught a brief whiff of smoke. This was not unusual when Uncle Heikki was home occupying the room separated only by a wooden door from the one which, until just a few months ago, Onni had shared with Väinö. The strong odor of his uncles rolled cigarettes would often trespass into his room.

But this wasn't the smell of cheap cigarette smoke. Onni peeled his eyes towards the door. His eyes traveled down to the narrow gap underneath this door. The bedroom was still illumined by sunlight. But Onni thought he detected an unfamiliar flickering of red coming through the gap.

He stepped out of his bunk and quietly called through the door to his uncle. There was no response, so Onni raised the volume of his voice. Still no reply. So Onni reached for the doorknob in order to open the door into Heikki's room. But he immediately and violently jerked his hand away from the ceramic doorknob. He waved his hand in the air intensely in an effort to alleviate the blistering, burning pain in his right palm.

Simultaneously, above his own howling at the searing pain in his hand, he could hear the sound of crackling, sizzling, snapping, and popping coming from behind the door.

Onni shouted out to his parents who slept in the room on the far side of the *tupa*. Even before it struck him that they probably couldn't hear his shout, he darted in a panic out of his room towards their room, all the while calling out for them.

"What is it, Onni?" a bewildered Tyyne exclaimed, jumping out of their bed. Martti was just raising his head from the pillow.

"Come! Hurry! I think there's a fire in Uncle Heikki's room! Hurry!"

"My dear God! Martti, get up! Onni says there's fire in Heikki's room! Get up! Go with Onni!"

When the three of them ran into Onni's room half-dressed, they were forced to stop at the threshold. The door separating Onni's room from Heikki's was aflame from top to bottom. Flames had spread to Onni's room and begun to engulf the wooden set of drawers Martti had built when Väinö was a small boy. They stood at the doorway, paralyzed in utter shock. Suddenly they had to jump backwards into the *tupa* as the flames exploded from the set of drawers and ignited the mattress and bedding on Onni's bed in a flash and climbed up to the top bunk and then the ceiling.

"Get back! We've got to get out of the house before the flames dart into the *tupa*! Don't delay! Get out!"

"But what about Heikki, Martti? We can't just abandon him in his burning room, for sweet Jesus' sake!" Tyyne shouted.

"It's too dangerous to try to avoid the flames in Onni's room to get to Heikki's! There's no time! Maybe he's climbed to safety out the window in his room! We have to get out! Now!"

By then, the handmade curtains in Onni's room were ablaze, and the flames had started to burn the wallpaper.

"Come on, Tyyne!" Martti barked. "We can't wait any longer! We'll be engulfed in flames if we don't!"

"I've got to go back our bedroom to get mother's and father's photograph!" Tyyne insisted. "If this house burns to the griound, it'll be only thing I have to remember them by!"

Martti grabbed his wife firmly by her arm and shook her. His teeth were clenched and his face hard as he snapped at her loudly.

"Tyyne, listen to me, for God's sake! By the time you get to the bedroom, grab the photograph and get back out here, this room will be blazing! You've got to believe me! Let's get out!"

Tyyne relented and reluctantly ran out the door behind Martti and Onni. They could see Pentti Toivola and his teenaged son Pekka running from their place towards them, each carrying two wooden buckets. They had seen the flames which had ascended and burned through the dry shingled roof which went up like tinder.

Martti shouted to Onni, "Go to the sauna and get a couple of buckets! Then draw water from the well and join me at Heikki's window! I'm going to see if I he's managed to climb out . . . or if I can climb in and pull him out."

"Martti, that's too dangerous!" Tyyne exclaimed.

"We've got to try and get him out!" He grabbed the shovel from the mudroom.

When Martti went around the house to the window to Heikki's room, he wasted no time smashing the glass with the shovel. Immediately, flames jumped through the window, causing Martti to drop backwards to the ground. The smashed window allowed a stream of oxygen to enter the room and feed the ravenous flames. Martti knew he couldn't climb in the window.

When Onni arrived at the window, breathless from the effort to run carrying the buckets of water, Martti ordered him to throw the water on the flames exploding out of the window. But the flames defied the water intended to extinguish them and seemed to burn with even more vehemence. Martti and Onni could only take a few steps back and stand and regard the fire helplessly. The heat was overpowering.

Pentti and Pekka had tried the same at the front of the house, with similar results. The whole lot of them – Martti, Tyyne, Onni, Pentti and Pekka – gathered in the middle of the yard, watching in disbelief as the flames engulfed the entire house. Martti was breathing hard. Tyyne had her hand over her mouth, shaking her head despondently as awareness grew of what they were losing. Onni could barely watch. It seemed as if he were observing himself staring blankly at the flames.

For almost an hour they maintained their desolate vigil. The adrenaline rush that made his escape from the burning house possible had caused Onni not to notice the palm of his hand. It was beginning to throb with pain now.

Pentti reached out his hand to shake Martti's. Pentti looked Martti empathetically in the eyes but didn't utter a word. Pentti's wife Lempi put her arm around Tyyne and began to lead her towards Toivola.

"Come, we'll have some coffee. I'll make beds for you. There's nothing more than anyone of us can do tonight."

Without replying, as though in a paralyzed trance, the Syrjälas silently obeyed their compassionate neighbor and formed a solemn, disbelieving parade to Toivola. Not one of them looked back at the smoldering heap of destruction that had been Kuokkala.

~ ~ ~ ~ ~ ~ ~ ~ ~ ~ ~ ~ ~ ~ ~ ~

Sheer exhaustion finally allowed the family to fall asleep. As soon the sun rose over the horizon after its few hours in hiding, Martti tiptoed through the Toivolas' *tupa* towards the door and his boots. Onni was only partially asleep and heard Martti's movements, and decided to follow.

The men didn't say a word to each other. They crossed the Toivola yard and then the road and eyed the damaged house.

"My God!" Martti uttered, a phrase Onni had never heard his father utter before.

Rivulets of black smoke were still rising from the charred remains of the house. The men stopped at their property line before continuing.

They headed immediately to the window to Heikki's room. Wispy spills of smoke were wafting out the window. Martti tried putting his head through the window, careful not to scratch his face against the sharp jagged edges of the broken glass, but couldn't make out a thing.

Then Onni tried. He squinted, to avoid the stinging smoke, and to focus his eyes. Gradually a form registered in the nerve endings in his retinas and in the neurons of his brain. It was the terribly scorched human form on the ashes of a mattress that had burned almost entirely. The posts of the bed that had supported the mattress were now just a pile of blackened timbers. The form's grotesque face with the mouth gaping wide open was burned beyond recognition. But who else could it be but Heikki?

"I think I see him. The unfortunate fellow has burned to death in his bed. Oh, dear Uncle."

Onni was struck by how inevitable his report to his father sounded, how thoroughly mundane. His father's only brother, now just a distorted, cremated mass amidst the tragic ruins of Kuokkala.

Martti and Onni didn't proceed to inspect the rest of the charred rubble. They had ascertained what they had tiptoed out of the neighbor's house to discover. It didn't feel anywhere near real yet, but both understood in the uttermost depths of their hearts that the lives of the family had been reduced to zero.

~ ~ ~ ~ ~ ~ ~ ~ ~ ~ ~ ~ ~ ~ ~ ~ ~ ~ ~ ~

The Syrjälas were persuaded to stay another night at Toivola. They had spent a part of the day rifling through the sad remains of their home. Teuvo Parkkanen, the village policeman, arrived in a motorized white van with an official from the funeral agency in Oulu. The official put on white cloth full-body overalls and rubber gloves, as did Parkkanen, and carried an empty cloth stretcher. They climbed over the timbers of the burned head beam of the door into Heikki's room. About an hour later, they emerged carrying a white bag on the stretcher. Tyyne burst into tears of anguish when she saw that.

Onni found his way cautiously into what remained of his room. There was nothing left of the wooden set of drawers or bed. The traditional peasant tapestry that Fredriikka had woven and that had hung on the wall near his bed had evaporated completely. He stood speechless in the middle of the devastated room. He realized suddenly that he was holding his breath. He let out his breath. The foul, filthy stench of burned wood was almost overwhelming. His eyes welled up with tears.

When his anguished survey of what was left of his room explored the floor in the corner of his room, he saw his beloved globe. It looked so forlorn, but still intact, miraculously still a recognizable sphere, its surface charred and indecipherable.

He walked over to the corner, and first gingerly touching the globe with the tip of his finger to determine if it was still hot, picked it up in his hands devoutly as though it were a sacred object. He knelt holding the globe, and wept uncontrollably for it, and for all else the family had lost irretrievably.

~ ~

Aukusti and Martta had rushed over in their horse cart right after they'd heard about the fire from Pertti Laakso when he delivered the mail the following morning. Martta wrapped her arms protectively around Onni.

"Oh my dear boy! What sorrow! How devastating! The only home you've ever known! What in heaven's name has been brought down on all of you? What could someone possibly do to deserve this?"

And then, shaking her head incredulously as she scanned the wretched sight of the house, and looking over at her one remaining son, asked, "Could there be anything salvageable from such a mess?"

Onni thought it odd for his grandmother not to ask about her other son, Heikki. Perhaps she had heard from Laakso the news that he had perished in the flames. Or maybe it was just too painful at the moment to acknowledge her loss.

"A house we can rebuild somehow," Tyyne chimed in as she pulled Martta into her embrace, "but poor, God-forsaken Heikki! He's gone forever! A human life cannot be replaced."

Martta said not a word, perhaps could not, or maybe there was no word that could do the tragedy justice. Or, did she resent Tyyne for stating the obvious and rubbing salt, inadvertently or not, into her wound of grief which she was trying to staunch? She just continued to shake her head as though that were the only way she could express her shock and sorrow.

Onni noticed how it seemed almost as though Martta was resisting her daughter-in-law's embrace, like a cat being held against her will on someone's lap.

Aukusti finally spoke.

"God almighty! You'll all come to stay at our home. We'll make room somehow."

He hadn't look at all towards Martta for her approval. Martti didn't look at his wife either when he replied, almost resignedly and with emotional tiredness in his voice,

"I guess there's nowhere else for us to go. We'll have to try to not get in your way. But thank you."

Chapter Eleven:
Peurajoki
Summer 1938

The three Syrjäläs were given the *pirtti*, a smallish
sitting room between the kitchen and Aukusti and Martta's
bedroom. There was a single daybed for Onni on which
Aukusti was accustomed to using for his afternoon nap.
Martta laid down several quilts on the rag rug on the floor
in the corner opposite Onni's bed. Until Aukusti or Martti
made a mattress out of straw in the barn, the quilts would
have to do as a mattress for Tyyne and Martti.

Tyyne was not at all reserved in her prolific thanking her in-laws for all they were doing on their behalf in
their time of distress. Martti and Onni were grateful, too,
but at times it seemed to Onni that his mother's expressions
of her appreciation were bordering on obsequiousness if not
servility.

One evening early in their stay at the elder Syrjäläs',
Tyyne said quietly to Martti, "I know it feels like our life has
been reduced to zero – no livelihood, all our meager supply
of clothes burned, the old rocking chair I inherited from my
mother, everything gone."

Her voice was cracking now. Martti remained as silent as stone. Onni listened with interest, his own eyes welling up with tears as well. His parents were on their backs in
their makeshift bed on the floor. Tyyne rolled over on her
side and placed her hand tenderly on Martti's chest.

"But we're *not* at zero! Not at all! We have your
parents, Martti. Where would we be now without their support? Dear One, we mustn't lose hope. And we have one another! By the grace of the Almighty, the three of us *survived!*
Thank God Onni was still awake reading! If he had been
asleep, none of us might have been spared."

Finally, Martti chimed in, as though he hadn't heard
a word of hers. "It's going to be very hard living here in

these tight quarters, five people in a cottage intended for just two."

Then he added, "I don't know where and how we'll get the money. But I'm damn well going to clear away all that charred rubble and build a new and better home for us, by God!"

"I know you will, Martti. I know you're not afraid of hard work. Maybe Lindholm will have compassion on a former tenant farmer of his and give us a loan." After a brief pause, she added, "Just take a few days, a week maybe, to get over the shock of what's happened."

"Don't you see? What good will it do just lying about? It's when I'm using my hands that I get over things like this? It's by the sweat of my brow that I am able to forget."

There were to be other assets that raised the family above zero level. The rector and his wife came over to the cottage and brought a liver and carrot casserole and freshly-baked rye bread for all of them. The rector was even brave enough in this cottage where he had never been invited before to offer a prayer for renewed strength for the family.

The rector handed Martti an oversized brown envelope as they prepared to depart. "This is for you and the family. Some of the women of the congregation gathered a small amount of cash. It's not a lot, but it's to let you know that many are with you in your loss."

Pentti Toivola and his wife came, too, with the customary food offering. But he also offered to help Martti if he had plans to rebuild over the footprint of the old house. He would come over in the evenings after planting the potatoes or harvesting the hay crop during the day. Alma's husband did so, too. Armas Pakarinen extended a similar offer, even though he and Martti hadn't had much to do with each other since their school days.

Onni could see how uncomfortable such offers of help made his father feel. Martti was more prone to extend help to others than to have to accept the help *of* others. He himself had contributed a small sum in 1934 when the Ketolas' farmhouse had suffered the identical destruction as theirs. He and Tyyne didn't have much to give, but it made Martti feel good to be able to pitch in the little they could. Undoubtedly Martti had been envisioning working the long summer days alone on the house, or with Onni. Onni suspected that his father would have preferred just that.

But perhaps it was the healing effects of time, even though the tragedy had occurred just a week and a few days prior. Maybe the harsh reality of what they had lost had begun to find an acceptance in his mind and heart. Possibly these tangible and kind offers of help from neighbors started to give him more confidence in the goodness of life in spite of his reluctance to be on the receiving side of assistance and aid. Or might it have been Tyyne's earnest words to him that night, and her perpetually hopeful outlook and ability to find the good in the bad? Whatever the cause, Martti's face began to take on a less despondent aspect. He became more animated and vocal than before at the dinner table, and Tyyne seemed relieved.

Onni recalled his father's words from years ago when together they observed the whooper swans returning from the south, about how can fly through even the more turbulent storm and into the fiercest wind because they stop flapping their huge wings and allow the air to hold them up and carry them.

Onni himself had been in a deep reflection and discernment mode. The fire had added a new complication to his life. It was understood by all, including himself, that while Väinö was fulfilling his military obligation, Onni would be his father's deputy, as it were, on the farm. Then when Väinö was discharged and returned home, Onni would pass the batôn to his older brother and head off to the technical college in Oulu to prepare for a career in journalism.

Now it appeared that he would be his father's deputy, his aide-de-camp, alright, but in the project of rebuilding a family home. Onni recognized that that would require more skill with a plane and hammer than he had. Whenever he had helped his father with carpentry projects, he knew he was trying Martti's patience. The best Onni could do was to hand his father the planks or tools as he requested them. Martti obviously would have preferred Väinö as his help-mate, and his older son would have been infinitely more productive. Onni was resigned to that fact, and it didn't par-ticularly hurt his pride excessively now as it used to.

It was as though the fire had burned a huge irrepa-rable hole through the fabric of the family's future. They were still alive and together, to be sure, and they still had the cows for milk and the barn and shed to store the hay. Their new home was going to be built over the ruins of the former one. Yet in some profound, ineffable way, everything seemed *different* now. It was as though his future had been tossed into the air and in its descent it had shattered into small fragments.

But as Onni considered where the pieces may be falling, he realized they could, with some imagination and ingenuity, form a new configuration now. What he had al-ways assumed would be the shape of his future did not *have* to be the only one possible. For generations, the future of all the men in the Syrjälä and Kuokkanen families was limited to the size of their small farm. It was understood by all that the future of the oldest son would be to assume the farm un-til he, in turn, aged and passed it on to this eldest son. The future of any daughters was to marry a man, most likely a farmer, who could provide shelter for them. If there were any younger sons, they would be headed for employment in the lumber camps that dotted the countryside of that part of Ostrobothnia.

Onni, however, had heard a beckoning from distant horizons since he had been a child. He hadn't allowed him-self to pay the call much heed before. Why should he have? To leave to explore distant terrains was just a childish fan-tasy, the voice of his inner adult told him. But now as the fragments of his future continued to fall back to the ground again, Onni discerned the faint outline of a future arranged differently than before.

The thought occurred to him that perhaps he could begin his professional education in Oulu that fall and not have to wait a year until Väinö was back. The thought filled him with a measure of guilt, of course. He'd be abandoning his father at a time when he really needed help. But then again, Alma's husband and Toivola and Pakarinen had offered to lend a hand, and they had demonstrated the requisite skills and know-how on projects on their own properties. His father would not be without help.

Onni shook his head as though trying to return to the here and now, to tear the thought about a new future for himself loose and jettison it from his brain.

However, the thought continued to grow in intensity and clarity in his mind. He could go to school in Oulu and come back to Peurajoki on school breaks and help his father.

But echoing in the chambers of his mind was another voice, this one no less adult than the one that was trying to get him to plant his feet firmly on the ground in front of him. He imagined it to be the voice of his maternal grandfather Aatu, a voice that he had never actually heard because Aatu had died before Onni was born.

"Your imagined world is too limited, boy," the voice said. "The journey that is beckoning you in your depths is longer than the fifty kilometers between Kuokkala and Oulu. The journey I envisage for you - if you are brave enough to pursue it - will require you to board a train and then climb the gangway onto an ocean-crossing vessel. I did that once, boy, and in spite of all the hardships at my destination, I have no regrets."

Chapter Twelve:
Peurajoki
June 1939

Over a year of cohabiting the small cottage had un-
covered some fissures in the new family alignment. The men
seemed to get along and not get on one another's nerves.
Martti talked in a relaxed manner with his father whenever
he had an update on the condition of the farm and fields,
which Aukusti seemed to be increasingly content to be in
Martti's purview now. Other than that both men retreated
into a comfortable taciturnity that bore no hint of tension,
even though Martti was quite anxious about approaching
Lindholm for a loan to rebuild his house.

The tension between Martta and Tyyne, however, was
almost palpable. Onni seldom heard an explicit argument between the two. They probably kept any negative feelings towards the other or the crowded conditions tightly under
wraps for the sake of Martti and Onni. Soon the two women
opted to take turns preparing the main meal of the day separately rather than cooking together. Martta had her own
mental recipes for stew or pea soup, and Tyyne had the ones
she'd learned from her own mother. Whenever they had tried
to cook the meal together, Onni could see the look of disapproval on Martta's face if Tyyne added too much salt into the
stew or cooked it too long so that the tiny pieces of beef in the
stew were too well-done. It was obvious that Tyyne was ex-
pending a lot of effort to trying to please her mother-in-law,
or at least not displease her in any way. She was apologizing
for what Onni thought were terribly minor infractions of an
unspoken but powerful kitchen code, or no breach at all.

There was even one occasion when the preparation
of the meal the men was complete, and the men were given
the signal to come to the table, Martta simply exited the
kitchen without saying a word and, slamming the door just
loudly enough to be heard by the others, closed herself in the
bedroom.

Tyyne's face was red with anger. Martti's displayed irritation at his mother. Onni shifted in his chair to try to alleviate his discomfort in the wake of such open emotional tension.

Aukusti tried to lighten the mood and turn Onni's attention to other matters.

"We don't have much food to eat these days. But, Onni, I can remember when times were even more desperate."

"You're not going to bring up the story from the civil war days about how you had to eat rats, are you, father?" Martti asked a bit irritably.

"What so bad about that?" Aukusti asked. "The boy hasn't heard the story. Let him learn a little about how things used to be." But Aukusti took the hint and stopped himself before launching into the story.

~~~~~~~~~~~~~~~~~~~~~~~~~~~~~~~~~~~~~

A few evenings later, Onni lay on his side on his bed, trying to avoid tossing and turning and waking up the rest of his family. Sleep wouldn't come.

The sun had finally escaped behind the horizon. It was almost midnight, but it was a tentative hazy twilight as though night wasn't totally convinced it wanted to descend.

Onni was in the delightful nether space between wakefulness and sleep when the body finally relaxes and begins to surrender and the mind is hushed. Faintly at first, Onni began to hear sounds from the direction of his parents' makeshift bed on the floor. Tyyne was moaning softly. At first, Onni wondered if she was weeping quietly over the tensions with Martta. But the realization grew in him that the sounds indicated another kind of moaning, a kind that accompanies pleasure. It had been so long since the sound of joy and pleasure was heard within the family that it seemed so foreign.

73

Even though he was trying to muffle his voice, eventually Martti erupted in a stifled groan, the kind of sound Onni had heard his father make when he was lifting a heavy weight onto the wagon with all his might, as though the expulsion of a deep groan would somehow add strength and power to the effort of the muscles. Then he heard Marti exhale deeply, contentedly.

He recognized Martti's groan followed by silence as something he himself had experienced, not with an actual girl or woman, but in private moments of his own when he fantasized about Anna-Liisa, visualized her in her underclothing, or even unclothed, and did what young men engaging in such daydreaming do when alone. At the point of climax, he had let out a similar groan, stifled because he hadn't wanted his parents or grandparents in the neighboring room to hear.

Onni pulled his head underneath the covers. Hurriedly, he placed his hands over his ears. He didn't want to hear what he now realized he was hearing. He had a pretty good idea of what had taken place. He knew, of course, that for his parents to have conceived four children, somewhere along the line they had to have had sexual intercourse. But he couldn't picture his parents actually engaging in the act. His father and mother hardly ever touched each other, and only once or twice could Onni remember his parents embracing in front of others.

Then there followed some shifting on the mattress, probably the straightening out of sheets that had been tousled. Then silence.

Onni turned over onto his back. He could hear Martti's subdued snoring. He could even hear his mother's restful breathing as she slept.

This cottage is too small for five of us. The two families are related by blood, true, but we're as different as oil and water sometimes. The sooner we're back in a home of our own, the better.

Only, Onni had begun to wonder seriously if he could wait that long.

Chapter Thirteen:
Peurajoki
August 1939

Even apart from the silent strain between the females in the cottage, there was a distinct element of tension in the air all over Finland. Both Martti and Onni had read articles in the *Kaleva* in recent months about gathering storm clouds in Europe. Hitler of Germany and Mussolini of Italy had formed an alliance, and the language and tone in their public pronouncements and speeches were increasingly shrill and strident. In March 1939 Hitler had engineered his *anschluss* into Austria, declaring a profound lust to unify all the German-speaking peoples on Europe. Austria was added to Greater Germany.

Stalin and Hitler had signed a non-aggression pact, in effect dividing Europe into two spheres of influence. Finland was assigned to the Soviet sphere along with Estonia, Latvia and Lithuania. What the two dictators meant exactly by "sphere of influence" was a mystery. to the Finns certainly, and perhaps even to Stalin and Hitler themselves. But having been a part of the Russian Empire from 1809 until 108 years later, Finns had their fears and suspicions as to what Stalin at least had in mind.

"The bastard thinks he can walk all over Finland again," Martti said as he slammed the newspaper down on the table beside the reading chair.

"Isn't that something," chimed Aukusti from where he was sitting. "They're two peas in a pod, aren't they? Hitler and Stalin? They deserve each other. Not much to choose between them, is there? A treaty? God, neither of 'em would know how to keep his word."

"I get nervous every time Stalin shifts positions in his chair," Martti added. "The Commander-in-Chief must feel the same way. Otherwise, why order all conscripts limited to their base? Call up this year's 19-year-olds when last year's

76

haven't yet been discharged? For Christ's sake, Väinö was supposed to come home in February."

"Can the army really keep him indefinitely like this?" Tyyne asked.

"Not unless there's a real threat of war," Martti said with obvious resentment. "Stalin and Hitler are sure as hell making certain there will be one. Stalin's God- damned people are starving, and he's out there raising an army."

"Don't you think people can work it out?" Tyyne asked, desiring reassurance more than information. "Surely both the Russians and Germans haven't forgotten the horrors of the last war. It's only been a little over 20 years."

"Mankind has a habit of remembering only what's convenient to remember, and then forgetting the rest," Aukusti opined.

Martti shook his head at the situation. Tyyne, Martta and Onni eyeballed one another with a silent look that said, desperately, "I hope to God for Väinö's sake that he's wrong."

Lightening Martti's mood and alleviating his stress was the fact that old Lindholm had agreed, however reluc- tantly, to give a loan to Martti to begin rebuilding the house. Martti knew that such news would make Tyyne especially happy: there was light at the end of the tunnel. The prospect of getting back into her own proprietary space soon lifted her spirits and caused her, consequently, to be more pleasant in Martta's presence.

Without telling his parents, on one of his errand rides to the church village, Onni had made a side trip to the post office, housed in the cooperative store, and enquired of post- master Lagerquist about the procedure for applying for a passport.

"Is the young Syrjälä intending to go on a trip?" Lagerquist asked with a mischievous glint in his eye. "A cruise to Germany, or France, or England, perhaps."

Onni was reluctant to give Lagerquist any more information than necessary, for he inevitably had contact with just about every adult resident of Peurajoki and the environs served by his his branch of the Finnish National Postal System. Onni had no idea of whether Lagerquist could be trusted to be judicious with the information that he possessed in his omniscient position. He knew Pentti Laakso was capable of being a leaky source of intelligence about the comings and goings on other farms if it were pried out of him by a hot cup of coffee or a glass of *Schnapps*.

"Nothing particular right now," Onni replied. "I just think it's always good to be prepared in case."

"In case of what, may I ask?"

"Oh, I don't know. In case I have reason or a desire to go to another country."

"I can't think of what reason we'd have to go anywhere these days. The world's not much better anywhere else."

Onni managed to wrench out of Lagerquist the information that he would have to go personally to the Oulu Provincial Office to apply for a passport and have his picture taken.

As he was preparing to leave, he thanked Lagerquist, and just as he was almost out the door, added, "Mr. Lagerquist, I don't want to alarm my parents just now or cause them to suspect something that very well may not happen. I would appreciate if we kept this conversation just between you and me for the time being."

78

With each passing day, Onni was more certain of the plan he was considering and had started pursuing. The question was, whom to tell first of the plan, and for that matter, how to put it. Tyyne would be the more receptive of the two to his idea, he knew, but she also had the better ability to cause him to change his mind.

Onni chose the customary Saturday evening session in the sauna as the time and circumstance in which to inform Martti and Aukusti. The sauna had always been the place where he and Martti could talk about matters without being self-conscious with a female audience.

Onni knew Martti was a practical man who wanted to get to the point rather than beating around the bush. Perhaps Martti would be in a good frame of mind with the difficult conversation with the former landlord behind him.

"Father, I've been thinking very seriously about our family's situation," Onni began.

"It's going to get better now. We'll get started on the rebuilding right away and get the foundation dug before the frost."

"You know that I've thought about going to Canada since I was little."

"*Canada!?,* Jesus Christ! Aukusti blurted out. "Like old Aatu Kuokkanen? You're as crazy as he was."

"I have been thinking of studying journalism in Oulu at first," Onni continued. "But since the fire, and our lives have changed so and become uprooted, I've been thinking, maybe this is an opportunity for me to forge a new path through life, a once-in-a-lifetime opportunity."

"You have all the opportunity a boy needs right here," Martti countered.

"I know you want me to lend a hand with the rebuilding."

"It's a big job, son. Too big for one man. Pappa is too old now to do much to help."

Martti sent an apologetic glance in Aukusti's direction.

"No offense, Pappa. I'm just naming the facts."

"But you know yourself that I wouldn't be of much help, either," Onni inserted. "Toivola and Pakarinen and Alma's husband have said that they would help. Now that the hay is almost all in, they'll have more time to help you."

Onni disliked the boyish tone of desperation in his voice as he spoke. It reminded him of times when as a child he had pestered his father to buy him licorice candy and Manninen's store when they had gone there to purchase supplies.

"If you're going to run a farm someday, boy, you'll need to learn some building skills."

"I know, father. But I'm not the firstborn son. Väinö is, and when he gets home from the military, he'll be ready to begin taking over."

"Then you'll need to learn a trade," Martti said, his voice beginning to show his growing annoyance.

Marti scooped a ladle full of cold water from the wooden buckets and tossed it on the hot rocks on the heater in the corner of the sauna. Onni felt the rush of heat on his skin almost immediately.

"But I don't think I'm suited to learn a trade," he said.

The look on Martti's face suggested he wasn't inclined to disagree with his son's self-assessment.

"I want to be a journalist and write articles for the *Kaleva*."

80

"Leave such things to people who don't have a farm-house to rebuild."

"To be as honest as I can be: I don't really want to spend the rest of my life running a farm, father."

Again, to his own ears, he sounded like the little boy who protested to his parents years ago that he didn't want to eat the turnip casserole.

But he felt instant relief that he had gotten it out. He couldn't look his father in the eye at first as a tense silence ensued. He was concerned that his words had offended Martti.

"I'm sorry I feel that way," he inserted in an effort to mollify his father. "I don't mean to hurt you. You're the best farmer in Peurajoki, father. But I don't think I can do it, or enjoy it if I did become one."

Now Martti's face was beginning to redden. He raised his voice and responded, "We poor Finns don't have the luxury of *liking* our work. That's just what it is: *work*. You do what you have to do to put potatoes and milk on the table."

That seemed to put at a punctuation point on the conversation. A silence dripping with tension ensued.

"Goddamit, boy! You ruined a good session in the sauna."

At that, Martti stepped down onto the floor angrily and disappeared through the door. Onni and Aukusti were left behind to finish their sauna session in awkward silence.

But Onni remembered Heikki's advice: *"Don't settle for reading about life in a book. Go out and live it first-hand."* That seemed to fortify his faltering confidence and courage.

When Onni and Aukusti came back into the *tupa* from the sauna, their hair wet and faces red from the heat, Martti wasn't there.

81

"Is father coming in later?" Tyyne asked innocently.

"I imagine he'll be in shortly," Aukusti said, looking at Onni who looked hopelessly repentant.

It was almost an hour before Martti came back into the house. He gave no explanation. He walked directly into the *pirtti* that constituted their bedroom and put out the light.

Tyyne sensed immediately that something had occurred in the sauna to send Martti into one of his periods of silent glowering. Tyyne had been on the receiving end many times.

Onni was too uncomfortable to remain in the house. He, too, wanted to lie on his bed and replay the exchange with Martti in the sauna. But he knew that Martti needed to be alone. It would be terribly uncomfortable for the two of them to be sulking silently on two beds just a few meters from each other. Onni stepped out into the August night that despite the lateness of the hour was a pale twilight.

Now Tyyne knew that whatever issue Martti was stewing over involved Onni.

"What happened out there tonight?" she asked Aukusti.

Aukusti answered, "I'd better leave that for one of them to tell you."

~~~~~~~~~~~~~~~~~~~~~~~~~~~~

In the morning, Martti still wasn't talking. He got himself a pickled herring from the pantry and went out in the direction of the last hayfield that hadn't been harvested yet.

Bringing in the hay was a light enough job that Aukusti could help. He walked out into the field with a pitch-fork and rake in his hand. He raked some cut hay on the ground into a pile, and then lifted the pile with his pitchfork onto a raised erect stake. At first, father and son said not a word.

82

Then Aukusti broke the silence.

"Maybe the boy has a point, Martti."

"Don't tell me you're siding with him," Martti shot back. "Didn't you hear how juvenile his notions about writing for a newspaper are?

"Does it have to be a competition between you two? It's an unfair contest because you have all the power."

Aukusti left a pregnant pause to let his words sink in.

"Besides," he added after a while, I wonder if some of those writers for the *Kaleva* might be farmer's sons. And how many of them might have had similar difficult conversations with their fathers as you and Onni are having right now?"

Martti still looked determined and fixed in his opinion. But he was feeling chided by his father, now.

Aukusti continued, "People aren't going to be farming until kingdom come. It's all you and I know. But the world is changing, Martti. The young folks in Finland aren't forever going to want to get callouses on their hands from physical labor."

"Then who's going to grow the food for them if they don't grow it themselves," Martti retorted.

"Come on, son. We ourselves don't grow everything ourselves that we eat any more. We don't have any cucumbers growing in our vegetable patch. And yet Martta had some on the table yesterday afternoon. Martti, farming is changing, even in poor old Finland."

"Maybe that's the problem these days. The young folks are all about change."

"It's hard to let go of all that we've known for so long."

At this, Martti slowed down his frantic pace of raking and lifting piles of hay. He came to a complete stop.

"Things are hard enough," Martti said. "It would be so much easier if things just stayed the same."

"Mummu and I had to let go of *you* once, too, Martti."

"What do you mean? I stayed right here nearby, doing the same thigs you had been doing all your life. I didn't run off somewhere where I could *like* my work."

"No, you didn't. But I wonder if times had been different, you might have given it some thought."

Martti didn't have a rejoinder. He hung his head slightly as though in defeat.

"Maybe it's time you let your younger son go now, too. It's *his* life, after all."

Martti divulged the contents of his conversation with Onni later that evening to Tyyne when Onni was out checking on the livestock. He didn't mention his later conversation with his own father, however.

Her responses, predictably, were much the same as Martti's earlier, only tinged with more emotion, especially fear. Martti simply relayed to her Onni's answers to his objections.

Finally, after a pensive pause, Tyyne remarked, "He's going to leave one way or another, Martti. Every boy has to make his own path."

Martti remained silent. She could tell that the idea of Onni blazing his own path hit a nerve.

She continued to press her point.

"You yourself have spoken for some time now about how the dark clouds of war are gathering. Onni is two years away from being called up into the military."

Martti could sense where this was headed.

Tyyne continued. "It must be because the powers-that-be know there's going to be war with Russia that Väinö has been held back and not allowed to come home. I'm really afraid that he'll be dispatched into the war."

"The fatherland is going to need all hands on deck," Martti said.

"The poor Varjanens lost both sons in the civil war. I don't want that to happen to us. At least Onni can be safe from the danger of war in faraway Canada."

"He didn't say anything about going to Canada to *escape*."

"Maybe he's not thinking of that at all. But I am."

Onni was rather surprised in the days ahead how little resistance he was encountering to his stated notion of emigrating to Canada. Tyyne was tearful the next morning, but she seemed to be resigned to the idea. Surprisingly, Martti turned positively affirming. Since he had received he generous loan from Lindholm, he handed over the money that had been given to him by neighbors and other villagers in the wake of the fire for Onni to use for the fare and other expenses incurred in preparing to travel.

Onni rode the bus one day, that had just begun service to Oulu a few months earlier, to the provincial office in Oulu to apply and pay the fee for a Finnish passport. The functionary at the office raised his eyebrows when Onni asked for the application form.

"There aren't many applying to leave the country just now," he said. "You're not trying to evade your military service, are you?"

"I'm only seventeen," Onni rejoined a little defensively, as though his courage and patriotism were being questioned. "I will probably be back by the time it's my turn to serve."

"Do you have your parents' permission?"

"Yes. I can get it in writing if necessary."

"It's not up to us, you understand?" the man continued. "We can issue you the passport. But both the United States and Canada have tightened their borders considerably in the past few years. They're not as interested in immigrants from Finland, or anywhere else, for that matter, as they used to be. It would help if you were a Limey. Canada will always take them."

Onni was a put off that this stranger was presuming to pour cold water on his plan.

"My grandfather spent a few years in Canada and did all right. I'll take my chances"

Chapter Fourteen:
Peurajoki
Early September 1939.

Onni wrote to inform Väinö of his imminent departure. He realized that though the two of them were different in so many ways, Onni would miss Väinö – had been missing him already when his discharge was delayed. He was eager to hear from Väinö stories of life in the barracks. He worried more about the possibility of Väinö's being retained for active duty should war break out than he had admitted to himself.

In early September, there were signs that Germany was preparing for an invasion of Poland. That was violation Number One of the so-called non-aggression pact Hitler had made with Stalin. Not at all surprisingly, Soviet troops were marching towards Poland as well. Violation Number Two. Field Marshall Carl Gustav Mannerheim contemplated the mobilization of Finnish forces under the guise of additional refresher training while the two big powers were looking the other way at each other.

Väinö's Joensuu battalion was ordered north to Kajani. Was this the writing on the wall the whole family had dreaded?

Onni had ordered a third-class ticket from Hanko to Halifax by mail and was waiting for the actual ticket to arrive. He had purchased a brown cardboard suitcase in Oulu once he had passport in hand.

There was still one preparation to make, one that he had been delaying: he wanted to say goodbye in person to Anna-Liisa.

A couple of afternoons before his scheduled departure on the train to Helsinki, and from there to Hanko, he resolved to face the inevitable. He walked to the Huhtamäki farm. As he approached, he spied a solitary figure in one of the fields raking up the remnants of this season's hay crop. It was Anna-Liisa, dressed in an old and worn peasant's smock, a kerchief around her head, and black Nokia boots on her feet.

She saw Onni approaching. Her complexion turned a beet red. She, too, had been dreading this moment. She felt the urge to flee, so embarrassed was she in her dowdy field outfit and with no opportunity to prepare emotionally for this encounter.

Onni opened the gate, closed it behind him, and took steps towards her. Anna-Liisa continued to ply her rake on the ground to give the impression that she hadn't noticed him. Her thrusts of the rake to the ground grew more determined, her swings of the rake lifting the strands of hay to the wagon beside her more ferocious. She kept her eyes peeled to the earth beneath her feet and continued raking as before, only more intensely.

Onni couldn't see her face which was turned away from him. He continued his approach until he was about two meters away from her, and then paused in his tracks, wondering if now was the time to speak. But she appeared to be so inattentive, perhaps even unaware, that he was there.

"Anna-Liisa."

"Well, at least you haven't forgotten my name," she hurled back with a sarcasm that stunned him. He had never heard her speak in such a sardonic tone, at least not to him.

"Just a tiny bit more to do to bring haying season to a close, eh?" Onni knew it was a perfectly inane remark, but he couldn't think of any other way to begin the conversation.

Anna-Liisa stopped her raking for a moment and gave him such a look of contempt that said loudly, "That's so obvious a question I'm not even going to answer it." Then she resumed her furious raking. The movement of the rake on the ground caused the familiar aroma of damp hay to rise to Onni's nostrils.

Since he hadn't been expecting such a frigid welcome, the look of contempt didn't register with Onni whatsoever.

"I wanted to come by and say goodbye. I'm leaving on the train south from Oulu is a few days."

"Oh, I didn't know."

But it was obvious to him that the lack of surprise or concern in her voice revealed just the opposite.

"Yes, I'm going to give life a try in Canada."

"Well, why wouldn't you? Here's nothing for you here, I suppose."

Her tone sounded angry, which again surprised him, but he thought he discerned a hint of hurt as well.

What's going on here? I'm totally confused. I was dreading this because I was afraid she'd cry, and then that would cause me to cry like a baby. But she seems so angry. What is this?

"I'm going to miss you, Anna-Liisa."

"Well, I wouldn't let myself feel too badly about it."

"I'll write to you from the ship and when I arrive in Canada to let you know I've arrived safely."

"You're a man now, Onni. You can take care of yourself. We'll take care of ourselves here."

"You don't want me to write, then?"

She didn't respond right away. Her face was still turned away from him, but if it hadn't been, he would have seen that her eyes were closed tightly shut as though by sheer frce of will she were holding back tears.

She took a deep breath to fortify herself and then said, "If you want, Onni. You're a free man. Who am I to tell you what you can or cannot do."

"Well, do you *want* me to write?"

At this, she ceased her obsessive raking and turned her face towards him. She was on the verge of tears, he could see. Her look and her voice softened

"I don't think your letters would give me much comfort, Onni. Quite opposite, in fact, I fear. I don't think I could bear to read them and know I'll most likely never see you again."

"But you will, Anna-Liisa. My grandfather went to Canada for a few years, but he came back."

"Life in Canada will be so much better. You'll want to stay; I just know it."

"That's not my intention."

"The best laid plans . . ."

"You don't believe me?"

"Onni, life here in Peurajoki is simple and predictable. I'll be a farmer's wife like my mother, and like her mother before her. But in the rest of the world right now, life's not so simple. You can't predict anything. Things are going to change, and plans and intentions will have to change with them."

What she said was true, he could see. Her words sounded so wise, so adult. He felt a little juvenile himself by comparison. Her words were laced with pain, and resignation to the pain. She was angry that his decision to leave Peurajoki was, without her control or approval, effecting irrevocable changes in what she had dared to fantasize as a possible future She regretted now that she had allowed her imagination to contrive a future that might include him even though he was virtually the first and only boy she had ever liked. Foolish, foolish girl!

There was a silence, a kind of interlude or stalemate during which Onni looked away towards the adjacent hayfield, as if sensing that Anna-Liisa wanted privacy.

Finally, he broke the silence. "I'm sorry that my decision is hurting you and making you angry. I wasn't really sure if I meant anything to you or not. I have a lot of affection for you."

"Then you're not very smart, Onni Syrjälä, that's all I can say."

He knew now that he couldn't kiss her goodbye as he had envisioned in his plans for this encounter. That would have bound her more firmly to him than she could stand.

"I think you had better go now," she said, her voice hardening again to its previous aloofness.

Onni stood still for what seemed like a long, awkward moment, wanting to say something comforting and reconciling so that they didn't part with such an emotional distance between them. His lips parted and he took a breath to say something, then thought the better of it, and just said "Goodbye, Anna-Liisa," and turned and headed back towards the gate and the road home beyond it.

Had be looked back, which he dared not do, he would have seen that she had stopped her raking and turned her back to him, and was shaking as she wept bitterly.

Chapter Fifteen:
Peurajoki
Early September 1939

For the several remaining days at Kuokkala, Onni felt the weight of his awkward farewell with Anna-Liisa. He had totally misjudged how it would go. He lay on his bed trying to go to sleep, but her distant voice, her indifference to him, her surprising anger gnawed at him and he was unable to fall asleep until he read long into the night. How little he understood, he realized, about matters of the heart. He still felt acutely the pang of embarrassment and confusion as much as he did at the time of rejection itself.

Tyyne noticed how downcast he was. At first, she hoped that he was having second thoughts about the whole idea of traveling to Canada. Then she attributed Onni's sadness the painful anticipation of missing his parents and brother and sisters. Finally, she landed on the realization that Onni's farewell to Anna-Liisa had not gone well and that his melancholy was actually lovesickness. But she didn't say a word about it to Onni. She knew that nothing she could do would really help with that malady.

The morning of departure arrived. Possessing one of the three automobiles in the whole village, the rector offered to take Onni to the Oulu train station. Tyyne, Martti and Martta waited in the front yard with Onni, who stood self-consciously beside a single suitcase that was to be his companion and containing all his resources for the journey of at least two weeks, maybe three. He had packed a couple of his books to read on the train.

He was dressed as though he were going to church. He wore the suit he had inherited from Väinö, the sleeves a little too short. One corner of the collar of his white shirt was curled untidily over the collar of the coat as though he'd dressed in a hurry. His mother smiled and reached up to straighten the collar and tuck it underneath the suit jacket's collar.

The rector's Skoda turned onto the property. From inside the car, the rector nodded his wordless morning greeting. Onni wasn't as happy to see his arrival as he had anticipated. Martti kept his eyes riveted to the ground and extended his right hand to his son and shook it and said, "Have a good journey, son." Martta gave him an awkward embrace and tearfully said, "Surely the Creator will take care of His own."

Tyyne went back into the house, and came out holding a brown paper bag and a book. Handing the bag to Onni, she said, "There's rye bread and a boiled egg, a piece of cheese, and some herring in the jar, for you to eat on the train."

Then, after pausing, she handed Onni the book. He opened it to find all but the first page blank. He noticed that the first page was in his mother's familiar handwriting.

"I know you like to write. This is a blank diary for you to record what you see and hear and experience on your journey. Perhaps when you arrive safely, you can send it to us to read about your adventures. But only if you like."

She then enveloped Onni in her arms and said in a voice barely above a whisper, "I have been praying that God keep you safe and that you are happy, come what may."

She spoke the last words of the sentence very quickly, her voice rising in pitch in a herculean effort not to burst into tears and embarrass her son on the occasion of his departure on his pursuit of his dream.

The rector had stepped unseen out of his car and stood silently at a respectful distance from the family. When he sensed that the sad domestic drama before him had progressed sufficiently past its climax, he asked Onni if he was ready to go.

Onni nodded without a word and stepped solemnly into the front passenger seat through the door that the rector thoughtfully held open for him. Once seated, Onni turned his head towards his family and, avoiding looking at his mother, gave an uncertain smile.

In a final gesture, he waved his right hand as the rector pulled out onto the road and quickly disappeared from the family's view.

BOOK THREE:

BEGINNING

AGAIN

"And suddenly you know: It's time to start something new and trust the magic of beginnings."

— *Meister Eckhart*

Interlude
Suomussalmi, Finland
January 10, 1940

Who *were* these eerie, mysterious, motionless statues in olive uniforms in the middle of a silent forest in northeastern Finland?

No matter how many strides Riihimäki took on his skis, no matter how close to the unnerving group of silent figures he approached, they did not move. When he was within a few meters of the figures, he lowered the rifle and let out his stifled breath. His eyes widened in wonder bordering on fright. In the middle of the grouping, there was a circle a meter or so wide of small granite rocks, and in the center of it a pile of charred remains of a campfire. The faces of the frozen figures looked vaguely and hauntingly human, though distorted into grotesque caricatures and rendered colorless by the freezing cold. One of the figures was erect, as if standing by a fire to warm itself.

Or, was it warming *himself,* a human being*?*

The partially consumed carcass of a horse off to the side repulsed him. The remaining three figures lay motionless in the snow near the campfire as well. He tried to turn one figure over, the overcoat as hard as sheet metal, but it was frozen to the ground beneath. An unfamiliar recognition and terror pulsed through Riihimäki and settled in the pit of his stomach.

These were Russian soldiers! In their panicked retreat back to the Russian border from Siilasvuo's ferocious counterattack, the poor bastards had frozen to death while stopping to warm themselves and cook the flesh of their packhorse horse.

Without warning, an abrupt and unbidden *crack* echoed throughout the forest. Instantly, Riihimäki crumpled onto the snow, his face distorted in shock and sudden pain and resignation to his fate. His hands clutched his breast. A stain of bright red spread on his white snowsuit.

Another explosive *crack,* and Riihimäki's limp, lifeless corpse was propelled backward half a meter on the frozen ground like a little girl's doll lying on the floor kicked irreverently by a malicious brother.

Chapter Sixteen:
Oulu
Early September 1939

As the steam locomotive began to chug and emit dense black smoke into the blue sky, Onni looked out the window of his coach. He came to the realization that while he'd been to Oulu several times, he had never been to points the least bit to the south of the provincial capital. The terrain was just as flat as in Peurajoki, although the harvested hayfields were still green as they neared Seinäjoki, not the faded brown that they had turned at Peurajoki after the first frost earlier in September. The farmhouses had several coats of bright red or yellow paint, as well. Despite their familiar shape, these farmhouses were so unlike the ones in Peurajoki where, if the farmsteads had ever been painted before, they looked sadly faded and weathered by life. In spite of the decade-long depression, some people in Finland were apparently doing better than merely surviving. Some were enjoying and creating beauty, a rare commodity in the more impoverished villages in the north like Peurajoki.

Onni sat alone. Small groups of young men in the grey uniform of the Finnish military, just boys a couple of years older than Onni, but not looking very much older at all, boarded the train at Ylivieska, and Seinäjoki, and most of the stations afterwards until the train pulled into the station in Helsinki. A few of the uniformed men talked to each other in hushed voices. The ones who boarded singly remained silent the whole way, as did many of the ones who came aboard in pairs of small groups. Each one looked as though he were contemplating something immense, some invisible threshold into the unknown they were crossing. They all had their gaze focused on the floor.

At Seinäjoki, Onni noticed a very plainly-dressed mother step into the train holding the hand of a four or five-year-old boy. She noticed the young soldiers, and then seemed to make an intentional choice to seat herself and her young son in seats that were as far removed from the soldiers as possible.

She made short eye contact with Onni and smiled at him.

The quiet was punctuated only by the click-clack of the steel wheels on the track below. Instead of fighting his urge to sleep, he closed his eyes and used the beat of the train's forward progress as a metronome until he was lost to the world.

When he awoke, he couldn't remember where he was until he saw the fields and farmhouses receding in the window. In his initial excitement about launching the journey, he had forgotten about the blank journal book. He suddenly remembered his mother's nimble handwriting on the first page. He figured that enough time and space had passed since he left Kuokkala that he could read his mother's words without their inviting the wistfulness he had stuffed down into his chest since he and the rector drove off from the front yard of the farm to rise to his consciousness and give birth at such an early stage of the journey to any feelings of regret or homesickness. He took the book out of his bag, turned to the first page, and read his mother's parting words:

Dear Onni.

Through my tears, I want to express my pride in the courage and curiosity you are exhibiting by your venturing on this journey. I can't put into words how much I will miss you while you're gone. But you know that I have always had admiration for my father for his going to Canada before I was born, and now I feel that same vicarious joy in your pilgrimage to the New World.

Of course, my father returned and resumed life here in Peurajoki. I do not presume to know if you will do the same or even if I have any right to expect you to come back. But you know, Onni, that the doors to your home (she had written "our home" then crossed it out the word "our") *will always be open.*

It's a big and perilous world you are entering. I pray that the challenges and temptations of the world do not erode the gentleness and kind-heartedness of your beautiful nature.

I know that you are too sensitive and perceptive to make a life here on the farm, or to be happy in such a life. I pray that you are able to discover a way of life that suits your thoughtful and tender nature that will make you happy, in Canada, or back in Finland, or elsewhere in God's world. If I know that you, or any of my children, for that matter, are happy, then I am happy.

Your father and I have not been the best parents, but I do pray that some of our example has left a positive mark on your spirit. A parent always feels that he or she could have, and should have, done more to guide his or her children in the way they should go.

I made my choice to marry your father when my own mother hoped for more for me. But I have been satisfied with my choice, which is why I want to be supportive of your right to make choices for your own life now, even if your choice puts many kilometers and a vast ocean between us. I pray that love can make a bridge over the Atlantic.

Allow me to be the mother just one more time.

Be sure to eat heartily to remain strong. Don't let yourself get worn down and then get sick. Choose your companions wisely and well. If and when you meet a woman with whom you can make a life together, love and cherish her and treat her as well as your father, as conventionally unromantic as you know he is, has treated me and his children. Do not dishonor your elders, as you have been taught. Be prepared to lend a helping hand to your neighbor as you have seen your father do.

Oh, and when you wash your clothes, be careful not to wash your white garments in the same bucket of water as your clothes of another color.

My heart is heavy with sadness, but I must not be selfish and try to cling to you or hold you back. You will be far away in Canada, but nevertheless, always near at hand in my heart. May God bless you, Onni."

Love, Mother.

Onni hadn't noticed that tears had formed in his eyes, and once he did notice, he closed the book and looked around the coach and hoped that the other passengers, especially the army recruits, hadn't noticed the forming tears.

Onni glanced ahead to the seat where the mother and her son were seated. The young boy had lain his small blond head against his mother's gray woolen raincoat which she had not taken off since she stepped on the train. The mother was smiling knowingly at Onni, and he noticed that she, too, had the beginnings of tears in her eyes. She had not read his mother's words in the journal, yet she seemed to comprehend their contents and import from where she was sitting. She gave a subtle nod to Onni before she closed her eyes to join her little boy in sleep.

The bench on which Onni sat had just a sad, thin cushion hardly more substantial than a piece of worn carpet. He couldn't find a comfortable position to get to sleep again. When he tried to fall asleep, his mind raced ahead to questions and anxieties about the next leg of the journey, or else back to the parting scene at Kuokkala a few hours earlier and his mother's words in the journal. He was relieved that his mother didn't seem to interpret his decision to leave for Canada as any kind of rejection of her or his father. He was familiar enough with her essential selflessness that he felt her acceptance of his right to decide his future for himself was sincere, although he was sure it was not an acceptance at which she had arrived without tears. Her words made him sad, but he could smile through his tears because they also gave him confidence in what he was embarking on.

He needed all that confidence when the train pulled into Helsinki station early the next morning. The station at Oulu had been straight-forward and easily navigable. But he found but the cavernous central station in Helsinki to be absolutely gargantuan. Other passengers seemed to know exactly where to go. Others took a quick reference glance at the huge signboard in the center of the spacious main ticket hall to check for their connection for parts elsewhere along the Gulf of Finland coast. Most were heading straight for the exits to the station square. Pedestrians buzzed by, walking at a pace that Onni found dizzying. Onni lingered, looking up at the signboard, trying to decipher it and find the track number for the train to Hanko. A middle-aged man carrying a leather brief case accidentally bumped Onni's right arm holding his suitcase, but the man didn't stop to apologize even after Onni dropped his suitcase to the floor as a result.

Onni didn't want to walk up to the information desk and ask for the track number when others around him seemed to find the information they needed quite quickly. He'd study the board and find "Hanko" by himself. If he wasn't able to find his way to a town in his own country, he thought, how fit was he to make a journey to a place as far away as Canada.

Chapter Seventeen:
Hanko
September 1939

Entry in Onni Syrjälä's journal:

September 19, 1939

The central station in Helsinki was big. But I think the biggest single thing I have ever seen in my whole life is the *S.S. Arcturus*. That is the name of the ship which I climbed up onto on the gangway today in Hanko harbor. It is operated by the Finnish Steamship Company, and was built in 1898. I don't remember, mother, from the things you said about grandfather's voyage to Canada, but this may very well have been the same ship that he sailed on.

I carried my suitcase on foot from the Hanko train station. When I came around the corner from *Kulmankatu* to *Satamankatu*, my eyes beheld the massive white steamer waiting in the harbor to accept its passengers. I knew that to cross an ocean we would have to be on a ship bigger than the ferry from Oulu to Hailuoto Island. But seeing the *Arcturus* for the first time almost took my breath away! It is almost 90 meters long, just about as long as the soccer pitch in the church village. Even from the level of the loading dock, it looks as though you could pile several Finnish farmhouses on top of one another and the still wouldn't reach the height of the third deck (which is the highest). You can't see how much of the ship is below the eater, but they say that it's at least 6 meters. The part of the hull you can see looks a little beaten with dents from all the voyages it has made.

If grandfather indeed sailed on this ship or one like it, he would have been in third class. Third class passengers in those days, I'm told, slept in the lowest level of the hold of the ship in bunk beds, men in one large room, the women and children in another. My ticket is "tourist class" because they don't call it third class any more. I am more fortunate than grandfather and those who traveled to Canada or United

States even just twenty years ago because tourist class passengers are housed in small cabins with three single beds crowded together and a small sink between them. I'm a short man, but if I were twenty or so centimeters taller, I'd hit my head on the heating and water pipes just below the ceiling of the cabin. The three of us will have to take turns standing up because there isn't room on the floor of the cabin, what with the three beds, for all three of us to be standing up at the same time.

Since we're below the level of the water's surface, we don't have a porthole to look outside. That means we don't get much fresh air either.

As we were boarding, stevedores were carrying the luggage of the first class passengers, and one tried to take mine from my hand and carry it up the gangway to my cabin. I told him that I am strong enough to carry it on board myself. But of course I said so in Finnish, and the stevedore looked at me uncomprehendingly, although he did say "Finnsk" to me, then hit his chest with his hand and said, "Norsk".

I was afraid I was doing the wrong thing by refusing the help. But one of my cabin mates, a fellow Finn named Eino Komulainen, (I'll say more about him, a lot more, I suspect, in another entry) told me, in his slow Savonian drawl that comes close to making me laugh, that I was smart of refuse the help because the stevedore would be expecting a big gratuity for his efforts. Eino told me that he's even heard that sometimes the stevedore will not leave the bag in your cabin if the gratuity isn't to his liking, and will take the suitcase with him until the "customer" antes up. I am an inexperienced traveler, and I'm trying hard not to do the wrong things that will identify me as such.

The ship departs from the harbor at daybreak tomorrow after all the non-passenger cargo has been loaded onto the ship. I am very excited about the prospect of sailing out of the Gulf of Finland, into the Baltic towards our first stop in Copenhagen. From there on to Hull, England to discharge some passengers and take on new ones. Then we will venture out full steam ahead into the North Atlantic, called the most dangerous ocean in the world.

105

An entry in Onni's journal:

September 20, 1939

We are on the North Sea today, on the way from Co-penhagen to Hull. It was thrilling to push off the from the dock in Hanko. Most folks in all three classes were out on their respective decks, waving back to the hardy souls who had come down to the pier to wave goodbye to their loved ones.

As I observed my fellow third class passengers, I con-cluded that most of us are people of the soil. Most of the men have necks whose skin has been reddened and hardened and furrowed by the sun after many years in the fields. I guess in the case of the Italians, it would be many years in the vine-yards. With their rough hands and dirt underneath their fin-gernails, the women have the look of farmers' wives as well.

Like them, I have lived my whole life on solid ground. When we set off from Hanko, we exchanged our familiar ex-istence for one that is totally new and alien to us. We found ourselves on a deck that has a floor beneath our feet, yet it is not the safe, solid floor of our farm dwellings. We had been accustomed to walking freely and unhampered in our fields and vineyards. Now we were in a space with railings to indi-cate the limits of our existence. We are accustomed to looking to the east or west and beholding a birch forest, and north or south to see our neighbor's fields or farmhouse. You look in any direction out on the sea and all you see around you are is an infinite expanse of grey ocean.

The skills we'd learned and honed as people of the soil aren't of much value on the fickle waves.

I thought of this as I watched Copenhagen harbor, and eventually the Danish landmass, become ever smaller and eventually disappear completely from our view from the deck. I wondered if many of the other third-class passengers were thinking the same thing. We were leaving the known behind, and trusting the fickle sea to bear us up for the remainder of the voyage.

But I find it's hard to trust something as vacillating and unstable as the sea.

I felt fine physically while were still in the Gulf of Finland, and even the Baltic. But yesterday, once we were on the North Sea, the winds picked up and the waves grew to nearly two or three meters high. None of us in our cabin rose up from our bed except to go down the corridor to the toilet when necessary. It was just about impossible to walk without being tossed against the wall of the corridor. I became extremely nauseous. Eino told me, for God's sake, to make my way out onto the deck, or at least to the toilet, to vomit. Unfortunately, I didn't make it in time, and the contents of my stomach from breakfast came spewing out and onto the floor of the corridor. I was still bent over, staring at my own vomit, when a member of the ship's staff was on site with a pail and mop to clean it up. This happens so often, especially on the first day on rough seas, that the ship has a whole team on the staff whose unpleasant task it is to clean up passengers' vomit from the floor before someone else steps in it or slips.

In spite of the best efforts of the cleaning staff, nevertheless there's a slight odor of vomit in the corridor even the next day.

I didn't think about it at the time, but now upon reflection on a calmer sea, these stoic men, many of them Norwegians, who form the staff of this steamer are the opposite of us third-class passengers. They are men of the sea in the same way we are people of the soil. Once we get to Halifax, they will have a brief respite, and then get back on board with new cargo and sail back to Hanko. They live much of their life on the waves. They are at home on it. They can navigate the corridors with steady feet. I suppose they have a domicile on solid ground somewhere, in Oslo perhaps, or Bergen. But I venture to wager that the moment they do get there, their heart begins to yearn for the open vistas of the sea – even if one of their duties will be to clean up the vomit of the tender people of the soil.

When I staggered back to the cabin, Eino asked if I'd made it, and I told him I hadn't, he broke into a hearty laugh. I was rather offended at first, but eventually joined him in the laughter. I felt better after vomiting, but even better when I could laugh about it.

An entry in Onni's journal:

September 21, 1939

Eino is a very interesting roommate. He reminds me of Ossi Kantonen back in Peurajoki – about the same age approaching sixty perhaps, the same short stocky frame, even a voice that is similar to the baritone of Kantonen. His hair is balding, but along the front hairline, not in the back of the head as is the patterns of the Syrjälä men.

Eino has experienced a lot in his life, I can tell, but he doesn't seem to take any of it overly seriously. He seems to have the enviable quality of letting his troubles roll off his back like water off a duck's back. There are about twenty of us Finns on board. They try to keep the Finns together in the same area so that we can communicate with one another. Mind you, our roommate, Jaagup, is a late thirty-something Estonian, but the guys in the next cabin are Finnish. Jaagup got past his Russian "protectors", as he sarcastically calls them, and escaped to Finland in a fishing boat. That's a story I want to hear more about.

Even though he's much older, I find conversation with Eino to be informative and interesting. His view of life and the world seems rather jaded and world-weary. Many of his remarks are couched in a sort of ironic, almost sardonic, humor. For instance, he told Jaagup the other days that Estonian is a second-rate language because it's stolen from the Finns, but to disguise their plagiarism, they drop the final vowel of words and cut the word off with a consonant I guess after all Jaagup has endured, he's not about to let a little good natured ribbing from an older Finn bother him.

108

One of the steamship staff in our area is named Charles. Eino insists on calling him "Charlie Chaplin". But because we Finns have difficulty making the "ch" sound, it comes out as "Sarlie Saplin". Charles went along with it for a while. But since Eino always greets him with a "Good morning, Sarlie Saplin", and then walks by him imitating the tramp character from the movies, seems irritated. In our very basic dining room, there is a server named Dominic – obviously Italian – but Eino keeps calling him Luigi, much to the server's chagrin. "Luigi, some vater, please," he calls out.

Me he calls *Epäonni* – Misfortune – but I tell him that in my own quiet reserved way I feel my given name describes me quite accurately – Onni – Good Luck – and that if he wanted some good luck on this voyage, he'd better stick by me.

"On the contrary, Misfortune," he retorted after he'd finished laughing, "If you want to get by in life without barely a scratch, just stick near Eino Komulainen. My parents should have named *me* Onni!"

Eino is actually going *back* to Canada. I don't know all of the story yet, but apparently he came to Canada originally as a young man the first decade of the century and worked at various jobs in northern Ontario. But he says he never met or heard of Grandfather.

There were supposed to be several hundred passengers from Russia on this ship, but Stalin has closed the borders to keep his subjects in. Eino says that since the Russians eat so much borscht and devour their cabbage, the ship will smell infinitely better because we will be without the farting of the Russians.

There were also supposed to be some German passengers, but Hitler, they say, is just as stingy with his citizens.

"He's going to need fresh meat every day to send out to the front to be slaughtered," Onni says cynically.

An entry in Onni's journal:

September 23, 1939

We were awakened by the sound of Jaagup's glass smashing against the wall above my bed and shattering into a thousand little pieces. He had left the glass on the tiny counter by the sink after brushing his yellowed teeth last night. I awoke up with small shards of glass all over my blanket. It was very early in the morning. Jaagup's beaten old suitcase was forced from out under his bed onto the middle of the cramped floor so that it seemed as though it were trying to force itself under my bed. When it hit the frame of my bed, the impact had broken the little metal hasps and allowed much of the meagre contents of his wide-open suitcase to come pouring out onto the floor.

I was too dazed from having been awakened in such an alarming manner to feel any fear. But within seconds, I felt overwhelming terror such as I have never experienced before in my life.

Funny, that I didn't experience even a hint of seasickness. Perhaps my stomach was so tight with fear that it didn't have the capacity to feel nauseous. Or is there a threshold beyond which this storm had taken us where we aren't susceptible to something as trivial as seasickness?

Jaagup was sitting up in his bed looking more confused than scared. He seemed to be barely emerging from the effects of the vodka he swigs from a small bottle he keeps under his bed. I noticed a clear liquid oozing out from under my bed. His vodka bottle must have rolled out, or more accurately put, been shot out as from a cannon, from under his bed and smashed into the wall under my bed. Within minutes, the smell of vodka saturated the air in the cabin.

We looked over at Eino's bed, since we both knew he had had much more experience in the open seas than either of us. We were of one mind of looking to him for guidance on what this was all about and how were to survive it.

110

But Eino appeared to be sound asleep. Jaagup and I looked at each other in abject disbelief. How was it possible to sleep through the violent rocking of the ship? Was Eino made of some kind of non-human substance that was immune to the terrors and discomforts of a storm like this and allowed him to sleep through it?

Rocking is not exactly the right word. Had some angry or malevolent god agitated the waters of the North Atlantic to watch the *Arcturus* being tossed about violently and mercilessly on the crests and in the troughs of the furious waves?

Up until now, I had known the sea as a pleasant splash against the hull at night. But now it had transformed itself into a beast with thousands of seething claws coiled around our ship. All I could hear an uninterrupted roar from the other side of the hull, like thunder after a bolt of lightning, the breathing of the beast.

I never was especially good at geometry in school, but I'd have to say that the ship was rolling at least 45 degrees to one side, and the before you could get your balance, it rolled back another whole 90 degrees to the other. Through the ceiling, we could hear items smashing against the walls of the second class berths directly above us. Unlike our cabin, the second class cabins have dressers into which the passengers can unpack the contents of their suitcase keep them in good condition during the voyage. The thunderous grinding sound along the floor above must have been the sliding of such an unanchored dresser, followed the deafening crack of its being obliterated against a wall.

In an effort to alleviate my growing sense of panic, I threw off my covers and put my feet on the floor. I succeeded in standing up in spite of the almost irresistible force of the ship's ferocious swaying and shaking.

"Where the hell do you think you're going," Eino asked. "For Christ's sake, get back into your bed! This is no time to go for a bloody walk. Your bed is the safest place right now"

111

I was back in my bed and prone under my covers before Eino had finished shouting his command.

So, Eino was awake after all, or at least now.

"What the hell did you guys expect? A quaint dinner cruise in Copenhagen harbor? Didn't they tell you that the ocean often gets angrier than a bull for no reason at all except that it's huge?"

His words seemed to be tossed about the cabin by the raging storm so that I might have missed hearing a few of them. Seeing that I was having trouble hearing, he raised his voice almost to the level of a shout.

"This storm may last all day, hopefully not more than two or three. It's stronger than you or me. But this ship has weathered them before and survived. So unless you've got to go to the crapper, I'd advise you to stay in your bed and just wait it out."

I was ready to do anything Eino said at this juncture. The strapping Jaagup obeyed his orders as compliantly as a little boy as well. We had, after all, looked to Eino as the experienced one, so we were prepared to heed his advice. The uneven swaying of the ship made reading impossible. So I lay there until I, too, fell asleep, trusting, as Eino did, that the engineers who designed the *Arcturus* had made allowance in their plans for occasions like this, and that the captain and his staff weren't rendered as paralyzed and impotent as I was.

I lay there listening to the breaking waves. They roared and splashed as they broke over the deck above us. After each wave, the S.S. Arcturus miraculously escaped the jaws of the beast. She was still afloat.

As I lay on my back, I remembered being struck in confirmation class while studying the New Testament gospels by the remarkable episode in which Jesus is found sound asleep in the hold of the fishing boat, like Eino now, when the disciples come in a panic looking for him to save them from the raging storm on the lake that was threatening to topple and submerge their boat and them with it.

"Have ye no faith?" Jesus askes them almost casually.

I recalled just then the rector's words to us in his confirmation sermon: "I weep for the person who doesn't have a solid rock on which to stand, a mighty fortress in which to take refuge, an anchor to steady him or her when the seas of life get stormy." Something like that.

It didn't seem particularly relevant to me at the time. But suddenly it was terribly pertinent.

"Have ye no faith?"

I wasn't really sure if I did. I don't think about God very much from day to day. I don't ask myself often if I have faith. But I wonder if just the fact that in the middle of such a violent storm, I should remember a New Testament story from a confirmation sermon years ago, and that the rector's words should rise from my dim unconscious, are indications that I do.

Chapter Eighteen:
Aboard the *S.S. Arcturus*
September 25, 1939

An entry from Onni's journal:

We've been 7 days out at sea now, and today was one of the first when it was not too foggy or windy and cold to go out on to the deck. The seemingly endless fog in the days prior had made me a little claustrophobic, as though we were imprisoned in some dreamy, misty insubstantial world. The sun was shining for a change and its beams shimmered off the surprisingly calm waves, such a welcome change. It lifted my mood.

I glanced up towards the brilliantly blue sky, and what did I see but a flock of birds passing over the bow of the ship from the starboard to port side? They weren't flying so high up that I couldn't recognize that they were arctic terns not unlike the ones we have near Peurajoki in the summertime.

Eino joined me on the deck after a while. I pointed out the terns to him. He was impressed that I could recognize them.

"By Jesus," he said, "that means that we aren't far from shore."

It had been so long since we'd seen solid ground that I had forgotten about it. I admire his resourcefulness, even though his schooling had been interrupted by the civil war and then marriage and emigration to Canada.

He said those terns hug the Labrador coast on their way south. The air near the coast is warmer. That means Labrador is nearby, and then Halifax not much farther.

The terns will continue to fly south until they come near the South American continent and finally Antarctica.

"After the bitter winters I experienced in Soviet Kare-lia, I can't for the life of me see what attraction of Antarctica has for these birds," Eino remarked.

That caught my attention. I asked him if I'd heard correctly. Did he say he's spent some winters in Soviet Kare-lia? I thought he had been in Finland.

Eino looked as though he wished he hadn't made that remark. Then he launched into a tale that I still find incredi-ble. I don't mean I think Eino made it up. Rather, it's that I find the experience he described as absolutely astonishing and almost inconceivable.

He told me that in late 1933, his wife Lyyli had con-vinced him that they should pull up stakes in Timmins where they lived, and move with some other Canadian and Ameri-can Finns to Soviet Karelia. Lyyli and her friends had heard a speaker at the workers' hall describe conditions in Soviet Ka-relia as a "worker's paradise".

Eino said he didn't really believe that. But his wife was so adamant about going, and even threatened to go alone without him. So to save the marriage, Eino went along.

To make a long story short: when they got to a lumber camp on the other side of Lake Ladoga where they were going to live and work, Eino found that it was anything but a work-ers' paradise. You can imagine what conditions must have been like. Eino says that the Russian Karelians had not ad-vanced much beyond their situation in the czar's days.

Things only got worse for the Finns who had been duped into coming over. Do you remember reading about Stalin's friend Sergei Kirov, a communist party big-wig in Leningrad who was assassinated in 1934? Stalin began to blame the Finnish leaders whom Stalin had placed in com-mand in Soviet Karelia. A certain Edvard Gylling had been one of them. Stalin had Gylling and several others rounded up and thrown in prison, and eventually executed.

After a while, all Finns in Karelia were suspect.

Eino tied to persuade Lyyli to leave while they could. However, Lyyli didn't believe that Stalin could afford to turn against the Finns who were keeping the lumber industry in Soviet Karelia going and thriving. Besides, she said, the Soviets had confiscated their Canadian passports "for safe keeping" when they arrived. They couldn't leave without one.

Reluctantly, Eino decided he'd have to leave alone. He conspired with a fellow Finn whose job was driving the finished lumber from the camp to Petroskoi, the nearest port. The man himself didn't want to risk the penalty of death if he was caught leaving. But he owed Eino a favor. He hid Eino among the lumber on his truck one day, drove past the guard at the gate of the camp. Once he had driven the truck a certain distance into the forest, and was sure no one could see them, the man dug Eino out from amidst the lumber, handed him some bread and cheese, and wished him Godspeed.

Before Eino found his way to the border between Soviet and Finnish Karelia, he navigated himself through the woods at night, and lay low during the day. He scavenged for food in abandoned lumbering or hunting shacks.

At the frontier, he found a space in the high barbed wire fence that someone before him had cut. He did cut a gash into his leg on the barbed wire, however.

Once in Finnish Karelia, he took the risk of approaching an older couple in their forest home, where he was given more food and dressing for his wound. But even in Finnish Karelia, he couldn't trust anybody. He couldn't know who was spying for the Russians and who wasn't.

He made his way on foot all the way to Imatra. From there he was able to bum rides to Helsinki. He headed straight to the Canadian embassy, got a new passport, and was given a ticket in the *Arcturus* to return to Canada.

Eino was exhausted from relating his tale and retreated inside I was bushed just from listening to it and marveling at the tremendous courage packed into this very ordinary-looking Finnish man. I wondered if I would have half

116

the courage and inventiveness to act as decisively in a time of crisis like that. Have you ever heard of such a thing?

I stayed on the deck and continued to bask in the sheer joy of sunshine against my scalp and face. The terns were beating their wings energetically but smoothly. I remember father's lesson about the terns, how such graceful beating of their wings portends favorable weather. Ironically, it's when the terns stop beating their wings and rather hold their wings out to catch a current of air that signifies the approach of windy or stormy weather.

Before this voyage and on it, I've had my moments of apprehension about my new life in Canada. I thought we were history when that beastly storm hit. But I've been trying to learn the art of simply commanding my wings to relax and letting a current from somewhere beyond bear me up on the days when I begin to become anxious about my new uncharted life.

When I returned to the cabin, Eino had lain down for a rest, but his eyes were open. He said that he'd heard from Jaagup that the Estonian foreign minister has been invited to Moscow.

"Invited, my ass!" he added. "More like 'summoned' or 'ordered'!"

I knew that wasn't a good thing.

Eino said he doubted that Stalin is inviting te Estnian official for purely social reasons. He thinks Stalin is starting to get paranoid that Hitler will eventually send his army east. Stalin wants to suggest strongly to the minister that the Estonians dance with the *Russians*, and become very unwelcoming to the Germans.

Who's next? Will Stalin annex Latvia, too? And then Lithuania? Will he bypass Finland completely?

We can only pray.

I was too tired to even think about it, and fell asleep.

When Onni awoke, Eino had already gone to the dining room for the midday meal. There was no sign of Jaagup.

When Onni entered the dining room, Eino waved him over to his table where he had been saving a place, for Onni it turned out.

"What delicacy are they giving us this time?" Onni asked as he took the seat.

"It's got the color of pea soup, but I haven't come upon many peas or any ham yet," Eino said in his usual flat, resigned manner. "But I've been meaning to ask you. Where will you be headed once we land in Halifax?"

"I'm hoping to go up north to where my grandfather was before World War I. He was near Sudbury."

"Oh hell, boy! And do *what* for a living? Go down and spend your day in a dark, damp nickel mine? That's no way for a smart kid like you to squander his youth, let me tell you from experience That, my dear boy, would be a waste of your intelligence."

Onni was gratified that Eino considered him to be intelligent. Eino had his own kind of practical intelligence, too, a levelheaded ability to assess a situation, a down-to-earth intuition to take an accurate measure of a person. Onni admired him for that, and was pleased that Eino had judged him worthy of his mentoring.

"I didn't know exactly what I'd do. I thought I'd wait and see what's available," Onni said.

"That's precisely the problem. There's not much work in Sudbury, or Timmins, or just about anywhere in Canada these days. Ever hear of the Great Depression, boy?"

"Well, yes, of course. But I was hoping things will have improved by the time I get there," I answered, feeling a little green and naïve.

"That's what's so good about being young; they're filled with optimism and hope. Not a bad thing, unless you have to go hungry."

"You've never told me where *you* are going," I countered. "I guess I just assumed you're going back to Timmins."

"Nah, there's no work there, as I say. Besides, I'd get such a hard time from some of my old buddies about having wagered everything on Stalin's workers' paradise in Karelia."

"Where, then?"

"A place called Holland Marsh, north of Toronto. The Dutch grow most of Ontario's vegetables there. People always have to eat. I suspect there's always work there, although I don't know if this damned dilapidated body of mine can take all the bending and lifting any more. The hard labor at the forestry camp in Karelia just about did me in. But I don't have an education or trade, so if I want to eat, I don't have a hell of a lot of choice."

He paused and took a bite of his bread. Onni didn't know how to respond. Besides, this information about the lack of work in the north caused his thoughts to be turned upside-down.

"But as for *you*," Eino continued, "You've still got a chance for a better life. If you want my advice, I'd get off the train in Toronto and stay there. There's more opportunity in the city, if you can get used to the noise and dirty air. I know there are other Finns there. In fact, many have come down from the north because of the worse situation up there. If you run out of options, you can always come up to Holland Marsh, and I'm sure they'll put you to work."

"I was hoping I didn't have to revert to farm work. I could have stayed in Peurajoki and done that."

119

"Well, whatever you choose as your end goal, you'll have to pay your dues at first with some kind of shit job."

Eino stopped to scoop up some of what the kitchen staff passed off as pea soup. Jaagup walked in and took a seat at a table to our right. He looked hung over and crusty.

"We all thought you were accompanying your foreign minister to the Kremlin, but here you are, after all," Eino shouted to Jaagup over the din of voices and cutlery.

Jaagup didn't think it was very funny at all. "Shut up, old man!" he slurred.

Eino got the message, and didn't dare say another word to Jaagup during the meal.

Eino picked up his discussion with Onni. "Since the Canadian government passed a tough immigration bill back in '31," it's very hard to get into the country. You've heard, I'm sure, about the Jewish wretches."

Onni had read in the newspaper back in Finland that the ship *St. Louis* had departed from Antwerp harbor in Belgium with over 900 Jewish passengers who were trying to flee Germany before Hitler shut the door completely on any Jews who wanted to leave. The ship sailed for North America. The American authorities in New York harbor wouldn't accept them.

So the ship steamed on up to Halifax. But on June 9, 1938, the Canadian immigration officers did as the Americans had. Britain sent word as well to Halifax that the ship need not bother stopping in Britain either because it wasn't interested in 900 Jews walking its streets and crowding its tenements and stealing Brits' jobs. So the ship sailed back to Antwerp where it had originated and disgorged its human cargo to who knows what fate.

"But I'm not Jewish, Eino," and Onni added, "Obviously."

"Yeah, obviously. I've caught a glimpse at that tiny dangling thing between your legs when you change into a clean pair of underwear. No sign there of your being Jewish. But that doesn't matter, really. Canada's not accepting much of anything right now, unless you're a subject of the Empire on which the sun never sets, or the U.S. The Italians and the Greeks they let in because they are willing to work in the fields, like the Holland Marsh, where a native Canadian wouldn't be caught dead."

"I thought they knew that Finns are hard workers at whatever they do."

"Yes, but in their wonderful logic, they think of all Finns as Reds. The old Finns in the north have been labor trouble-makers for a couple of generations now. Besides, the suits know that a portion of the Finnish immigrant population had run off to Karelia. Now all Finns are suspect."

He paused again, probably for effect to let it sink in.

Then, he added, "But don't let it discourage you. Just stick near Eino Komulainen in the immigration queue, and you'll be alright."

Chapter Nineteen:
Halifax, N.S. Canada
September 27, 1939

An entry in Onni's journal:

Sure enough, Eino was right, not that I doubted him much. We had, indeed, been close to the Canadian coast when I saw the arctic terns. The old but dependable *S.S. Arcturus* moored in Halifax harbor.

Once he saw the ship's staff no longer dressed in their blue surge and had changed into almost tropical-looking white uniforms, Eino knew that we were within a few hours of Halifax. I'm so grateful that Eino has attached himself to me; or is it me to him? He knows the drill so very well that as I follow and imitate him, I must look to the others as a knowledgeable veteran seafarer. I feel sorry for some of the other passengers – the Italians mostly – who look so stunned by it all. I'm glad that I can at least give the appearance that all this is just routine to me.

Once Eino told me that arrival was on the horizon, I want down to the cabin and gathered all my belongings, packed my bag, and put on the cleanest shirt and the pair of pants that looked most like they'd been ironed. There'd be no one waiting for me and greeting me when we got off the boat, of course. But I wanted to look respectable for the immigration officers, and to honor what might very well become my new country.

We third class travelers had to wait on deck while the first and second class passengers disembarked in their finer clothing. The men wore grey fedoras and had matching grey overcoats folded neatly and draped over their left forearm, and expensive Zeiss cameras slung over their necks. The women were decked out in what must have been their finest and more expensive jewelry, their hands nestled in delicate white gloves, their heads crowned by natty dark wide-brimmed hats with the feather on one side. I surmised they were native Canadians returning to their homeland from Europe, or middle class English and Scottish residents either visiting relatives in Canada or wanting to establish residence themselves.

I was so close to fulfilment that I could taste it, the Canadian soil almost within the reach of my feet. But the wait to disembark felt almost interminable. Even the ships stewards seemed impatient for the disembarking process to be finished.

It was finally our turn to go down the gangplank. But at the very first steps on solid ground, I stopped in my tracks. I felt dizzy. The ground under me rolled exactly as the deck had done. Giddiness made me stumble a bit until Eino grabbed me by the elbow. Now that I finally made it to solid ground in the land I had been dreaming of, a confounding dizziness overtook me. and my legs were like flaccid rubber. I couldn't understand it. Perhaps eight days on the waves had caused me to forget how to walk on solid ground, and I'd have to learn again from the beginning as I did as a toddler.

But in this new land, I must stand firmly on my feet and put one foot in front of the other.

Once we were on Pier 21, the scene was rather chaotic. Passengers of every class dodged one another trying to find their luggage along the long rows of suitcases and trunks that had been carried off the ship. Our third-class row was the smallest since most of us had our suitcases with us in our cabins. But the number of suitcases and trunks in the first and second class rows was something to behold. My whole family in Peurajoki wouldn't have enough clothing to fill one of the trunks of some of the first-class passengers

I have to be honest and confess that my very first impression of Canada was disappointing. Our quarters in the ship had not been luxurious. But as I looked at the crude wasteland of the pier and the surrounding harbor, with its rusting ships and windowless warehouses, I felt let down. Everything looked so old and worn. I had expected, perhaps childishly so, that every building and facility and amenity in the New World would be brand new.

~~~~~~~~~~~~~~~~~~~~~~~~~~~~~~~

Many of the first-class passengers hired longshore-men to carry their ample baggage through the immigration and customs lines, and then into the automobiles that many had waiting for them on the street beyond the pier. Eino, Jaagup and Onni stood in the interminable line holding their single piece of luggage. Onni held his suitcase in his right hand, but Eino and Jaagup, being escapees who had come to Finland with nothing but the shirts on their backs, held only cloth bags that were smaller even than Onni's humble suit-case. Eino kidded Onni that with his "huge" suitcase, he was as bad as the first-class passengers.

"Surely, you could have left some of your luxury items at home instead of schlepping them all the way to Canada."

By now, Onni understood Eino's sense of humor. At the beginning of the voyage he wouldn't have known whether or not to take him seriously.

Onni didn't realize how long the queue for immigration and customs was until we made it through the huge brown doors into the immigration hall. What they had been part of outside was only the *beginning* of the queue, it turned out, further sinking his heart. But at the same time, it eased the tension in his stomach. He did see ahead that one or two individuals or couples walked back with heads bowed, their children looking confused, from having talked to the immigration officials in their kiosks.

"Those, my friend, are people who have probably been rejected passage into Canada," Eino said when Onni asked about them. "They're on their way to a holding area where arrangements would be made for their prompt return to the point of departure."

That didn't make Onni's stomach any calmer.

What if I get to the kiosk and I'm sent to that same holding area as well?

124

The ceiling of the hall seemed a mile high. Despite that, it was a cavern of almost impossible humidity. Sweat rolled down Onni's face, and his shirt was sticking to his back.

"Is it always this bloody hot and sticky so late in September? He asked his companion.

"It's been known to be."

The heat will take some getting used to.

Jaagup had found some other Estonians and had gone to stand in the queue with them.

When Onni and Eino were only the fifth or sixth people in the queue away from the kiosk, Eino said,

"Your face is as white as February snow in Lapland."

Onni's mouth was completely dry as well.

"Relax, kid," Eino said. "I've got things in control. Just let me do the talking."

Onni took a deep breath when it appeared he would be next with the immigration officer.

Next!" the officer growled.

He was a man of late middle age, a little portly, his head balding, his round face streaked with red

Eino stepped up to the immigration officer's counter with Onni, although Onni was ahead of him in the queue.

"No, not you, sir," the officer said gruffly to Eino. "One at a time, please."

"Sir, with all due respect," Eino said addressing the official, "this young man doesn't speak a word of English. He is from Finland, as am I. I am serving as his interpreter."

It impressed Onni that Eino spoke so confidently, not at all bearing the demeanor of the aging backwoods lumberjack or miner that he was. Onni had not heard him speak much English before. Onni was astonished by how faint his Finnish accent became when he did.

Will I ever be as fluent with this strange language?

"Well, then," snarled the burly official, "let me see your passport first, please."

It was clear this man was as tired of dealing with all these people in the queue as were those standing in it.

Eino handed his unblemished passport to the man.

"But this passport is barely a month old. Where do live, sir."

"I am employed by the DeGroot family in the Holland March in Ontario, sir. I live in the company housing there."

"How long have you been a citizen of Canada, sir?"

"Since . . . oh, let me think . . . since 1921. Yes, 1921."

"How, then, do you explain a Canadian passport that's just one month old?" The man looked at Eino with suspicion. I didn't understand the conversation until Eino replayed and translated it for me later on the train to Ontario. But the look on the official's face made me very uneasy about not just Eino's prospects of getting back into his chosen country, but mine as well.

"I misplaced my original passport, sir. That was very inconvenient, it's having happened just a few weeks from my scheduled return to Canada. But your very fine colleagues at the Canadian embassy in Helsinki took care of giving me a new one very promptly with no trouble."

The man's visage softened somewhat.

"And your traveling companion, his passport, please."

Eino translated the order for Onni, and he handed his passport to Eino, who relayed it to the man in the kiosk.

"This is a Finnish passport."

"Yes, sir," Eino confirmed.

"He must know that the Order-in-Council 1931-695 restricted immigration into Canada by applicants other than those from the British Commonwealth or the United States, assuming they can verify that they have the means to be totally self-supporting financially. The last time I checked, good sirs, Finland was not a member country of the British Commonwealth. This is a problem."

Onni didn't understand a word, of course. But Eino didn't seem to be too perturbed or distracted from his mission by whatever he man said to him so earnestly.

"Yes, that is true, sir. You know your geography very well. But as I recall, if I am not mistaken, exceptions could be made at the discretion of the Ministry of Immigration or his staff in the case of persons from other countries who intend to be engaged in agricultural labor."

"Yes, sometimes that is true, but only rarely, mind you. Your friend, he intends to be engaged in agricultural work? What experience does he have?"

"Yes, I have arranged a job for him with DeGroot. Onni, here, has helped his father run the family farm in Finland. He will adjust to vegetable farming in the marsh with no problem."

The man seemed to be considering whatever Eino had said. He picked up both passports in one hand and was tapping them in the palm of the other hand as he pondered. Eino gave Onni a quick puckish look in the eye, as if to indicate a furtive, invisible thumbs-up. But Onni wasn't feeling thumbs-up at all.

The officer leaned his head out of the kiosk and turned it to his right and asked another officer in the corridor nearby, "Hey Joe, is Laz in his office, and is he occupied?"

After a few second, Joe sent back his answer, "Yes, and no. He's in his office, and he isn't occupied."

"Good. Thanks, Joe."

Then he handed Onni and Eino their passports and said, "You'll have to see my superior to discuss your friend's situation."

He pointed them in the direction of the corridor with a nod of his head.

Onni was confused, not having understood the conversation one bit.

"Is he sending us to the holding area for those who have to return?" Oni asked Eino nervously.

His heart was sinking fast.

Had I come all this distance on a voyage I'd been waiting for since I was a little boy, only to be turned down and sent back home in disgrace?

"Don't worry, boy. Eino Komulainen has this situation under control."

They were shown into a very plain and drab office. In the middle of the room was a huge navy grey desk, and behind an even more burly and red-cheeked officer than the officer in the kiosk. He held out his beefy hand to indicate that they should sit down in the two serviceable unpadded metal chairs in front of his desk. He introduced himself as Harry Lazarenko.

When he was asked what our concern was, Eino proceeded to repeat the account he had given the first official. The corners of Laz' mouth shifted upward slightly as he took

128

down the details of Eino's explanation Onni feared that Laz was finding Eino's story rather far-fetched. Surely, he must have listened to hundreds of implausible tales pitched to him by immigrants desperate to make their case for entry into the country. No doubt Mr. Lazarenko saw commonalities in Eino's deposition to the many other alibis he had heard.

"I see the boy has a Finnish passport."

"Yes, that's right, sir."

"He must speak Finnish then."

"Right again, sir."

"Let's see if that's the case, then."

He turned his eyes to Onni and said, *"High's da paschal"* and laughed.

Onni was stunned, first of all that he addressed him and not Eino, but also because of what Onni thought he said. Eino was stifling a laugh.

"My neighbor Harri Kari taught it to me when we going to school together as kids in Kapuskasing," Mr. Lazarenko explained. "He told me that if I ever run into another Finn, I should say *high's da pascha* to him. He never told me what it means. But from the little Ukrainian I learned from my grandmother, I know *pascha* refers to Easter. So I presume the Finnish greeting he taught me meant 'Happy Easter'."

"Not exactly, sir" Eino offered. "But yes, in certain circumstances it can be a good way to greet a Finn."

"You people are hard workers. Harri's father never let an idle moment go by. When he grew up, Harri was the same way. He was my best employee at the filling station I ran for a while in Kap. When the Depression came, and it was clear that I'd have to shut down the business, Harri moved to Toronto hoping to find work. I lost track of his after that. But he was a tireless worker."

"Well, Mr. Lazarenko, that describes this young man, Onni, to a tee. He'll be the best worker at DeGroot."

"If he's anything like Harri, then I'm sure you're right."

He looked at the passport again and paused before speaking again.

"I will use the authority vested in me by the Minister of Immigration of the Dominion of Canada to allow Mr. Syrjälä entry into Canada as an agricultural worker."

He then slammed his rubber stamp down on Onni's passport emphatically, smiling at him and extending his hand.

"Congratulations, Mr. Syrjälä! Welcome to Canada! *High's da pascha!*"

Oni was so relieved that he responded spontaneously, "*Joo, haista itse paska!*".

Eino let out a wicked laugh and hit Onni playfully on his shoulder with his fist.

Onni felt a little shame that he had thanked the kind immigration offiver and friend of Finns to go and small his own shit!

Eino had it all under control.

Chapter Twenty:
On the Train towards Toronto
September 27, 1939

Onni and Eino found their way to the Halifax train station and purchased one-way tickets to Toronto. They boarded and found second-class seats in the fourth coach. Eino gave the window seat the Onni.

"Well, this train doesn't have the luxury of the Orient Express, but it's certainly an upgrade from the damned piece of crap from Leningrad to Petroskoi," Eino remarked as he settled in the mildly cushioned bench seat. "Count yourself fortunate, boy."

Onni didn't register much of a response. The next time Eino looked over, he beheld an open-mouthed Onni asleep with his head leaning on an angle against the glass of the dirty window. Eino closed his eyelids as well and celebrated his return to Canada with a thorough nap.

When Onni awoke, he looked out the window. He saw farms; or at least vast open fields where hay or grain had been cut at the end of the summer. There were just a few farmhouses scattered far apart from one another, which Onni fund strange. The barns that were visible bore a different shape from the small and rectangular ones with the steep sloping rooves in Peurajoki or elsewhere in the Finnish landscape. The rooves on these Canadian barns were high and with a sheet metal polygon shape, held up by walls of simple wooden planks.

I wonder if father is out in the barn right now. Did all the hay crop get taken in before the snow flies? How's he doing with the construction of the new house? . . . And shouldn't I be there helping him now instead of here?

Onni continued regarding the view out his window, still recovering from his nap and the fatigue of the long voyage on the *Arcturus*, and especially the anxiety in the immigration hall. He laughed to himself quietly as he recalled Laz only phrase in Finnish. Harri Kari must have been a mischievous fellow as well as a hard-working one to have taught his neighbor such a crude expression.

He regarded the farms once again.

Eino muttered a few garbled words in his sleep and then regained consciousness and quickly wiped some droll from the corners of his mouth. The two sat side by side in silence as if still partially asleep.

Finally, Onni asked Eino, "When will you start work at the Holland Marsh?"

Eino gave an inexplicable chuckle. "I don't rightly know, as a matter of fact. But that's because I don't really *have* a job waiting for me, at Holland Marsh or anywhere else, to go to."

"But that's what you told me on the ship. Didn't you tell the immigration officials that Holland Marsh is where you are headed, and that you will work for some farmer there."

"DeGroot? I don't really know him. He's an invention of my imagination. But whoever Mr. DeGroot is, I'm sure he's of Dutch extraction"

Onni fell silent for a moment.

Eino noticed Onni's pensive demeanor.

"Oh, don't fret, boy! I'm pretty sure that even if there isn't a real DeGroot, there's some other Dutchman like him up there who will hire me in spite of my fifty-some years. I may not always end up in in the most high-class situations or the executive suite, but I usually land on my feet. Don't worry about Eino Komulainen."

Onni continued to look at Eino pensively as though the boy was trying to figure out how this new information could be made to fit his still boyish sense of right and wrong.

"What you've got to learn, boy, is that some of us weren't born into privilege, and sometimes we have to get inventive and creative in getting by. You're out in the big world, now, Onni, and sometimes these are the ways of that world."

Onni nodded wordlessly.

Eino looked at the boy. "You've got to remember," Eino thought to himself, "that he still just a boy. He hasn't even been in the army yet where the smooth edges of his moral foundation would be rendered more ragged. Take it easy on the boy."

"I know what you're thinking," Eino continued after their mutual silence. "Just the typical roguish Savonian, right? What do you expect? Well, I'm not defending myself, but I am warning you that you'll run into characters who will see your lack of English and your immigrant's different way of carrying yourself, however subtle or disguised, as an opportunity to take advantage. Learn from this, boy."

Again, Onni nodded while he considered this.

Eino felt the lesson wasn't finished.

"Life is about telling the difference between those who do want to mislead you, and those who don't. But don't think that you'll never take a moral short-cut yourself."

Eino's last sentence for Onni was food for thought for a long while. Eino remained silent, too, for a long stretch, fearing he might have said too much that Onni wasn't ready to hear or absorb.

But then he thought to himself, "Hell, Eino, the boy's not made of fragile glass. He has to be equipped with some practical smarts to match his book smarts if he's to make his way in this country, or anywhere else, for that matter."

A night passed, the another day. Onni's and Eino's conversations turned to more practical matters, like fetching sandwiches from the dining car, the discomfort of trying to sleep while sitting up, and observations about passengers who came on board at various stops along the way.

"Doesn't that lady look as though she's leaving a no-good drunk of a husband back home in Moncton?" Eino asked, pointing with his head towards a rather frumpy middle-aged woman in a grey overcoat. I wouldn't want to be caught in a dark alley with her."

Onni chuckled. She didn't look too friendly at the moment.

There were stops in Saint John and Fredericton, places Onni had seen on his globe. Then came the names of towns and cities with French names, like Rivière-de-Loup and Québec, then after spending what seemed like an eternity in its outskirts, Montréal.

Eino leaned over to Onni when they stopped there, and intimated, "I thought about getting off here. There are a lot of Finns in this city, and maybe I could make connections with them and find work. But I don't want to put up with those Frogs."

"Frogs?" Onni asked, picturing the small and harmless critters he had played with on the banks of the Peura River when he was a boy.

"Not the animals. The French Canadians. That's something you'll learn about for yourself if you stay in this country long enough."

Then came stops in Cornwall and Kingston, Belleville and Port Hope.

"Well, Toronto's next, Onni."

At this, Onni's heart beat faster, partly out of excitement that his new life was closer to realization, or at least beginning, than ever, but partly also out of apprehension of what lay ahead. This irritated Onni. He didn't want his enjoyment of the anticipation to be tainted by any nervousness.

134

The train slowed down in an area where the water of Lake Ontario could barely be seen behind warehouses and factories built along its shore.

"I'm going to go on up to the bus station to catch a bus up Highway 11 to Bradford near the Holland Marsh," Eino said. "Here, take this piece of paper. I've written the address of a good boarding house in the city and walking directions to find it. It's run by Iida Pyykkönen. She's a widow who takes in a lot of young, single Finns, or at least used to when they were actually allowed to come into the country. She runs a tight ship, but you can be assured that its clean and safe, which you can't say of all the rooming houses in Toronto. Tell her Eino Komulainen sent you, and she'll treat you really well."

It suddenly struck Onni that he and Eino would be parting ways. This awareness got him down for the moment. He had become so dependent on Eino's help and example. Onni felt like a bird being forced out of the nest and made to fly with his own wings.

An entry in Onni's journal:

September 28, 1939

It's so ironic. Here I am on the cusp of a new adventure in my life, full of excitement and joyful anticipation. But sadness, too, simultaneously. This moment reminds me of the one in the front yard of Kuokkala. I was impatient to get going on my venture, fulfilling my life's dream, but I was grieving the unavoidable farewell and separation from my parents, sisters, brother, Anna-Liisa, and the only way of life I had known. Eino would say that life's like that, a series of comings and inevitable goings, endings and beginnings again.

I was frankly disappointed with myself while I regarded the farms in the Canadian countryside. The whole time, I was comparing them to farms in Finland and judging the ones I saw from my window on the train to be inferior.

Why should I judge them to be inferior just because they look different? I'd have to say the ones I saw here so far are less attractive. But how do I know if they're inferior or less productive than the ones we had back in Finland?

Is it just because I'm so tired from my journey that I jump immediately to judgmental and negative thoughts about the very first sights I see in my new country? Is this some kind of permanent distortion in the Syrjälä clan's heritage? For all the good that father has passed down to me, it always bothered me when he behaved and thought in that hypercritical way. Remember how I vowed that I wouldn't let myself approach life in that way? That I would learn to withhold judgement? That I would be open to what's new? Isn't that precisely what this journey is about? Is there some perverse kind of inherent assumed arrogance in our family make-up that always presumes that ways that are customary to us are superior to those of others if they differ from ours?

Or is it bigger and more profound than just my particular family makeup? Is this come blemish on the Finnish character itself that immediately finds what's wrong with an object or place or person instead of perceiving and valuing what is good?

Or, for that matter, is it deeper and broader still? Is it a more universal human tendency?

In any case, I left Finland with an attitude of exploring a new country, encountering new customs, and meeting new people. I have to rediscover that mindset, and soon.

Chapter Twenty-One:
Toronto
September 29, 1931

Toronto's Union Station did not feel to Onni to be any larger, and not especially any grander, than Central Station in Helsinki. It just simply felt more confusing, that's all.

As much of a whirlwind as Onni experienced Central Station to have been, a least the signage was in a language he could read, and the announcements over the loud speaking system were in a tongue he could understand.

But as Onni stepped off the train at Union Station and tried to find his way to the street, he was met by direction signs written in words he could not read.

WATCH YOUR STEP

WASHROOMS ON MAIN FLOOR

PEDESTRIAN WALKWAY TO FRONT STREET

EXIT TO BAY STREET

Suddenly Onni understood that he would need to learn to read all over again. It had been thrilling to learn to read the first time as a child; now the thought of having to learn to read this strange language seemed overwhelming. Here he was, a young adult at age seventeen, yet he felt like a little schoolboy again.

It bothered him also that a female voice was making announcements in a language in which he knew only one or two words. People were rushing to the street or to the designated track for the continuation of their journey and didn't seem to be listening to a word the woman was saying. But Onni figured that what she was announcing must have important, and he wanted in the worst way to hear. But hearing the words and understanding them, he could see, were two entirely different things.

All this he had thought about before while still in Finland. But it had all been theoretical then, so far in the future, that he had put it to the back of his mind. Now the realization was not abstract and theoretical any longer. He felt it in the pit of his stomach.

He did recognize the word "Front Street" on the signs, however. The directions Eino had scribbled for him on paper mentioned Front Street, so he managed to follow the signs and found himself on a broad sidewalk outside Union Station. He followed the Eino's directions to Queen Street.

It was surprisingly hot for this late in September on the unfamiliar streets of Toronto. Back home, the leaves on the birches and aspens will have dropped to the ground to make room for the approaching winter. Onni took off his jacket as he carried his suitcase along Queen and took out his handkerchief to wipe the sweat from his brow.

It struck him suddenly that these were *Canadians* he was seeing on the sidewalk. Most who walked past him in the opposite direction seemed to be in a hurry and so took no notice of him. One or two looked at him with benign curiosity, recognizing, he surmised, that he was not a native Canadian. Several gave him what to Onni felt like at least mildly hostile stares.

These were people who were settled. He imagined that some of them were descendants of immigrants from somewhere. But some might have been settled in the country for generations going all the way back to when the French first landed and established New France or when the British won possession of the land on the Plains of Abraham.

They all had homes to leave in the morning and return to in the evening. All Onni had was a name and an address of a landlady he didn't know, but as yet, no home. For the moment, he felt as homeless as a Gypsy.

Here he was, from a tiny farming village in northern Finland where everybody knew everybody else. The only time Onni could remember that he ran into a face he didn't recognize in the church village was when a clan of Gypsies stopped to supply their caravan at the cooperative store. After a while, even some of them became familiar, although not altogether welcome faces.

But now he was on the streets of Toronto where he knew no one. Not a single soul. Every face he looked at was that of a stranger. That had been true in the central station in Helsinki, too. But There every face exhibited the familiar, characteristic features of Finns. But on Queen Street in Toronto, some faces were what he imagined the English to look like. Every now and then he'd come across a broader visage with the same shiny jet black hair as the Italians on the *S.S. Arcturus.*

He looked down for the umpteenth time at the little piece of paper Eino had given to double-check the address. "31 Beverley Street." He had been adhering strictly to Eino's directions on the paper: "Walk 3 blocks west to John Street on Front Street from Union Station; 8 blocks north on John Street to Queen." Now he was on Queen. The journey and the unfamiliar stifling heat exhausted him. He was eager to find Beverley Street, which the directions indicated was only one block west of John Street.

Onni read Eino's directions: "No. 31 will be on the right-hand side as you turn right on Beverley Street, about a half block north of Queen."

Onni stopped in front of the reddish brick house with the big dark door connected to two other houses. A set of stairs leading to the small landing and front door was set parallel to the street and connected directly to the cracked concrete sidewalk on which he stood. There were a few automobiles parked on either side of the street. A portly man, probably in his fifties, who was sweating profusely came out the front door and turned around to lock the door behind him with a key from his trousers' pocket. He greeted Onni with a mildly irritated glance. From the high cheekbones on the man's face that made his eyes look like tiny slits, Onni surmised that he was Finnish.

"Excuse me. Is this the boarding house run by Mrs. Pyykkönen?" Onni asked.

"This is it," the man replied "It's not much, but it's a place to lay your head and have a decent meal. But it's hotter than hell in there today. I've got to get out of there and go to Simpson's cafeteria to stay cool. They have air conditioning."

The man used a Finnish term that he had never encountered before: air conditioning. Onni didn't really know what that was. But the man seemed to be in such a hurry to get to this Simpson's place that he didn't ask the man to explain.

The man sauntered down Beverley Street.

Onni pressed a button on the jamb of the door. When he released his finger from the button, he heard a shark, high-pitched ringing sound from inside the house. No one came to the door for what seemed like the longest time, so he pushed the button again.

After a while, the door opened and a petite grey-haired woman of about sixty-five appeared from behind it.

"Excuse me, "Onni began. "I'm looking for Mrs. Pyykkönen."

"Yes, you've found her," she replied a mite suspiciously.

"I'm looking for accommodations. Mr. Eino Komulainen recommended your place to me."

"Eino, you say? Good Lord, what's the character up to these days? The last I heard through the grapevine was that he was in Russia, of all places."

"Well, he was . . . in Soviet Karelia, actually, and his wife still is. But Eino felt he had to leave, and so he came to Finland."

"You know him from Finland, then?"

"No, we met on the ship from Finland . . . actually it was leaving Hull, England when we met. We came together on the train from Halifax, and now he's gone on to what he calls the Holland Marsh."

"Going to pick vegetables, is he? He's a man of many talents. And, I hope, a strong back."

Mrs. Pyykkönen asked for Onni's forgiveness for her not having opened the door and letting him inside.

"Please step inside. It's so hot out there."

Onni stepped into the foyer of the house. To him, it didn't feel much cooler than it had on the doorstep.

"Recently arrived from Finland, then? We don't see many arrivals from the old country anymore these days. Not like the old days when a week wouldn't go by without several requests for a room."

Onni could see that the lady was relaxing a bit and warming up to him. Yet all the same, Onni felt that he was being gauged by this woman, most assuredly his suitability as a tenant being assessed on the spot.

"Where are you from back home?" she inquired.

"From the north country. A place called Peurajoki, actually. In northern Oulu province."

"Good Lord, this bustling, noisy dirty city must be difficult for you to make sense of."

"Actually, I just arrived; all I've seen of it is between here and the train station."

"Will you be working? I've had it up to here with boarders who can't pay the rent because they were laid off from their jobs."

"Oh, intend to find work, Mrs. Pyykkönen. I assure you of that."

141

He was hoping that she was, indeed, assured, even though he had no clue where even to begin looking for a job, or even what he would do.

"We'll see about that. Times have been rough for the last ten years. Do you have funds to pay the first week's rent?"

"Yes, I still have money from home. But how much is the room?"

"Seven dollars per week. That includes two meals a day, laundry on Mondays, and use of the bathroom and living room."

She paused to give Onni some time to consider the offer

She continued. "You look like a fit young man. Osmo Kettunen was our coal man until he died last week. If you'd be willing to shovel coal into the burner every morning in the winter, then I can reduce your rent by two dollars."

Onni seemed satisfied with that, although he had no basis of comparison of the cost of rent in rooming houses in the city. He had heard of coal, of course, but in Finland, only people in the apartments in Helsinki and Turku used coal to heat their living space, so head never seen it, much less handled or shoveled it.

"I should have mentioned that old Osmo didn't die from shoveling coal, in case you're worried. He died on his daily marathon walk to and from High Park. That must be at least 10 miles! That's about 16 kilometers to you. He had bad heart, and the stubborn mule wouldn't give up the task of shoveling coal when I offered to find another tenant to take over. But he was just so afraid of his money running out. Aren't we all?"

"Can I see the room?"

"Oh, of course. You have several to choose from since I'm a little short on tenants these days. Please follow me."

She led him up a set of stairs covered by a faded red carpet with a floral pattern. On the second floor, they passed several closed doors, which Onni presumed were those to rooms of other boarders. A little way down the corridor, they passed an open door which revealed tiny room not much larger than the cabin shared by Onni, Eino and Jaagup on the *Arcturus*. Beside the single bed stood an older woman who eyed Onni suspiciously.

The landlady greeted the woman, "Good day, Mrs. Kyllönen.", to which the woman responded with a barely audible, "Good day."

"That's Aune Kyllönen," the landlady confided in a hushed voice. "She came here from Viipuri about ten years ago with her husband who has since died. She moved in here after she was finally able to sell her own little bungalow on McCaul Street. You'll find she doesn't say much, at least to other boarders. Don't take it personally."

They proceeded up another flight of stairs, bare and not carpeted this time, to the third floor. Onni noticed that it was a great deal hotter up there than it had been on the first floor.

"This is the room I have in mind for you, Mr. Syrjälä. Mr. Pellonpää and Mr. Urbanski are your neighbors up here. You will share the bathroom with them. Does this suit you?"

Onni's eyes scanned a room at least slightly larger than Mrs. Kyyllönen's downstairs, with a metal frame single bed covered by a bedspread of the very lightest hue of faded green that Onni suspected had served many other boarders through the years. There we thick reddish curtains on the small window that looked out onto Beverley Street. A simple, serviceable set of wooden drawers were housed in a dresser against one wall. Underneath the window there was a plain wooden desk painted in a cream color. When he saw it, Onni thought about writing immediately.

Without seeing or knowing what was in the other rooms available. Onni said, "This will do just fine, Mrs. Pyykkönen. Yes, this will be just fine."

Handing him a key on a key ring advertising a local drug store, she said curtly and businesslike, "I serve breakfast from 7:00 am, to 8:00am.; supper from 5:30 pm. to 6:30 pm. But that's all. If you can't make it at those times, I'm afraid you're out of luck. I simply can't work around every boarder's idiosyncratic schedule. If ever you won't be joining us, I always appreciate word ahead of time. We eat in the dining room on the first floor. We'll see you today at 5:30 pm?"

Onni hadn't had what could be called a full meal since he and Eino disembarked from the *Arcturus*. He realized that he was hungry for one.

"Yes, Mrs. Pyykkönen. I will surely be there . . . and on time."

After she left, Onni put down his suitcase on the rag rug that covered the wooden floor in the familiar Finnish style. He threw off his shoes, and laid his body down on the bed. Within a few minutes, in spite of the heat, he was sound asleep.

Several hours later, Onni pulled himself erect on the bed. Out of his pocket, he pulled out the pocket watch that Aukusti had given him as a farewell present, and noticed that it indicated that it was 6:10 pm. He swung his legs out of the bed and onto the floor. He swept his hand through his hair tousled by sleep and damp from sweat. He ran his hand down the front of his trousers to give them an illusion of being ironed. He dashed out of his room and started to run down the staircase in a panic that he had missed supper.

When Onni entered the dining room almost out of breath, there were five others seated around the table. They eyed him with curiosity. He was a source of novelty for these veterans of the boarding house who hadn't seen a new face in quite a while. Mrs. Pyykkönen gave him what Onni interpreted to be a "I thought-you'd-do-better" look.

144

Onni recognized the portly man who had gone to Simpson's to keep cool in the air conditioning. The man held out his hand and introduced himself as Tauno Pellonpää.

"He's one of your neighbors on the third floor," informed Mrs. Pyykkönen.

"Glad to meet you," Pellonpää said after he'd finished chewing on his food. "I apologize for my lack of hospitality earlier this afternoon out front. But it's just that I can't bear this bloody heat. I had to get to Simpson's and the cool air."

"No offense taken," Onni assured him. "Can you tell me what this Simpson's is."

"Oh, you'll soon get to know Simpson's and Eaton's," Mrs. Pyykkönen interjected before Pellonpää could respond. "Everybody in Toronto is familiar with them."

Pellonpää looked a little irritated that his landlady presumed to answer for him.

"It's one of the two big department stores in town," Pellonpää appended to Mrs. Pyykkönen's comment. "Eaton's Annex is a good place to buy cheap but good clothes."

"Mr. Hutari, here, works in the mail order department at Eaton's," Mrs. Pyykkönen added.

She nodded towards a thin shy-looking Finn of about 25, who said "Hello" rather mechanically without looking up and making eye contact with Onni.

"Reino gets to be in the air conditioning at Eaton's all day long," Pellonpää commented. "He likes his job because he can go practically all day and doesn't have to say a word to anyone. Right, Reino?"

Pellonpää let out a hearty laugh and gave a light tap Hutari's shoulder beside him. Hutari looked around the table. Since everyone else seemed to be laughing at Pellonpää's remark, he decided the best way to deflect attention from himself was to force a laugh, too.

145

Two other burly men were at the table, too, but were not participating in the conversation or laughter. In the course of the table conversation, Onni learned that one, Kalle, was Estonian.

Onni nodded politely at Kalle, and greeted him, "Tere".

Kalle's eyes lit up at hearing Onni speak his mother tongue. Without hesitation, Kalle eagerly launched into a few sentences in Estonian. Onni raised his hands, palms up, to indicate that "tere" was the extent of his fluency in the language of Finland's southern neighbor across the Gulf of Finland.

The other, the brawnier of the two, Dmytro, was a Ukrainian. Onni didn't know so much as a greeting in Ukrainian, so he simply smiled and nodded at the man politely. The others spoke enough English that they could include Kalle and Dmytro in the conversation from time to time, but for the time being at least, Onni's communication with them would have to be limited to sign language.

There was one other person at the table who had remained silent: the lady in the room on the second floor, Aune. Kyllönen. She was going about the task of eating supper rather nervously, as if her focus was somewhere else. She didn't even look up more than once or twice during the meal. She took a half-hearted tiny bite here and there of her bread and sipped an occasional small spoonful of chicken soup from the bowl in front of her. She looked older to Onni in the brighter light of the dining room than she had in the semi-twilight of her room earlier. The corners of her mouth drooped downward slightly. Onni guessed that with the wrinkles that pitted her face, she was probably in her late sixties, like his *mummu* Martta.

Onni remembered Mrs. Pyykkönen's remark to him that she didn't connect much with the others. Mrs. Kyllönen was surely being true to that description at the table. No one made the slightest attempt to include her in the conversation.

"We don't see many new arrivals from the old country these days," Pellonpää remarked, looking in Onni's direction, presumably expecting an explanation from Onni for his presence.

"Yes, I arrived just the other day from Halifax. Well . . . from Finland, actually, From Peurajoki, up north."

"You're not trying to escape service in the army, are you, young man?" Pellonpää probed. "There's all this talk over in Finland, I hear, about call-ups in case Stalin makes a grab."

"I have a brother in the army stationed in Kajaani, as a matter of fact. But I'm just 17, so I don't qualify for the service yet."

"Ah, I've met more than a few at the hall who snuck over as teenagers just the avoid their military obligation," Pellonpää said reprovingly, as though he wasn't convinced of Onni's age, or his patriotism, either.

"They're probably all Reds who don't want to fight their ideological kin in Russia, or, more likely I figure, damned homosexuals who are too chicken-livered to pick up a gun and fight."

The others al looked up at Pellonpää after he had spoken. At Pellonpää's mention of homosexuals, Mrs. Pyykkönen rose from the table in a wordless huff. It was clear that by introducing the word, Pellonpää had violated an unspoken rule of the house, at least the dining room.

The boarders finished their meal and carried their dishes into the adjoining kitchen without speaking so much as another word during the duration of the meal. Onni conjectured that Mrs. Kyllönen and Reino Hutari were pleased.

An entry in Onni's journal:

147

It's certainly an interesting collection of individuals 1
here at 31 Beverley Street. It's not hard to imagine that Eino
made a home here once, however temporary. I would love to
hear his ironic Savonian description of each person around
the table. He'd find humor about each one, I'm sure.

Reino Hutari is a curious piece of work. His shyness
borders on the extreme, even for a Finnish male. Kalle, the
Estonian chap, and Dmytro, the Ukrainian, are total mysteries
to me, since there are very few options for communication
with wither one. I was able to make out some things that
Jaagup said on the ship, so I might be able to get better ac-
quainted with Kalle. I'm curious about his story

Of course, Aune Kyllönen is the really inscrutable
one. She's of a much different generation than the others except the landlady, my grandparents' generation, really. Her
appearance reminds me of mother's mother and so many
other of the church ladies back in Peurajoki, and seeing her
here made me taste a little homesickness, as reluctant as I am
to admit it.

There seems to be such suffering written on her face.
I wonder what he story is. She carries herself so self-consciously and so nervously as though she were made of paper.
I may never know her story since she's not the communica-
tive kind. The poor woman had such trouble eating as though
she were nauseous and was about to throw up. But I suspect
it's more than mere nausea that is eating at her.

Pellonpää strikes me as more than slightly bigoted. I
was very uncomfortable with his asking me if I was in Canada
to evade military service. I found, in fact, his mentioning
knowing others who have come here for precisely that reason, and his obvious disdain for them, to be threatening. I've
been pondering his remark ever since supper. As I hatched
my plan back in Peurajoki to sail here, the thought of ab-
sconding from my military obligation didn't even enter my
mind. At least, I don't recall that it did.

But the fact that his remark bothered, and continues
to bother, makes me curious. It introduces an element of
doubt, in fact. I didn't come here for that reason . . . did I?

148

I admire Väinö greatly for not only his willingness to serve in the army, but his downright eagerness to do so. I recall my parents' mixture of pride and anxiety as he departed. But I have seldom pictured myself in a grey woolen uniform with a rifle in my hand. When he left home for the army, I was sincerely happy for him because I could see that it was a fulfilment of a dream for him.

But I also recognize that I have come for the fulfillment of my dream, too, only it's a very different dream from his.

Chapter Twenty-Two:
Toronto
October 12, 1939

Onni carved out a routine for himself almost immediately after finding the room at 31 Beverley Street. Since he and Aune Kyllönen were the only ones in the house who didn't have to rush off to a job right after breakfast, he lingered over his morning coffee served in what at first struck Onni as very large cups, not the more delicate demi-tasses that were more common in Finland. The mute Aune usually got up the leave the table even before the men decided it was time to leave for work. Some days, it was just Onni in the dining room, except for the bustling Mrs. Pyykkönen, who hustled back and forth to and from the kitchen and dining room carrying dirty plates and leftover toast on a platter.

Several times he tried to engage the landlady in conversation, hoping to hear more of her experiences as an immigrant to Canada in the first decade of the new century. She was polite enough in her responses, but they were short, indicating thereby that she had her own routine – clearing breakfast, grocery shopping, cleaning the house, and preparing supper – and conversation just interrupted her routine and delayed her schedule.

Onni did ask her once if she received the Toronto newspaper, which Onni would have been eager to examine even though he didn't read a word of English. She replied that she didn't have the luxury of spare time to devote to reading either *Toronto Daily Star* or *The Evening Telegram*. She grumbled that *The Globe and Mail* was the rich business people's paper for the folks in Forest Hill and Rosedale, so there's no way she'd subscribe to that.

He added daily walks downtown to his routine. He walked east on Queen Street usually, stopping every now and then to inspect the wares that in the autumn sun were still being laid out on portable tables in front of the stores. He had heard from Pellonpää about Esther's Café, owned and run by a Finnish woman of Mrs. Pyykkönen's vintage, and he sometimes stopped in to have another cup of coffee, a slice of fresh *nisu,* and to overhear the lively conversations among the mostly older male Finnish customers.

Fortified by his snack, he would continue on Queen Street towards downtown, past the Canada Life Insurance Company building on University Avenue. The insurance firm provided a public service by installing a beacon light at the top of the building, green to indicate fair weather ahead, red to warn of imminent inclement conditions. As the son of farmers, Onni didn't need to be told what kind of weather was pending. He could see it in the type of clouds in the sky, or the feel of the wind against his skin. But he made a point of looking up at the beacon light anyway.

Just before Bay Street, he beheld the city hall, an imposing edifice of dark brown stonework with the green copper roof that loomed over the downtown. That's where he noticed Pellonpää's infamous Simpson's across Queen Street. October had brought brisker days, so that even in the direct sunlight, Onni didn't feel a need to go hunker down for yet another cup of coffee in the Simpson's air conditioned cafeteria.

His destination on this particular day was the tall, sleek Canadian Bank of Commerce building, which he understood to be the tallest building in the British Commonwealth. He paid a few dollars to the lady in the ticket booth in the impressive, almost intimidating lobby and joined several others in an elevator that would take them to the observation deck on the 31st floor.

High atmospheric pressure governed the weather that day, so the view from the deck in every direction was breathtaking. Onni had never been at such a height. The tallest structure in Peurajoki was the windmill along the church road. The sensation he felt on top of this skyscraper was that of being a celestial figure watching over the city. To the south, beyond the piers and warehouses, he could see the great lake, the waves shimmering in the sunshine. In every other direction, Onni was struck by how colorful the scene was, how dwarfed the private homes and almost all of the stores and businesses were by the maples, elms and oaks, now turning into a riot of red, orange and yellow. He thought of the

151

birches and alders of Peurajoki, which turn a bright yellow in September, and would be bare of leaves by now.

Onni looked west and tried to locate 31 Beverley Street. He spotted what he figured must be the park a few houses north of the boarding house. He stretched his right hand in front of him, and used the tip of his thumb to trace an imaginary line southward from the park, stopping just before Queen Street to mark the location of what was becoming his new home.

The sun, refreshing weather, and the almost transcendent height above the city on the deck caused a giddy sensation like an electric current to flow through his body from head to toe. He felt almost as if he had to pinch himself to make sure this experience was real and not a daydream.

Who would have thought eighteen years ago that someday I would be standing on the tallest building in the British Commonwealth, in a country almost 7,000 kilometers from where I was born and raised, with my whole undefined and open-ended future still ahead of me? It's so good to be alive!

As Onni was walking to the elevator to take him back down again, he beheld a sight that for him, was truly novel. Waiting for the elevator, resting his gloved hands on the rim of a cart on four wheels about three feet high, was a man – a *black* man. The man wore a shirt with his name Desmond stitched in letters on the left breast. On the right was the logo of the Canadian Bank of Commerce. It was obvious that Desmond was an employee of the bank, probably on the maintenance or cleaning staff. Best Onni could figure, the cart was used to collect and haul refuse from the various offices in the building.

Onni had seen pictures in his geography textbook at school of black people, usually Africans. The *Kaleva* sports pages had been plastered with photos of Jesse Owens on the medal stand at the Berlin Olympics in 1936. But he had never in his life encountered one in the flesh before. He tried not to stare at the man, but he was very curious and had a hard time keeping his eyes looking straight ahead at the closed elevator door. The man nodded his head and smiled at Onni in greeting, and uttered a few words politely which Onni thought must mean, "Good day". The contrast between the brilliant white of the man's teeth when he smiled and the dark color of the rest of his face was startling. Similarly, the whites of the man's eyes stood out and seemed to shine out like a light from the black background into which his eyes were set.

When the elevator arrived, Desmond extended his palm to indicate that Onni was welcome to enter first before him and the cart.

As the elevator door closed for the ride down, the very proper operator, a prim woman of about fifty, asked Onni, "Which floor, sir? Not comprehending his question, Onni merely smiled and replied, "Yes."

Desmond shrugged his shoulders, and even though he hadn't been asked, told the operator, "Ground floor, please."

Again, Onni did his best to keep his eyes focused on the blank door in front of them that was closing. Every few floors the elevator would stop to pick up new passengers. On one floor, another maintenance staff member entered, a white man this time, and greeted Desmond with some kind of comment that, of course, Onni didn't understand. It must have been a friendly comment, because in response to the other's greeting, Desmond let out a lusty laugh, and continued to shake vigorously with laughter. The other man joined the hilarity. He looked at Onni, perhaps inviting him in on whatever the joke was between him and Desmond. Onni could only smile politely to give the appearance that he knew what was up. The elevator operator didn't crack so much as a smile.

Outside, Onni headed west on King Street and retraced the steps he had taken the day he arrived and trekked back to the boarding house.

Interesting encounter, that was. I wonder if anyone in Finland has ever seen a black man before. Maybe here or in the United States, but certainly not in Finland. He looked so mysterious, so exotic as though from another world, with that

153

*differently colored skin. And yet . . . when Desmond stood
beside the other man in the elevator, both of them in the gold
and purple work uniform, they didn't look terribly different
from each other at all, only in the color of their skin.*

When Onni arrived back at the house, it was almost
the appointed time for supper. But no one was in the dining
room, and Mrs. Pyykkönen was not in the kitchen. Strange.
Had he been so determined to be back from his walk by the
strict appointed time for supper that he had arrived too early?

Onni heard men's voices emanating from a room in
the distance. He was pretty sure the voices were of Pellonpää
and Kalle. But the sounds were coming from the direction of
Mrs. Pyykkönen's personal living quarters. She had posted a
sign that read "Private" on the door leading to the corridor to
her flat, which made that one of the first words that Onni
learned in English.

Onni walked quietly down the corridor from the dining room. He put his right ear against the door. He heard Pellonpää's deep, scratchy voice from behind the door curse,
"Goddammit!". Onni wondered what he should or could do.
Why would Mrs. Pyykkönen allow – or invite – a man into
her personal quarters? He didn't think he should knock or in
any way make his presence behind the door known.

He had just lowered his ear and stepped away a short
distance from the door when the door opened suddenly. Kalle
came storming out, almost crashing into Onni. He was visibly
startled to see Onni where he hadn't been expecting him.

Then he blurted out, in Estonian, *"Seal saab olema
raske!"*. Having crossed the Atlantic with an Estonian as a
roommate, and in the few weeks he had been having breakfast and supper with Kalle, Onni had picked up enough Estonian to know that *raske* was the word for "trouble". Kalle had
already disappeared up the stairs, so Onni couldn't ask him
to explain his comment further.

*What trouble? Does he mean that I am in trouble for
snooping around Mrs. Pyykkönen's door? Or does he mean*

that trouble was coming for Pellonpää for trespassing into her
private living space? What?

Onni hadn't noticed till then that Kalle had left the door into her flat slightly ajar when he came out. Apprehensively, silently, Onni opened the door further and poked his head into the flat. His curiosity was too aroused now not to investigate the situation.

He saw Mrs. Pyykkönen, Pellonpää and the withdrawn Hutari sitting on overstuffed chairs in her living room, encircling her large radio console which dominated the living room and was making an indeterminate crackling noise.

"Oh, come on in, young man!" Pellonpää presumed to say very officiously when he spied Onni's face poking into the room from behind the door. He glanced at Mrs. Pyykkönen to conform that it was alright to allow Onni into the room as if asking for forgiveness after the fact rather than permission beforehand.

"We've been listening to Helsinki on the short-wave. Big news today! The Finnish delegation in Moscow met with both Stalin and Molotov yesterday. The buggers demanded the whole Karelian Isthmus for themselves! Their own part of the God-forsaken, swamp-filled, mosquito-ridden, not-much-good-for-anything wilderness isn't big enough for their inflated egos, so they insist on more! The ingrates! They want us to surrender some islands in the Gulf, and the Rybachy Peninsula. As far as I'm concerned, they can have that frozen little piece of shit in the Arctic. But to rub salt in our wounds, they demand rights to the naval base in Hanko. Can you imagine that? The greedy bastards."

Onni was stunned.

Mrs. Pyykkönen looked paralyzed, too, by the news. She continued to sit in sad silence and rock in her chair while Pellonpää railed and ranted.

"Kalle knows what this means. That's why he's angrier than a bull that sees red. The Russians started this way with the Estonians, too. First, they make a demand for land.

Then the bastards find some excuse to send in troops and claim not just the land they had the nerve to requisition, but *all* the land, every last hectare! They don't have balls, but they have nerve, the louse-infested bastards!"

At the mention of troops, Mrs. Pyykkönen asked, almost in a panic, "You don't think, do you, that they'd do the same with Finland?"

"Why not?" Pellonpää uttered. "Stalin has proven he's capable of just about any beastly crime."

Onni interjected, "My mother said in a letter that they had moved my brother's army unit from Joensuu to Kajaani. I wonder if this has something to do with it. Did Mannerheim have some inkling that Stalin would be up to something. But that's going in the wrong direction, isn't it? The border with Soviet Karelia is south and east of Joensuu, not north and west."

"Maybe even the Commander-in-Chief gets his directions mixed up sometimes," Pellonpää offered. "I hope to hell he gets it right, and very soon."

Chapter Twenty-Three:
Toronto
November 14, 1939

Onni realized that he was beginning to run out of the money his parents had given him. He grimaced internally when he remembered that the money had originally been given to the family by generous neighbors after the fire to rebuild Kuokkala. Now it was all almost used up. But it had given him the wings to get to Canada.

Mrs. Pyykkönen intuited that Onni might be reaching the end of his financial reserves. One morning, after the others had left for their jobs and Aune Kyllönen had retreated to her cell, she mentioned to him that business in the stores of Toronto was picking up, slowly, finally after almost a decade of decline.

"They're always looking to hire day laborers, you know, Onni? You get hired in the morning to work for that day. Usually to hand-deliver advertising notices to homes in the city. You know, the kind of fliers from stores that have started appearing at our front door the past few weeks. They pay $3.00 per day. You'll earn your rent in just a few days."

"I don't suppose I have to be fluent in English to do that," Onni responded, happy to have a lead for some productive activity after a month and a half of filling his days with sight-seeing and reading and sleeping.

"Oh, no, that's for sure. In fact, I doubt if many of the day laborers speak much English at all. More like Polish, or Ukrainian, or Hungarian. But you would need to learn enough English to introduce yourself and say to the man at the *Evening Telegram* printing plant, "I want work. Day labor.""

"I vant verk. Day leipo," Onni said, imitating her.

"Labor, it's labor, not leipo. Just add an "r" to leipo and you'll have it."

Onni went down to the plant early one morning at the beginning of the week. Since then he had returned to the house at twilight tired, his feet sore. He noticed that the shoes he had been wearing since he left Kuokkala would wear out in no time on this job. He felt the trickle of cold wetness in his right shoe whenever it rained, as it had done almost every day this past week.

When he arrived at the house one evening, he ran up to the bathroom he shared with Pellonpää and Dmytro to wash ink from his hands. When he got down to the dining room, it was almost empty. The others had finished their meal and scattered throughout the house to pass the evening. Only the reclusive Reino Hutari was remained in the dining room, seated in front of his plate of meat and potatoes at the table, facing Onni.

Onni gave a polite nod in Hutari's direction. As usual, when Hutari noticed, he turned his eyes immediately the other way so as not to make eye contact with Onni. Onni picked up knife and fork and began attacking the meal that Mrs. Pyykkönen placed before him, saying to him quietly,

"Just in the nick of time, young man. I hope it's still warm."

Onni saw Hutari out of the corner of his eye as he ate. He always felt that he was invading Hutari's secure personal fortress whenever he entered a room where Hutari had been by himself. Reino usually wrapped up his eating hurriedly so as not to have to risk any kind of verbal engagement with Onni, even if that meant leaving parts of his meal uneaten. Onni could understand shyness, for he himself was shy. But Hutari's obvious abject discomfort with company, and certainly Onni's, was beyond what Onni had encountered in even the most solitary backwoods loggers in Peurajoki.

But on this particular evening, however, Reino didn't rush his meal as usual in order to flee as quickly as possible to the safety of his secure, silent one-room retreat. Onni took a quick glance at Reino, hoping that it wouldn't be seen as too invasive. Reino seemed to have ceased eating completely, and was looking, almost staring, Onni thought, at Onni. As Onni glanced at him, Reino didn't dart his eyes elsewhere, but rather kept them on his dinner partner. Onni took another look to confirm his impression. Yes, by God, Reino was holding Onni firmly in his gaze as though he had never seen him before and was inspecting him for the first time.

Now, ironically, it was Onni who was feeling uncomfortable. He wasn't all sure how he should be reacting. He eliminated immediately the option of staring back, or acknowledging Reino's stare by smiling at him. That left the option of continuing to chew on his stew beef and potatoes as if nothing unusual were occurring. Onni had tried to engage Reino in conversation when he first arrived, just as he did the others, even Dmytro. But each time Onni had addressed Hutari with even the briefest and most perfunctory and conventional of greetings, Reino had acknowledged it by lowering his eyes and picking up his pace up the stairs or through the corridor to his room. What a strange and novel sensation now to have Reino's full, if mute, attention.

Only the awkward sound of Onni's jaw chewing the overly-well-done beef and sipping his buttermilk broke the silence.

Finally, as though even the mute one couldn't bear the silence any longer, Reino said in a rapid staccato, "They came back yesterday."

The remark seemed to have come from nowhere. Onni stopped chewing and looked over towards the source of the clipped sentence. Onni was disbelieving that it could actually have emanated from Reino's tongue.

"They came back yesterday," Hutari said again, just as quickly and machine-like as before.

"Pardon?" Onni queried rather tentatively.

"They came back yesterday. . . The Finnish delegation from Moscow. . . They came back from Moscow. . . To Helsinki. . . Yesterday."

Onni paused to consider how to proceed. Was Reino attempting to engage him in conversation? Or is it the case that he is mentally retarded in some way, or born with a speech impediment that could only speak in such hurried, mechanical phrases almost devoid of affect?

Hesitantly, very tentatively, Onni edged closer to the exchange. "Is that so? I hadn't heard."

He hoped that despite his lack of certainty about how to answer Reino, he had said it in a way that communicated his genuine interest in the political event itself.

But apparently, Onni had edged too close. Reino received Onni's words by averting his eyes once again, turning his head almost 45% away from Onni. He shoveled the rest of the food off his plate into his mouth, arose abruptly in almost military precision, and carried his dishes to the kitchen like a man on a mission.

As Reino passed through the dining room again, just as all he could see of him was his back, Onni said after him, "Thank you, Reino." Whether he was thanking the peculiar man for sharing important information about current events or for making the effort to engage him, Onni wasn't completely sure. But he was genuinely grateful on both counts.

And with that, Reino was out the door, and Onni was as confused and confounded as ever.

~~~~~~~~~~~~~~~~~~~~~~~~~~

An entry in Onni's journal:

The episode with Reino in the dining room today was absolutely bizarre. I had never experienced anything like it in my life. I had never before witnessed him actually talking with someone, anyone, let alone me. He usually sits facing Aune at the supper table over to the side of the dining room. They chew their bread contentedly, secure in their knowledge that the other doesn't want to talk, and therefore neither has to. I admit I had wondered silently to myself at first if perhaps

160

he was deaf, like poor Arto Heino back in Peurajoki, who can utter only indecipherable phrases.

I scratched my head for a long time after he left the dining room, as if in that way, I could make sense of what had transpired. But once I got over my being totally perplexed, I began to think deeply about it.

I felt deeply sorry for Reino. I see in him my own shyness mirrored back to me, only magnified many times.

The rest of us, however, even we taciturn Finns, consider his extreme shyness to be some kind of deformity, some malfunction of normal character. But I know how difficult it is to feel out of place, to believe that I have nothing valuable to offer, or that what I say will not be received well or welcomed. I think we are being too hard on poor Reino for being more shy than the rest of us.

Was this evening's episode an instance of an isolated soul's attempting to make a connection of some kind with another human being? I recall how relieved I was, overjoyed if I tell the truth, when Eino reached out and connected with me on the ship. I had been feeling so much like a stranger, so disconnected, before he took the initiative. Don't we all want connections to another human being, no matter how shy we are, and no matter how comfortable we feel being alone as well?

How is it that Reino chose me with whom to try to establish a connection? And why now? And does the Finnish delegation's coming back from Moscow have some special significance for him? Or does he sense that it is a matter of some importance to me, and so he wanted me to know about it?

I hope I will have another chance to connect with Reino, and that I have the sense to seize the opportunity.

~~~~~~~~~~~~~~~~~~~~~~~~~~~~~~~~~~~

It became clear a week later what Reino had been referring to. As usual, Pellonpää took great pride and pleasure in assuming the role of town crier who announced the news of important events, and chief editorialist who registered his opinion.

It had become almost an established tradition in the past few weeks for some of the residents to gather by Mrs. Pyykkönen's radio every day just before supper to hear the broadcast of the day's news from Finland. Every day in November seemed to bring a new and foreboding development in relations between their homeland and the Soviet neighbor. If Pellonpää had been able to contain himself and withhold his considered opinion about the events reported while they listened, then he would be glad to enlighten the other boarders at supper.

"Well, good countrymen, you heard for yourself what horse manure the Soviets are capable of dishing out for their people's consumption! To actually have the nerve to accuse the Finns before the nations of the world of having trespassed into Soviet territory. Pure unadulterated horseshit, I say."

Kalle, who understood a little Finnish, chimed in, "Here, here!" The rest remained quiet, knowing the pattern. They knew Pellonpää wasn't finished.

"So now Stalin has a pretext to withdraw from the non-aggression pact with Finland, which as you recall, I'm sure, I called a flimsy piece of paper that I wouldn't use even to wipe my ass, if you'll excuse my French. Does he expect the rest of the world to believe such crap?"

"*Maailma liidrid usuvad, mida nad tahavad uskuda,*" Kalle interjected in thick Estonian.

"You're absolutely right, my Estonian cousin. They'll believe whatever is convenient for them to believe and tell their people. If the Russkies trespass across the border onto Finnish soil, I wouldn't expect Lebrun or Churchill to lift a finger to help even though on paper, we're allies. They're too

162

preoccupied trying to halt Hitler's further advance into Poland. So-called 'allies', my ass!"

"Surely, the Russians wouldn't be brazen enough to march into Finland. They'd be foolish," added Mrs. Pyykkönen in a tone that seemed more like an uncertain question than a statement.

"My dear landlady," answered Pellonpää, as though he were the only one in the room qualified to respond. "I don't see any alternative. If Stalin wants the land he demanded, and if the Finnish delegation come home without agreeing to it, and if then the Finns file a counteroffer that Stalin throws into the fire, what else can it mean?"

Mrs. Pyykkönen appeared both disbelieving and disappointed in Pellonpää's answer and looked around the room at the others in search of someone to disagree with Pellonpää, who seemed so sure of the truth of his opinion. But no one spoke. Aune Kyllönen was rocking in her chair as usual, giving every indication that she hadn't heard a word that Pellonpää had said; Dmytro wondered what all of Pellonpää's unintelligible emotional steam was about; Reino looked down at the table before him as though there were some invisible secret inscribed on its surface. He did look up at Onni every now and then to read his reaction to the news.

For his part, Onni was thinking of Väinö, wondering if he was still stationed in Kajaani, or if his unit had been moved closer to the Karelian border. He felt a tinge of guilt that his older brother was on the precipice between peace and war, while he was thousands of kilometers away merely speculating about war.

"You know, the very first mention of my home village in the history chronicles," Onni inserted into the silence, "was when the Russians invaded it in 1486. What the heck would they want with a poor farming village in the frozen north?"

"They didn't want it, son," Pellonpää replied in a tone that struck Onni as at least a mite patronizing. "Don't you get it? If they had wanted your village, they wouldn't have raped the women and slaughtered the children and then set their houses on fire and gone on to the next unfortunate village."

That caused Onni's mind to make an unpleasant detour. Is there the possibility that some traces of Russian blood ran through his veins? Was an ancestor of his raped and impregnated with the rapist's child, who then began the Syrjälä or Kuokkanen lineage? How ironic would that be? What a repellent thought!

The news on the Finnish radio simply got more grave as the days and weeks passed. Not only had Russian troops crossed into Finnish Karelia, but they took the war to the skies as well. At the end of November, they dropped their first bombs on Helsinki. The next day, Stalin set up a puppet Communist government in Helsinki, the "Finnish Democratic Republic". Moscow radio had already declared Soviet victory on December 2.

Everyone in the rooming house was clearly on edge. Pellonpää's supper time editorials became louder and more animated. Kalle had a permanent scowl on his face, and Dmytro followed him around from room to room as though they were Siamese twins. Aune didn't appear any different, but Onni wondered what she knew and what thoughts might be spinning in her head. Reino remained his silent self, although Onni noticed that he looked up at him from his supper plate more often than before.

As he was wont to do when confronted by anxiety or worry, Onni retreated into silent contemplation and a book.

Mrs. Pyykkönen buzzed about the house, occupying herself with household duties, only more intently than before.

"Onni, are you a church person?" she asked him one day as he descended from his third-floor room.

"I wouldn't say 'church person', but I was confirmed."

164

"I'm going to church tomorrow. We Finns have our own church up on Huron Street. It's not actually a church building like the ones you see around the city, but a house that our men converted into a church. I don't get to go very often because I have this house and boarders to attend to, of course. But lately, I've been feeling the need to go to church. Usually Mrs. Aho who manages the building at No. 82 Beverley Street – you know, the one that has been turned into apartments – anyway, she usually goes with me. But she tells me she can't go tomorrow. Would you like to go with me, Onni?"

Onni hadn't really considered church very much since it seemed no one else in the house was involved there. But he had seen a Bible and daily devotion book on Mrs. Pyykkönen's coffee table when he had been there with the others to eavesdrop on *Yleisradio* from Finland.

He had been thinking off and on about God recently. It was hard not to with the grave developments in his homeland. He had made a few clumsy attempts to pray for Väinö.

He agreed to accompany Mrs. Pyykkönen to church the next day.

Chapter Twenty-Four:
Toronto
December 14, 1939

Peurajoki
14 December, 1939
Dearest Onni,

Thank you so much for your letter which arrived just a few days ago. It was so good to hear from you, that you are safe and doing well in your new country.

Mrs. Pyykkönen sounds like a wonderful landlady who treats you well. I have to admit that I feel a little jealous of her. She gets to mother you, while your mother is thousands of kilometers away, helpless to do anything but write letters. Oh well, I had my chance to mother you during your first seventeen years.

Father accomplished a lot on the new house in the fall. The foundation was poured and laid, the rough frame erected, the exterior plywood sheathing put in place to keep the rain, snow and wind on the outside during the winter. Pentti Toivola and Armas Pakarinen were a big help, especially in putting up the rough framing before the real cold weather began arriving last month. Father will work on putting in the rough plumbing pipes over the winter.

I'm glad that you have found work there in Toronto, and with a newspaper at that. Times have been so hard for a long time now that we were afraid (but didn't want to burden you with our fears) that you would find it difficult to find employment. What is it exactly that you are doing?

Have you been learning the English language? Don't let the others on your job teach you the wrong things to say – you know the kind of words and phrases you wouldn't use in your mother's hearing.

The big news back here – which I am sure you have heard among the Finns there – is the very real threat of our being thrust into another war barely twenty years after the civil war. We worry so about Väinö, though father keeps it to himself and doesn't like it if I voice my worries to him when he comes in from working on the house. And Väinö himself doesn't seem to be consumed by fear if what he writes in his letters is an accurate reflection of his heart. You know that his unit was moved to the barracks at Kajaani, which had been empty of soldiers. It's at least a little closer to home – if he gets leave, which unfortunately since the middle of last month, they are not permitting.

I feel so bad for the people and families in Helsinki who endured some violent bombing by the Russians a few weeks ago. Hertta Ukkonen has a sister in Helsinki. Her sister has written that she is well, but an apartment building on her block was hit and suffered serious damage. The residents of those apartments are now refugees in their own country. Why can't Stalin just leave us alone to live our lives in peace?

You may have heard over there that the Russian troops have now progressed far enough to see the whites of the eyes of the Finnish soldiers at their guard posts on our side of the border. In fact, they came over the border and surprised a small company of our soldiers at Suomussalmi, south of Kuusamo, and occupied the village. But father, especially, was overjoyed the other morning when *Yleisradio* reported that our forces had encircled the Russian troops on the frozen lakes near Tolvajärvi north of Lake Ladoga in Karelia. We did lose over one hundred men, however, which makes me sad, and some one thousand were wounded. But father reminded me that Russia lost over seven times as many men as we did.

But doesn't each one of those dead Russian soldiers have a mother worrying about him just as I worry about Väinö. Father chuckles and says that this is no time to get sentimental about the enemy.

Write whenever you can, Onni, and tell us about your life in the new world.

With all our love,
Mother and Father

This was the second week in a row that Onni and Mrs. Pyykkönen came to the little church house on Huron Street as a tandem. The broad-rimmed black straw that that she wore was at least five years behind current fashion trends. Pellonpää had muttered under his breath as they were going out the door at 31 Beverley Street, that her monstrous hat was at least twice the circumference of her head, and made her look even more petite than normal.

The worship service took place in what once was the living and dining rooms of a large, dark red brick house built in the early nineteenth century. It struck Onni as such a different setting for worship from the huge church in Peurajoki. The small electric organ which was used to accompany the hymns seemed so miniscule and inconsequential compared to the venerable pipe organ of which the citizens of Peurajoki were so proud.

Onni was surprised when the pastor, Leo Hepola, was standing at the rear of the room after the closing hymn greeting worshipers with a handshake. He had never witnessed that in the few times he had been to church back home. What impressed Onni even more was that Hepola had divested of the black cassock that he had worn to lead the worship and to preach, and was greeting people in shirt sleeves rolled up at his elbows and suspenders in plain view holding up his grey trousers. He couldn't imagine the rector in Peurajoki doing such a thing. But rather than be offended by such casualness, Onni found himself pleased by it.

Mrs. Pyykkönen introduced Onni to him when it was their turn in the line to greet the pastor. The pastor was youngish in Onni's estimation, compared to pastors he had seen in Finland. He might have been in his mid-thirties, although his sandy hair, which had likely been very blond when he was younger, was receding slightly in the front of his scalp. His body language gave off an image of youthful energy.

Hepola held out his hand and shook Onni's enthusiastically and said warmly to Onni, "I had heard that Maija

168

had a new tenant from Finland, and now I get to meet him in the flesh. Welcome, young man, and come again."

The next week, as Onni and Mrs. Pyykkönen were walking up the short flight of concrete stairs leading into the house, Hepola was at the door, greeting them heartily, and saying through a wide smile, "Welcome, Maija, and you, too, young Onni. I hope you've had a good week."

This was such a welcome difference from the emotionally restrained atmosphere at the Peurajoki church. Women of all ages greeted Maija keenly even though they had just seen her a week earlier. Onni could tell that Maija felt at home with these people. Men gathered in little clusters in the hallway before worship, but not one of them failed to shake Onni's hand before the morning was done.

All these men and women, presumably all born and raised back in Finland, now living a new life in a country far away. I marvel at that, truly marvel. Probably few of them could have imagined as children back in Finland that they would be living later chapters of their lives in a place they had barely heard of, a place that to their forebears and parents must seem like a misty dream. The river of life that carries us into the wider world keeps on flowing. I put my feet in that river just this past September. Each of them put their feet in it at some other time and in some other bend in the river. But the river has led all of us to this place. I don't know these people. But I feel that a bond as strong as iron ties me to them. They each have a unique story, although I am sure there are many threads and themes in their various stories that they share in common, even with mine.

Very strong coffee and *nisu* were served in an adjacent, much smaller room. Hepola made the rounds, greeting each person with a smile, and evidently inquiring of each person about his or her week. Onni could overhear a couple of the women mentioning others by name, absentees apparently, who were ill at home or in one of the hospitals. Hepola was jotting down their names in a tiny pad or paper and a small stub of a pencil.

It was a relief for Onni that Pellonpää's booming voice was absent.

There was another piece of 31 Beverley Street in the room, however. Onni hadn't noticed him during the worship service. But there, in a quiet out -of-the-way corner of the coffee room, dressed in a sport jacket whose sleeves were far too short for him, his long black hair nicely parted in the middle and slicked with an oily tonic, was Reino Hutari.

Onni had been approached by a jovial man in his fifties and was talking with him when he spotted Reino. He was fascinated that Reino would be at the church when he hadn't spoken a word previously that he had any interest in religious matters. But Onni didn't want to appear rude to the man who was interested in where Onni was from and where he was living, so he pulled his eyes and thoughts away from Hutari.

By the time the eager gentleman had finished his line of questioning with Onni, Reino had disappeared from the room as quietly and furtively as he had suddenly appeared.

Onni came back from the church feeling good. Hepola was so refreshing as the pastor, and Onni was warmly welcomed and received by members of the church with whom he felt a string bond. He had renewed hope that this church would help fill a void that he had felt ever since he arrived was growing in his core. On one level, it was a spiritual vacuum in a space deep within him that had been filled the first time at his confirmation. On another level, the letters from his mother reminded him that even if he would never acknowledge it to her or anyone else in Peurajoki, he was essentially lonely. He was glad to have ample time by himself, mind you, to explore his new city and to observe people. But ever since he and Eino parted ways, he was beset by a lack of meaningful human connection. On his solo reconnaissance expeditions into the city, Onni had even stopped by the bus terminal on Bay Street to investigate the fare and schedule to some town near Holland Marsh in the hopes of going and rekindling his friendship with Eino. But not knowing how to contact or find Eino once he got off the bus discouraged him from buying a ticket.

The time for supper was always moved up to mid afternoon on Sundays so that Mrs. Pyykkönen could enjoy one evening during the week when she was free from duties around the house. The menu usually consisted of something which they didn't have the rest of the week, often a beef or pork roast with roasted potatoes and vegetables which Mrs. Pyykkönen had fetched from the open-air Kensington Market nearby the day before.

Conversation was subdued on this particular Sunday afternoon as if even Pellonpää, who had abandoned his Lutheran faith and left the church behind, understood that it was a Sabbath, and that he should refrain from introducing opinions about the profane world of politics and current events into the serene environment. The boarders ate in monk- like silence, and then got up from their seats without a word and taking their used dishes into the kitchen. The only words spoken were "Thank you" to Mrs. Pyykkönen.

Onni had taken his time to savor the beef roast. He wasn't in a particular hurry to get back to his room, though he usually was. He noticed that on the other side of the room, Hutari was still finishing his meal.

Onni was still mystified by Reino's being present at the church, an equally, by his furtive and sudden disappearance. Seeing that Reino had taken the initiative a couple of weeks ago to begin a conversation with Onni, as clumsy and awkward as it had been, Onni felt fortified now to follow up and pursue further contact now. He took his dishes into the kitchen, and then on his way back through the dining room, he headed to the chair opposite Reino.

Reino visibly hunched his shoulders as if curling into a ball when he saw Onni approach and take a seat uninvited.

"Mind if I have a seat, Reino?"

For a short while, there was no verbal response as though Reino were reaching within himself for some rehearsed line of dialogue.

"Yes, it's ok." If Reino had spoken any more quietly and meekly, Onni doubted he would have heard him.

"No complaints, then?"

Reino shook his head slowly. His eyes were a big as saucers as though he couldn't believe what was happening.

"I saw you at the church today. Frankly, I was surprised." And then after a few seconds, added, "Oh, but don't get me wrong. I was pleased to see a familiar face. It's just that I didn't know you were interested."

Reino continued to site mutely, but attentive to Onni.

"Have you gone before? Have you been going on the other Sundays?"

"Once or twice," Reino replied docilely.

"Mrs. Pyykkönen invited me," Onni said.

Onni pondered his next sentence quickly in his mind.

Do I want to take the risk? It would be the polite thing to do, of course. Maybe he wants to go alone when he goes. But what if he says yes? What could we possibly talk about on the way there, or on the way back?

He decided to ask. "Would you like to come along with the two of us the next time? . . . Or, would you prefer to go by yourself?"

Reino looked a little more relaxed now. His eyes had returned to a normal size, even though he still had them riveted to the spot on the table in front of him.

"Yes, that would be nice," Reino said, but in a very rapid and clipped manner, as though he had to get the words out as quickly as possible, or else he'd lose nerve to say them at all.

"Good. I'll come by your door at about 9:30 next Sunday. We'll walk together to Huron Street, and if Mrs. Pyykkönen is able to join us, we'll make it a threesome."

Onni rose and pushed his chair back in its place by the table. He nodded a farewell to Reino.

"Next Sunday. . . The send-off," Reino said in the same mechanical monotone he used in their first aborted conversation.

"What's that, Reino? I didn't quite get what you said."

"Next Sunday . . . the send-off."

"The send-off? For whom?"

"The volunteers."

"Volunteers? I'm afraid I don't fully understand you, Reino. What volunteers?"

"The volunteers. . . For the war. . . The Finns."

Onni was getting a little frustrated that Reino could fill in only one short phrase of information at a time.

"The Finns are volunteering for the war?"

"Yes. . . At Union Station. . . Next Sunday. . . In the afternoon. I am going."

"To Union Station? Is that where the volunteers are coming?"

Now it was Reino that was growing slightly annoyed. Was it with Onni who didn't seem to comprehend quickly enough, or with himself for his inability to put a sentence together, to get his tongue and lips to shape the words he had in his mind?

173

"No, they're *going,*" Reino said in a slightly raised voice and insistent emphasis on the "going", like a child who is trying but can't get the grown-up to understand.

"Oh," Onni said, his face indicating that a light was going on in his brain. "I think I understand now. The volunteers will be getting on the train at Union Station?"

"Correct"

"And going back to Finland to join the effort against the Russians? Is that it, Reino?"

"Yes," he blurted, pleased that Onni understood. "Want to come?"

With that Reino looked even more intently at the spot on the table's surface. He appeared more anxious than before.

Onni wasn't sure he heard him correctly.

"Pardon, Reino?"

Reino looked downhearted and discouraged that he'd have to pronounce the extremely difficult, potentially explosive words again.

"Want to come along? . . .With me?"

Onni was stunned into silence. But he was careful not to maintain the silence too long, lest Reino think him ungrateful.

"Is it after supper next Sunday? If so, I don't have other plans. It'll be Christmas Eve; you know? My first Christmas in Canada. Sure, Reino, I'd be happy to come along."

174

Chapter Twenty-Five
Toronto
December 24, 1939

On the previous Sunday, Pastor Hepola had read the standard wording for the Intercessory Prayers from the handbook of the Church of Finland. But at the end of the assigned petitions, he added his own.

"Protect we beseech you, O dear beneficent Father, the sons of our dear homeland, Finland, who have been called forth from their peaceful lives into service for their nation. Keep them from harm or injury. Grant them your strength to withstand the assaults of the enemy. Fan their flames of love of their country and its people. Restore their spirits when they flag. Unite the people of the nation, divided as they have been by loyalties to opposing factions in previous decades, and inspire them to a new fervent and proud commitment to our one Fatherland in its time of peril and need. Sustain us all with the vision of the peaceable kingdom and the hope for peace infused in us by your Son, Jesus Christ, our Lord, the Prince of Peace."

Onni had been inspired by the genuineness of Hepola's prayer. After the service, he announced the farewell ceremony for the first contingent of Finnish-Canadian volunteers to join with the forces in Finland and Karelia fighting the Russians.

Later that afternoon, Onni and Reino walked side by side towards Union Station. Both wore their most formal clothing, Reino in his sports jacket that was too small, Onni with a blue sweater over white shirt and tie. It was, after all, Christmas Eve. Besides, Onni had reasoned, he wanted to honor the young men being sent off on their perilous project in the home country with the best he could offer.

Onni had to stop every now and then to allow Reino to catch up to him. Reino took short, almost childlike steps.

They could hear the muffled sound of a band playing familiar Finnish folk tunes inside the cavernous station as they approached down Bay Street. There was a small stream of other prototypical Finns entering the building off Front Street, most bearing small Finnish blue and white flags in their hands. Onni and Reino accepted a flag from a woman near the entrance and went into the central hall of the Union Station.

In the center of the hall, a stage had been set up. Sitting on folding chairs on the stage was a row of a dozen or so men, young, not much older it appeared, than Onni. Mixed in among them, however, were several slightly older men, in their early forties perhaps. Onni recognized one from the coffee hour at the church. He later discovered that these were veterans wounded in the War for Finnish Independence.

In front of these men was a podium, and seated behind it, three gentlemen, one of whom was Hepola. The emcee of the proceedings was a portly man of fifty or so. Later it was disclosed that this way Lindsey Graham, a prominent lawyer who was also the Consul-General for Finland in Toronto. He was effusive in his praise of the men facing them on the stage, their bravery, sense of self-sacrifice and love of homeland. They were, he said, among Canada's finest citizens, a down-payment and surety of other forthcoming Canadian support for the war effort in Finland.

He introduced an elegant-looking clergyman, the senior pastor of Graham's own church, Knox Presbyterian, to say a few words and give a blessing. He did so, and then invited Hepola to say a prayer and add a few words in Finnish.

Even though he had just met him a few weeks' prior, Onni was proud of his pastor, who came across as so humble and yet self-possessed, so full of grace and calmness, yet clear passion for the cause.

The makeshift band consisting of a trumpeter, drummer, trombonist and accordionist, accompanied the gathered assembly in the singing of "God Save the King". The men on the stage seemed shy about singing in front of all these people. But when the band broke into a less than perfect version of

Oi, Maamme, Suomi, even these reticent citizen soldiers joined in with unbridled enthusiasm and solemnity.

The brief formal program was brought to a close by Graham's making a plea for donations to the Finland Aid Society. Then the small crowd began to disperse as family members, wives and girlfriends of the men approached the stage to hug their loved one and accompany them to the stairs that led down to the trains to New York City.

As Onni turned to Hutari, he thought he saw moistness in his eyes reflected by the bright lights above. Onni remained silent as they both turned towards the exit.

"That was a great event, Reino. Thanks for inviting me to come along."

Reino struggled for what to say. He was clearly not used to being thanked or having his invitation or suggestion received with appreciation.

Finally, he coaxed a "You're welcome," out of himself.

"That was absolutely inspiring. I don't remember ever singing our national anthem with such pride and emotion."

Reino looked too overcome to respond. It was clear to Onni that Reino was still moved in the wake of the event.

"I have to admit I felt a little tinge of shame as well," Onni confessed.

Reino looked at him puzzled.

"I mean, my brother, and I am sure older brothers of my school buddies from Peurajoki, are in the army right now. I was too young to be called up when I left Finland, but I'll be eighteen soon. This farewell made me wonder if I should be going back to Finland along with those men on the stage tonight. I feel like a coward."

177

After the silence following his confession, he appended his remark with a question.

"Reino, you're just a little older than me, right? Are you at all considering signing up?"

Reino had a look of panic on his face. His brain seemed to be rushing towards an answer, but again his tongue and lips couldn't keep up.

After a while, he said, "I can't go. My eyes. My glasses. They won't take me."

"Oh, yes, I see."

Then with his left hand, Reino reached for Onni's right hand, and said very quietly, very solemnly, but very clearly, "Don't go."

Onni had trouble falling asleep that night. He didn't know quite what to make of Reino's softly-spoken remark that he didn't want Onni to sign up as a volunteer. Was it some kind of verbal gesture of a growing friendship? Or an unnatural dependency on Onni to fill some vacant space in Reino's life, which Onni in no way wanted. He wanted some kind of friendship in his new surroundings in Canada. But he didn't want to be responsible for someone else's happiness.

Or, did the remark possibly have a deeper, more profound and confused intent behind it? Certainly Reino's taking Onni's hand in his seemed to suggest that. Onni's first instinct had been to pull his hand away. But he was too confused by the suddenness of the gesture, the utter unexpectedness of it, to have the presence of mind to do so. By the time Onni had made up his mind to pull his hand away, Reino had already withdrawn his, and held it close to his side as though he was disciplining it for acting without permission.

He finally fell asleep without an answer to his wondering.

178

He was awakened, however, some indefinite time later, in the middle of the night, or early morning before sunrise, by a startling, haunting dream. An indistinct spectral figure approached him in his dream, trespassed uninvited into his sleep, and seemed to be speaking to him from out of a deep white mist that partly shrouded its face. The figure was trying desperately, like Reino, to articulate something. But it wasn't Reino. The face of the figure became a little more clarified as the mist seemed to evaporate. It had no color that was familiar or known. The eyes were large and round, almost too large to fit a human face. The figure moved its grotesque mouth, but emitted no sound.

The figure was robed in bleached white. A red stain on the soft surface of the robe near what would have been its chest glistened in the bright light shining from beyond the mist. The face grimaced in pain.

Still, the figure continued to move its mouth through the pain. But Onni was unable to read the figure's otherworldly, misshapen lips.

And then, Onni was awake with a start, his mind groggy and muddled, sitting dazed in his bed, shaken, mystified amid the rumpled sheets damp with sweat, on the longest night of the year.

Chapter Twenty-Six:
Toronto
January 10, 1940

Onni had mentioned to Mrs. Pyykkönen one morning after breakfast that he was impressed with her pastor, Hepola. She was pleased that Onni was impressed, for to Mrs. Pyykkönen, Hepola was the best thing to come along for the Finnish immigrants in Toronto in a long time.

"He cares about us and our lives. He lets us know that we are his people. He's younger than me by a lot of years, but he feels like a father.'"

She told Onni about the English lessons Hepola was holding at the church.

"Perhaps you should go and give them a try. You can't get far in this country if you can't speak the language."

Onni agreed that it was high time he started to learn English. After work on the evening of first weekday after New Year's, he walked to Huron Street and enrolled in the class.

After class was dismissed on the second or third evening, Hepola asked Onni to stay a moment. The others either gave Hepola a nod or a short curtsy and left the room.

"Onni, I'm so glad you have come to the class and to the church. I've been meaning to come over to Maija's rooming house and get to know you better. But with all the activity around Christmas, I haven't had the chance."

He asked Onni about his place of origin, the size of his family, and a brief summary of his journey. When Hepola asked him about any plans for his life in Canada, Onni started slowly and reticently. But his pace and tone sped up as he talked about his hope to study journalism and become a newspaper reporter.

"Well, it's good that you are beginning to learn English, then. It's pretty hard to study at the university where the classes are in English, of course, if you don't. And there isn't a market in this country for many Finish journalists. I write an article every now and then for the *Vapaa Sana*. But you can't make a living doing that."

"I get a free copy of the *Evening Telegram* every weekday because my job delivering fliers starts at the plant every morning," Onni volunteered. "But the newspaper is hard to read when it's not in your mother tongue."

"But it's a good habit, Onni. Keep it up. Bring a copy to the class next time, and we'll try to study an article together as a class."

Onni shook his head in concurrence.

"The *Evening Telegram*, did you say? I'll see what I can do."

Chapter Twenty-Seven
Toronto
January 21, 1940

Peurajoki
January 14, 1940
My dearest Onni,

Oh, Onni, the pain of it is too much to bear! I sit here at the table in the *tupa* with tears streaming down my worn cheeks and dripping onto this piece of paper. At first, I wasn't going to write you about this. You are so far away, and launching your own life. But father said it would be unconscionable not to let our younger son, and Väinö's only brother, hear the news from his own mother. And so, as painful as this is for me and surely will be for you, I obeyed father and now am sending you this unbelievably horrific news.

Onni, we received news from Väinö's company commander that on January 10, Väinö's body was found in the snow with a fatal bullet wound in his chest. That's right, dear Onni, your brother is gone, is no more. I am sorry that I could not think of a gentler way to tell you. It must be a terrible shock to you just as it was to us here when the commander's letter arrived. As soon as Pertti Laakso saw on the envelope that it was from the Finnish military, he kindly made a special trip to Kuokkala to hand-deliver the letter to us even though it wasn't our usual mail day. I'm sure he hadn't seen the letter, but you could tell that he knew.

Oh, Onni, I can scarcely believe it. It's too much for a mother to absorb. I shake my head all day long in disbelief. I go about the necessary chores totally unthinkingly, as though I am in a dream, a nightmare from which I cannot awaken. But then I realize that it's not a dream. I reread the commander's kind letter over and over again to make myself believe that it's really true, that our elder son is lost to us; he who had so much life ahead of him; he whom we relied on to take over the running of Kuokkala as we got to be too old. The plan's now all gone in ashes.

I can hardly write; my heart is in such pain. But I feel better writing you. It's as though you're here in the *tupa* beside me and I can reach out my hand and touch your arm, or your hair, and hold you close to myself.

The nice commander – Nurmi is his name – wrote that his company had arrived near Suomussalmi on January 7 as reinforcements for the Finnish boys who had liberated the village from the Russians in the weeks after Christmas. His company had been part of a battalion that made a final push out from the village onto the surrounding lakes and woods to flush out the few Russians who had not been chased out earlier. Captain Nurmi says that in the fierce fighting, Väinö had been separated from the rest of his company. The medics who found Väinö's body near an abandoned Russian tank on the frozen lake surface said that we can take comfort from the fact that someone appears to have tended to his wound, that he didn't die alone and without help. The medic found a makeshift bandage over the wound. But judging from the relatively rudimentary way the bandage had been applied, the medic said, it must not have been a medic who nursed him, but most likely a fellow soldier. But the medic adds, Captain Nurmi wrote, that even if the bandage had been applied properly by one of the medical corps, he doubts that poor Väinö could have survived a bullet so close to the heart and through a lung. No one in Väinö's company has reported having seen Väinö that day, much less having nursed him after he was shot.

I say it was Väinö's body that the medic found because that's not really Väinö any longer, just his outer shell. I believe the real Väinö is with my mother and father in the bosom of God, where I long to go, too, to be with them.

Oh, my dear Onni. The war was barely a month old when your brother was killed! The irony of it! My heart is so broken that I don't know how I can go on living. But for the sake of Hilja's and Alma's little ones, I must find a way to go on and begin life again.

This has been difficult for your father, of course, but he doesn't want to talk about it. Even though it's frigid cold, and there aren't many chores in the barn this time of year, he spends a big part of each day out there, or else at m*ummu's* and p*appa's* fixing one item or another. They know not to talk about Väinö's death in his hearing. *Mummu* just sits in the bedroom crying as I do, I know, and *Pappa* seems more lethargic than usual, as though he doesn't see much point in his usual routine anymore.

Väinö's body will be brought back here to Kuokkala as soon as they can get through on the snow-covered road. We'll keep him here in the barn until the earth thaws in the spring and then bury him in the church cemetery at that time. We know you will not be able to come.

Oh, Onni, my own flesh grows cold thinking about that. To be standing at the graveside of my child.

I am especially relieved and thankful to God that you are far, far away from this danger. I could not bear having two sons exposed to the perils of this war and the potential of being killed.

Elsa Varjanen, who as you remember, lost two sons in the civil war, has been so kind comforting me. She says time heals all wounds. But she admits there are still two empty corners in her heart that will never be filled again.

There will other households here in Peurajoki, I know, that will receive a similar letter from their son's commander with the horrible news. This war seems so needless. Why do the Russians want some of our land when it is the biggest country in the world, as you showed me so many times on your globe, do you remember?

But since the Russians started down this violent path, I agree with father and *Pappa* that we have to respond or else the whole nation will be lost. Our family can take pride in the midst of our profound grief that Väinö sought to do his part in keeping our fatherland free.

God keep you safe in His care.

With deepest love and longing.
Mother

Onni reread his mother's letter several times, just as she had Captain Nurmi's letter, to make sure that he had read correctly. The stalwart, fearless Väinö, shot? Dead? Never to speak or walk or laugh again?

He didn't go to his usual day labor that day. He didn't think he had the strength to walk the streets of Toronto, carrying a cloth bag of advertising fliers. He didn't see much point in the few dollars he would make. He couldn't muster the motivation. He didn't even try.

Instead, he sat much of the day in the silence of his room on the third floor. He sat holding his mother's letter in his hand for a long time, his eyes staring vacuously at the plain wall above the small wooden desk. He hadn't made a sandwich for himself in Mrs. Pyykkönen's kitchen to take to work as he usually did right after his breakfast. He was in no mood to eat.

Onni was disappointed in himself that the first emotion he had felt when he had read his mother's letter had not been grief, or longing for Väinö, but rather resentment. Väinö's dying, and in so doing, becoming a war hero summoned up again from Onni's unconscious the feeling of inferiority Onni had often had in his older brother's presence. By the benchmarks by which one measures a man – physical strength, mechanical aptitude, technical skill, proficiency in sports, competence with a rifle or fishing pole – Onni usually felt so frustratingly mediocre in comparison to Väinö. His parents had been careful not to seem to value Väinö's manliness more than Onni's penchant for the realm of the imagination and intellect. But Onni knew that it was Väinö's aptitudes that are considered essential in an agricultural society. On most days, he could accept that fact without jealousy and even have respect for his brother's pragmatic abilities. But on others, he resented his older brother for them. Now he felt ashamed of his resentment.

He sat in his room and relived some of those experiences from their boyhood. Foremost in his reminiscences on this day was the hunting expedition.

In the depths of the 1930s, the only meat that could be procured to add to the stew, without paying a king's ransom at the market in Oulu or Kemi, was the animal that gave Peurajoki its name – deer – or else rabbit or hare. When Martti was occupied with getting fields prepared for seeding in the spring, Väinö became the family's primary hunter in the patch of woods behind the cow barn.

Väinö would usually return from his safari carrying a hairy carcass or two of a rabbit, and occasionally even a fox or deer. As he got older, Väinö became accustomed to dressing the animal and cutting the meat into pieces small enough to throw into a frying pan to brown and then add to a pot of steaming stew.

Tyyne was grateful and Martti was visibly proud.

On one occasion in 1935, Väinö invited Onni to come along for a day of hunting in the woods. That was in 1935.

"Do you think you dare to be parted from your books for just one day and help feed this family?"

Onni had been taught by Martti how to shoot and care for a rifle, but he had always turned down his father's invitation to come along.

He had tired of Väinö's implicit mockery in his questions to Onni. If it would get Väinö to lay off and cease his teasing, then he'd go along this one time.

When they arrived in the woods, Väinö had suggested that they separate and go in different directions. Onni crept slowly and carefully to the left. After twenty or so minutes of near silence, Onni thought he heard the cracking of a large twig and the rustling of the fallen birch leaves on the forest floor. Onni stopped and listened. Eventually his eyes spied a small brown figure jumping about twenty meters in front of him. His shot echoed in the spaces between the tall spruce trees and denuded birches. The jumping ceased.

When Onni walked to see what he had shot, he saw a tiny ruptured slice of animal life splayed on the forest floor, no larger than the size of Onni's fist. The creature's eyes were open as though at its last breath they wanted to take in the wonder of the forest one last time. Blood oozed from its riven body and formed a small puddle before it was absorbed into the sandy earth.

It was a baby squirrel, one of this early spring's litter, no doubt, whose mother had perhaps forced it out of its nest so that it would learn to handle itself in the world.

Onni's head was spinning. He bowed his head in shame. He lowered his body onto his backside and sat beside the slaughtered animal.

When Väinö ran over to see what had happened, he found Onni slumped on the ground and weeping almost uncontrollably.

Väinö was relieved that the shot he had heard was not that of his younger brother accidentally misfiring or injuring himself. But his relief morphed into visible anger as he beheld his brother groveling there on the ground, weeping like an infant.

"God dammit, Onni! You're thirteen years old. Be a man! Christ, I wonder if you ever will!"

To Onni, it felt as though Väinö had just spoken those damning words yesterday. They echoed in his mind now as he remembered his brother. Did Väinö die thinking that his pathetic younger brother hadn't grown into a man even now? The possibility pained Onni even more than the fact that he'd never hear his brother speak another word again. To feel that way in the wake of his brother's death shamed him.

When the avocado green walls of his room began to crowd in on him, he grabbed his grey winter coat which he had found in the thrift store on Queen Street, and headed down the stairs. Mrs. Pyykkönen was carrying a basket of laundered sheets and towels to the closet on the second floor. As Onni passed her without saying a word in the corridor on his way to the stairs leading to the ground floor, she expressed her surprise that he hadn't gone to work.

"Are you not feeling well, young Mrs. Syrjälä?"

Onni's reply was almost at the volume of a hoarse whisper. "I feel well enough, thank you. I'm just going to get some fresh air."

"I noticed a letter from home in the mail this morning. Everything fine there?"

Onni would have preferred just to get outside without an intervening conversation with her, as genuinely warm as she always was towards him.

Reluctantly, he said, "Not exactly fine. Thank you for asking, Mrs. Pyykkönen, but I'm just not ready to talk about just now. Maybe later."

At that, she looked him in the eye, and then resumed her task in the closet.

"You go get some air, Onni. Then, when you come back, if you're up to it, just feel free to knock on my door. Sometimes it helps just to talk with someone."

She sounded so much like his own mother. But like his father, he doubted that divulging his feelings about Väinö's being killed at Suomussalmi would do much good.

Would it bring Väinö back from the dead? Would talking about it turn back the calendar to a date before January 9?

He put on his snow boots just inside the front door and exited the boarding house, turning right on Beverley Street, heading towards Grange Park. The little plot of green is usually filled with children in the summer time. But now in winter, the park was abandoned and eerily silent. Appropriately so, Onni thought. In fact, he felt that the whole world should come to a respectful halt, stand at silent attention with its right hand over its heart, in solemn acknowledgement of

188

Väinö's death and Onni's own bewilderment that had not yet translated to real grief.

He brushed the shallow coating of snow off a bench and sat on it in a daze for a half-hour until he noticed that he had started to shiver in the January air. He rose and started walking out of the park towards McCaul Street with no definite destination in mind. He just wanted to walk, to feel the frost-hardened ground of the park, colder than death, beneath his feet.

He continued his hike up McCaul Street, thankful that he didn't have to encounter any other pedestrians. He wanted the street to himself. He wanted to be immersed in his own private grief.

McCaul came to a "T" intersection at College Street and the edge of the campus of the University of Toronto. A couple of male students were bundled in threadbare coats, hunched and leaning forward against the wind that had started to blow from the north. But Onni was oblivious to the cold, unmindful of the gathering wind, unaware of any particular destination.

He crossed Beverley Street again as he navigated along the edge of the university campus. At the next intersection, he noticed that the street sign read "Huron St.". Without any thought or intent that he was aware of, he turned right and headed north up Huron Street. He came upon number 246 Huron Street almost as though he had been transported there without any willful assent or intent of his own.

He walked up the three steps leading to the front door of the church house, opened it hesitantly, not knowing what he wanted to encounter within. He walked very quietly, almost furtively, into the room that had been converted into a library for Finnish immigrants. Onni investigated the books on the shelves. Someone had had the good intention of shelving the books in alphabetical order by title. But either the individual who had started the project abandoned the notion of a tidy alphabetized library, or else people making use of the library had failed to abide by the volunteer librarian's example and simply returned books in some haphazard manner and according to a system idiosyncratic to each individual. Some books were stacked horizontally in unruly piles, making it difficult for the browser to establish the titles.

Most of the heavily-bound volumes were devotional works written by some Finnish pastors and bishops. One book that Onni noticed was worn from frequent reading and handling was a biography of Paavo Ruotsalainen, the peasant from Nilsiä whose pious followers founded the Awakened Movement in the early nineteenth century for others who were dissatisfied with the overly-fed clergy of the state church that was closely aligned with the aristocracy and landed gentry.

Onni hadn't noticed that he hadn't thought much about Väinö's death or his own sorrow since he came in from the sidewalk on Huron Street. But what he had noticed in that room surrounded by books, however, was a most welcome respite, a pleasurable peace within that had eluded him since receiving his mother's letter.

He walked over to a table on which lay several newspapers. One was the *Evening Telegram*, which he would have received had he gone to the plant to retrieve his fliers to deliver. Another was a new Finnish language paper, the *Vapaa Sana*, that had been established in Toronto at the beginning of the previous decade. Conspicuous by its absence in this makeshift library was the other Ontario Finnish language publication, *Vapaus*. Whoever was overseeing this library was seeing to it that the influence of the strong leftist element would not be felt there.

Onni had heard people at the church mention the *Vapaa Sana* which arrive weekly in their mail. He had never looked at it himself, however. So he picked up an issue, one dated December 4, 1939. He skimmed the headlines and quickly read a few stories. It was the lead editorial that caught and held his distracted attention. The editorialist was lamenting the start of the war in Karelia, and castigating the Soviet Union for the merciless bombing of Helsinki at the end of the previous month.

The editorial discussed the shelling incident at Mainila on November 30, the spark that lit the Russian powder keg. Pellonpää had spoken about it back at 31 Beverley Street, but it hadn't sunk in in Onni's consciousness at that time.

Mainila was on the eastern end of the Gulf of Finland, a little to the north of Leningrad, on Soviet territory. The Russians accused the Finns in no uncertain terms of shooting at the village from the Finnish side of the frontier. But, the editorial argued, the incident was probably not initiated by the Finns at all. Instead, the newspaper had argued, shots from across the border in Finland could not have possibly caused the kind of damage that had been inflicted on the seaside village. In fact, the Finns did not possess a weapon of any sort that was powerful enough and had the range to send a shot successfully over 800 meters over the border as far as Mainila. Therefore, the village must have been destroyed by the Russian forces themselves, not the Finns.

In the ruins of the village, however, Stalin had the pretext he needed within the international community for invading Finland, the alleged "aggressors". Pellonpää had been correct in his speculations.

Onni felt heat rise to his face as he read the editorial. He had been so overcome by Väinö's death that he hadn't thought about the Russian soldier who had fired the fatal bullet that struck his brother. But now he felt an anger growing in his breast, not so much for the nameless and faceless Russian soldier, but for the military machinery of the Soviet Union that in all likelihood had fabricated a deadly ruse to further its imperial aims. His brother's untimely death could be traced, indirectly at least, to Stalin's lie. Tears welled up in Onni's eyes as he read and contemplated the editorial, but they were tears of rage, not just of grief.

Pastor Hepola entered the library and was startled that there was someone else in the room.

"Oh, hello Onni. I'm sorry for intruding. I hadn't heard anyone entering the building."

"I'm sorry, sir," Onni said sheepishly, trying to compose himself. "I found the door open, and so I let myself in."

"That's perfectly alright, Onni," the pastor assured him. I'm glad someone is making use of the library."

He paused and took a longer, closer look at Onni.

"You look upset, son. Is anything wrong?"

Onni was taken aback by the pastor's question. Obviously he wasn't as practiced in masking his emotions as the other men in his family.

"Oh, I'm upset after reading this editorial in the *Vapaa Sana* about the Russians' staging an attack on their own people in Mainila and making it look as though we Finns did it. A war, instigated on a false pretext. Shame!"

"You found the editorial convincing and moving, then, did you?"

"Yes, it moved me to anger"

"I'm glad . . . because I am the one who wrote the editorial."

Onni was surprised.

"*You* wrote it?"

"Remember, I told you that I write an article every now and then for the *Vapaa Sana*. One day in early December, when I was in the *Vapaa Sana* office on Queen Street, I made a comment to the editor to whom I handed an article about the church for the next issue. I expressed my feelings about the incident and how I tended to believe the Finnish officials who were denying any Finnish responsibility for the attack, and my frustration with the Russians for denying the Finns' calls for an official inquiry. He knew I was from a small village outside of Viipuri. He could see how passionate I was

192

about the incident. And even though strong passion and emotion and good journalism often do not mix, he asked if I'd be willing to write the editorial since they are so short-staffed."

Onni was impressed by the pastor's abilities as a writer and his being invited to represent the editors of the newspaper with an editorial. The old familiar journalistic juices were starting to run in his veins again. Onni thought how much he would enjoy submitting an editorial someday. But immediately, he felt shame that he was lost in his own thoughts when his brother had just been shot. He sat in silence.

The pastor noticed and perhaps read Onni's thoughts.

"But I don't think the editorial, or the fabrication by the Russians, is what's really troubling you, is it, Onni?"

Onni lowered his eyes so that they didn't meet the pastor's which seemed to be peering right into Onni's heart. His eyes began welling up with tears. Onni was afraid that if he spoke now, he wouldn't be able to get far without bursting into tears. He felt embarrassed.

"Well, yes, there is something else." He couldn't go any further.

"Take your time, Onni. Say more if you like, when you feel able."

Onni appreciated the pastor's creating space and time for him.

"I don't know how else to say it other than to tell you . . . that my mother wrote . . . to tell me . . . that . . . my-older-brother-was-killed-at-Suomussalmi". He blurted the last words of the sentence as quickly as he could before he'd break down emotionally. The tears rose in his chest. For the first time since he was a little boy, he didn't stop them. He let them spill down his cheeks. Then he raised his hands to his face and shook uncontrollably as he wept.

The pastor remained silent. Onni was grateful.

After a minute or so, Hepola placed his left hand firmly on Onni's trembling shoulder. Onni's trembling intensifies initially until gradually, it stopped and he raised his head out of his hands.

"Mother says that they found him on January 10, but that he probably was shot the day before as the Finnish forces advanced out of the village towards the Russian units in the woods. I feel so grateful for the man who tried to bandage Väinö's wound and might have been with him when he died. I wish I could tell him how much Väinö's family appreciates it."

Onni launched into a new bout of weeping and shaking. Hepola handed him his handkerchief. Onni wiped his eyes and wet cheeks.

"That was a generous gesture by the man," Hepola said very quietly, almost in a whisper. "Is Väinö your only brother, Onni?

"Yes. He's three years older than me. Or was."

The pastor's voice and demeanor remained quiet and ever-so gentle. Onni felt himself relaxing, his heart beating a little more slowly, his throat stinging noticeably less.

"It hurts to lose your only brother," Hepola said.

"We weren't always close because we're so different," Onni offered. "But still, he was my brother. My only brother. I still can't believe he's gone."

"It takes time for the heart to absorb the loss and for the mind to grasp the news."

"But who knows, we might have grown closer as we got older? But now I'll never know."

"Death always has a way of cutting off relationships and short-circuiting potential."

Onni nodded his head thoughtfully. "The funeral won't be until the spring when the earth thaws. I don't know if I can afford the trip. But I feel such a need to be closer to my family."

"You don't need to decide that now. For now, it's important to just acknowledge your loss and to grieve. There's nothing shameful about sadness and tears. Tears are God's way of healing our hurt."

Again, Onni nodded his head slowly in assent.

"It's like Väinö and I have been playing the parts of Cain and Abel all our lives, or Jacob and Esau," Onni said.

"But if you're Cain, you haven't killed Abel, have you? You had nothing to do with your brother's death. But it's to be expected that when someone dies, we feel some guilt."

Onni sat in silence and pondered Hepola's words.

"Thank you, pastor. I feel better now. I haven't talked about this with anybody else yet. But I will write my mother and father and sisters so they can know that I share in the sorrow. Thank you, pastor. It was helpful to talk. I'm sorry I came unannounced."

Onni stood up and gathered his hat from chair. He looked one more time a Hepola. Then Hepola spread his arms and pulled Onni towards him and embraced him. This was totally unexpected for Onni, and a novel experience to be embraced by a man. Even by his own father. But he brushed aside his discomfort with the new, and allowed his body to rest in Hepola's embrace.

"God be with you, Onni, and with your family. God's loving arms will receive his precious child, Väinö Syrjälä. Be sure of it."

195

Chapter Twenty-Eight:
Toronto
January 20-23, 1940

Onni's heart felt much lighter as he headed for home. He turned down Beverley Street from College.

He was grateful for Pastor Hepola and his listening ear and calm manner. Hepola was at least fifteen years his senior. Onni wondered if Hepola had experienced the loss of a loved one. Surely, having been born in the first difficult decade of the new century, and having come of age in the tumultuous and tortured twenties, he must have lost someone to sickness, or accident, or surely the civil war. He sat by Onni's side and spoke with such authority, even if his speech was gentle, that Onni was sure the pastor was not unfamiliar with death.

He was grateful for the pastor's assurance that God would receive Väinö into his everlasting arms, even though he wasn't altogether sure he believed it thoroughly. He believed in God, to be sure, believed that there is a power greater than ourselves that in some mysterious, unfathomable way oversees all. He recalled the sureness of his faith on that Sunday after Easter several years ago back in Peurajoki, when he had walked Anna-Liisa home afterwards, even though on subsequent Easters the thrill of certainty was more elusive.

True enough, I believe there is a God. But if God is in charge, how could he allow Väinö to perish in the bitterly cold snow of Suomussalmi? Doesn't God have the power to intervene somehow, to provide a protective shield around Väinö and all the other soldiers who might have begun that day with a devout prayer for God's protection, so that they would not be lost? What about the prayers lifted up to God by the chaplain in the worship services in the barracks or out in the field? Were those prayers not heard by God?

Even though they're Russian Orthodox and pray in a manner different from ours, wouldn't the Russian soldiers have prayed the same way that morning for God's protection?

196

Wouldn't the Russian chaplain have uttered prayers not all that different from those offered by the Finnish Lutheran chaplain? How does God differentiate between those prayers? Does he choose a favorite? Or, since it's too difficult for God to deal with prayers by opposing armies, does he just abdicate and ignore the prayers of them all?

Onni had tried to have discussions about such unanswered questions, maybe utterly unanswerable questions, for that matter, with Väinö when they were younger. But each time, Väinö had simply waved off Onni's questions and speculations, saying it was time for his little brother to come back to earth and get to his chores as Väinö was doing.

My head says that we are just pawns in a cosmic chess game, that God has bigger matters to address than our prayers and wishes. In the back of my mind, I have doubts that God even noticed that Väinö was shot. He was just one of dozens who fell that day. He was just one of thousands who were victims of enemy fire that day in places like Poland where the Nazis had solidified their iron rule.

But today, I feel something stronger than the ruminations of my mind. Pastor Hepola's words penetrated deep into me and touched my heart. None of this makes sense to my mind. But my heart chooses to trust that all evidence to the contrary, God notices me, and wishes well for me. I choose to trust Pastor Hepola's assurance, that God will receive Väinö into his embrace.

Onni had been so immersed in his thoughts that he hadn't noticed how quickly the walk back home had gone. As he approached the boarding house, he noticed that Reino was standing out on the sidewalk in front of the house, looking forlorn and confused. He hadn't bothered to put on a coat to protect himself from the January chill. He wore only the one well-worn woolen sweater that he had been wearing practically every day since the fall. Reino was scanning the street in both directions rather anxiously.

Onni wondered why he was outside. When Reino spied Onni coming south on Beverley Street, he started running towards him, with a look of panic on his narrow face.

"Where did you go?" he asked Onni with a tone of desperation in his voice, the kind his mother had when they were in a store in Oulu together when Onni was five or six years-old, and had wandered off out of her field of vision.

"I went for a walk to the Finnish church. Why?"

"Mrs. Pyykkönen was worried. . . I was worried," Reino said, not meeting Onni's eyes.

"I had something to talk about with the pastor."

"You looked upset when you left the house."

Onni hadn't heard Reino put a full sentence together like this before that he could recall. Reino's face was a mixture of anxiety and relief.

"What's the matter?" Reino asked. "What's wrong?"

Since he had broken the ice by confiding in Hepola earlier, Onni didn't find it as difficult as he might have to divulge his news to Reino.

"I received a letter from my mother, informing me that my older brother had been shot and killed in the war." Onni was surprised how little emotion he heard in his voice as he shared the news with Reino.

Reino's body stiffened noticeably. His spine was immediately erect. His eyes increased in size and roundness. There was fear on his face. He turned his thin body almost 180 degrees away from Onni.

"I'm sorry if I startled you with this news, Reino."

"My mother died . . . many years ago."

Onni reflected on Reino's curious response.

"Did the death of my brother make you remember your mother's death, Reino?"

198

"Yes," Reino answered rapidly and tersely.

Onni was flummoxed as where to take the conversation from here.

"I'm sorry you lost your mother, Reino. Then you know how I felt when I heard that my brother had been killed."

Not knowing what else to say or do, Onni began to go up the steps to the front door.

"Don't go in!" Reino shouted. "Don't go in! It's not good."

Onni was totally bewildered.

"Why shouldn't I go in the house, Reino, and what is not good?"

"Bedbugs," Reino answered. "He's mad."

"Who's mad? And what bedbugs?"

Onni didn't wait for an answer but finished going up the steps and opened the front door. Immediately he heard the sound of urgent haste and raw anger. Mrs. Pyykkönen was coming down the stairs in a sweat from the upper floors with soiled bedding bulging out from her two-handed grasp.

"Onni, please go upstairs and remove all your bedsheets and pillow cases and bring them to me in the laundry room. They must all be washed, and washed again. These are Aune's. Please co-operate."

Before he could start ascending the stairs to his room on the third floor, he made way for Kalle and Dmytro who had their sheets and pillow cases in their hands. Kalle looked at Onni with a resigned look on his face that communicated, "You'd better do as the lady says".

Pellonpää followed on their heels. His sheets were dragging on the stairs behind him. He looked terribly agitated.

"It's all that retard's fault," Pellonpää shouted, pointing to Reino who had sheepishly followed Onni into the house. "It's that Goddamned retard's doing. He doesn't take care of his hygiene. Have you seen the fucking mess in his room? I'm surprised there aren't more critters in there than just bedbugs He ought to go back to his mother."

"Goddammit, Pellonpää, your insensitive oaf!" Onni exclaimed, red in the face. "Reino doesn't *have* a mother. She died a few years back, for Christ's sake."

Pellonpää was taken aback by Onni's anger and raised voice. He remained thoroughly unrepentant, however.

Onni looked at Reino, but Reino had slipped out of the house once again during this exchange.

"That's right, boy. Just go away and leave the mess you made for us to clean up and deal with," Pellonpää bellowed at the closed door.

"Mr. Pellonpää, would you please stop your ranting and bring your bedsheets to me here," Mrs. Pyykkönen's insistent voice emanated from the laundry room.

Onni ran upstairs two steps at a time and fetched his bedding and took it to his landlady who was trying valiantly to address the growing crisis that had befallen her house.

It was Mrs. Pyykkönen herself who first noticed the bedbugs. She had had more trouble sleeping than usual. At first, she attributed it to the usual worries about maintaining the household, whether or not the room and board fees would be paid on time, and whether their sums would be enough to purchase food and replace worn bedding. But she woke up with a nasty, persistent itch all over her back and legs one morning, and recognized immediately the cause. As a veteran landlady, this was not a totally new experience for her, even though she had been meticulous in her housekeeping. She knelt by her bed, stripped the cover off one corner of the mattress, and with her fingers inspected the mattress. Sure enough, the nasty intruders were crawling in the padding of the mattress. Upon closer inspection, she found bedbug eggs as well.

The rest of the day 31 Beverley Street was a veritable beehive of activity directed by Mrs. Pyykkönen. She was the queen bee, the others the drones. She hand-washed every single sheet and pillow case, using a scrubbing board in the grey ceramic laundry tub in hot, soapy water. Since Onni noticed that Reino wasn't inside, he went into Reino's room and fetched the bedding and took it to be washed with the rest.

She solicited the help of Dmytro to ring the surplus water after she had rinsed the bedding thoroughly, Mrs. Pyykkönen on one end of the sheet and Dmytro obediently at the other.

There wouldn't be sufficient fresh air in the basement where she usually hung the routine laundry on a rope line. They had to be put on the line in the backyard. She apparently wanted to punish the complaining Pellonpää because out of all the residents, she picked him to accompany her outside into the cold air and yard covered with patches of snow to help her hang the sheets on the line. It was a job that couldn't be performed with gloves on their hands, but with bare hands. The residual dampness of the laundry bit into their bare skin as even the slightest breeze blew on their hands.

She sent Kalle and Onni into the basement to fetch the grey rubber tarpaulins she kept there and to spread them out on the surface of the backyard. Dmytro and Pellonpää were dispatched to carry every single mattress down into the open air of the yard and place them on the tarpaulins in an effort to prevent the wintry moisture from climbing into the mattress from the ground.

Onni carried Reino's mattress to the yard.

Then Mrs. Pyykkönen instructed each resident to inspect the mattresses, especially the cracks and folds for bugs and eggs. When they found evidence of infestation, Mrs. Pyykkönen would attack the natural hiding places of the uninvited vermin with a misty dose of insecticide from a spray bottle.

The residents thought they were done. But Mrs. Pyykkönen gave an order for everyone to take their wooden beds apart and bring the loose parts out onto the tarpaulins as well. She ordered Onni to boil pots and kettles of water on the gas stove in the kitchen. After the water had boiled, Onni, Kalle and Dmytro carried the pots outside and poured the steaming water over the parts of the beds.

"As you can see, I haven't had time to prepare dinner for you," Mrs. Pyykkönen lamented when all had one inside to warm themselves by the stove. "But there are links of sausage in the refrigerator, and bread in the bread box if anyone wants to make himself a sandwich. I'm sorry. It's the best I can do. I've got to get down to Eaton's and Simpson's to buy new mattresses and sheets and order their delivery tomorrow."

"New mattresses? Sheets?   By tomorrow? What do we sleep on tonight?" Pellonpää inquired in utter disbelief and obvious irritation.

"I'm afraid we'll have to repeat today's extermination process every day for the next two weeks. God forbid we get a bad snowstorm in that time," Mrs. Pyykkönen informed the group. "We can't sleep on the bare floor more than one night, so we need new mattresses."

"Well, that's just *fine*," Pellonpää whined. "What trouble! All because of that Goddamned unkempt retard! Those mattresses are going to cost a pretty penny. I hope you don't raise the room and board because of the village idiot's grubbiness."

Onni turned emphatically and left the kitchen.

Pellonpää was speechless, for once.

Onni came back to the kitchen several minutes after he had stomped out.

"Reino's not in his room. He was outside at the front when I arrived. I looked, and there's no sign of him there. He knows his way around the immediate area. But if he's wandered off any farther than Queen Street or College, then he could easily get lost."

Pellonpää seemed to pay no heed. Kalle and Dmytro listened to their junior with growing urgency.

"We've got to organize a search party," Onni interjected. "Does anyone know where he goes when he leaves the house, or where he might be?"

"Probably the girly show at the Victory," Pellonpää volunteered, adding a cynical chuckle that no one else found funny.

"I'll go up to Grange Park and the art museum area and look for him there," Onni continued. "Kalle, you search south of Queen. Dmytro, you know the area west of Spadina pretty well. Look for him there, would you? Mr. Pellonpää, would you look towards Yonge Street?"

"Look, I'm too worn out from all this carrying the bloody sheets and mattresses down the blooming stairs," the rotund Pellonpää protested. "I'm in no shape to go running around town looking for the little turd."

"Okay, sir," Onni said almost defiantly. "As you wish. I'll go over towards Yonge Street as well as up to College Street." Sardonically, he added, "Mr. Pellonpää, perhaps you'd prefer to look for him down at the Victory Theatre, then."

Onni had lost his patience. He went out onto Beverley Street and retraced his steps earlier in the day to Grange Park. He had spotted Reino there several times before, although not in the winter time, best as he could recall. But it would be a logical place for Reino to retreat.

He walked around the perimeter of the park, then up and down the paths that transected it. No sign of Reino on any of the benches.

He went back to Beverley Street and waked hurriedly up towards College Street, inspecting every alleyway between the Victorian houses for Reino's shape. When he reached College Street, Onni was beginning to feel a panic rising from his stomach. Which way to turn to look for him? Which way would Reino go if he was on College. Or did he wander over onto the university campus?

Taking a shot in the dark, Onni turned right and started towards Yonge Street. At University Avenue, Onni hoped that Reino hadn't gone up into Queen's Park on the left because it was a far too large area to survey in search of him. Between Bay and Yonge streets, he entered the Central YMCA where Reino might have sought shelter from the cold. Onni remembered that Reino wasn't wearing a coat. Onni stopped and looked on every floor, the dressing rooms for the swimming pool and the gymnasium, in the game room, the billiard room. The place was full of men, young and old, but no sign of Reino anywhere.

When he arrived at the intersection with Yonge Street, Onni had a sudden hunch. The National, a cheap movie theatre north near Gerrard Street, might be a possibility. For a mere fifteen cents, Reino could have entered the heated theatre and sat in his seat for the duration of two "B" movies. Onni headed there.

He paid the admission price himself, passed through the meagre lobby, and entered through the swinging door into the spectator area. His eyes took a while to adjust to the dark. The dark was mitigated by the light from the huge screen in the front as the projector threw up moving images on it.

He stood in one of the aisles in order to get a look at the faces of the patrons, almost universally male, as the light from the moving picture on the screen reflected off them. An usher shone a flashlight into Onni's face and requested him to find a seat. Onni moved further up the aisle and went through the motions of looking for an available seat, but continued to scan the men's dimly lit faces.

There he is! That's Reino two seats away from the man who hasn't taken off his hat.

Onni begged the pardon of the patron in the seat nearest the aisle, and did the same with every patron in the rest of the row of seats, including the man with the hat, who seemed irritated about having to rise and allow Onni to pass to the seat beside him, which was empty.

Onni sat down but had no interest in whatever black and white movie was showing. He leaned to his left in his seat, reached out to take Reino's right arm, and said to him in a loud, excited whisper,

"There you are. I've been looking for your everywhere. Come on, Reino, let's go back home."

The patron in the seat to Onni's jerked his arm from Onni's grasp. In a gravelly voice, he said in a volume louder than a whisper, "Get your Goddamned hands off me, you faggot! I'm not Raymond, or whoever the hell you are looking for. Fuck off, will you, and let me enjoy the movie."

The man rose and took the empty seat to his left, creating as much room as possible between him and Olli.

"I very sorry," Onni said in his broken English, and got up to leave the theatre.

When he got back out onto Yonge Street, Onni shook his head in embarrassment, even though none of the other pedestrians on the sidewalk, hunching against the cold, knew a thing about what had just transpired. Then, the corners of Onni's mouth turned upwards into a smile as he replayed the incident in his mind, and let out a little silent laugh at the slapstick humor of it.

He continued down Yonge Street as far as Queen Street. He was beginning to be affected by the cold as darkness began to descend. His feet were aching and his heart slowing in discouragement that he hadn't found Reino, and now the rush hour crowds were beginning to fill the sidewalk.

He continued west on Queen to Beverley Street and a few steps north to No. 31.

No sooner had he entered the foyer than an anxious-looking Mrs. Pyykkönen asked eagerly, "Did you find him?"

"No, I'm afraid not."

"Kalle hasn't come back yet. Dmytro has, but with no news about Mr. Hutari. When Dmytro came back empty-handed, I decided to call the police. They assured me that they would put out a missing person alert to all of the downtown stations. They would also check the hospitals. Good God, I hope they find him soon, and safe."

A few minutes later, Kalle came in, shaking his big Estonian head. *"Mingit märki teda lõuna Queen."*

Pellonpää came down the stairs to the foyer in time to overhear the Estonian. "He says there is no sign of the louse south of Queen either."

There was nothing they could do but wait.

"I'm going to take Mrs. Pyykkönen up on her offer of sausage and bread," Pellonpää announced. "I don't suppose any of you bleeding hearts want to join me?"

Onni knew he couldn't eat in his state of worry. Kalle, however, headed towards the dining hall and kitchen.

"There, I knew someone would eat with me. I've never met an Estonian who doesn't like to eat."

The evening progressed terribly slowly. The evening was when Onni usually read or wrote home. But he was too distracted by his anxiety about Reino to sit in one place long enough to do either. He stared out over Beverley Street from the window in his room, now in gathering darkness, and made an effort to pray for Reino's safe return, and to ask for forgiveness for all of them, Pellonpää, Kalle and Dmytro, even Aune and Mrs. Pyykkönen, and himself, for their collective failure to be more sensitive towards Reino, more attentive to his uniqueness, more thoughtful of his limited abilities.

206

Except to go to the bathroom a couple of times, Onni continued to stare numbly out his window. The adrenaline that had fired him earlier had receded from his bloodstream, and he was sensing sleepiness.

Suddenly, an automobile pulled up against the curb in front of the house. The faint light from the outside bulb above the front door was just bright enough to allow Onni to read the words City of Toronto Police on the front door on the driver's side of the car. One person came out of the car from the driver's seat, and another from the front passenger side. But neither bore the thin body outline of Reino.

He heard the doorbell three stories below. Onni's sleepiness receded as he ran out of his room and down the flights of stairs to the foyer. Mrs. Pyykkönen had opened the door and was now standing in her flannel nightgown in front of a uniformed policeman. The officer acknowledged Onni with, "Good evening, sir."

"Ma'am, we located the young man. We found him lying in a corner on the floor in Union Station."

Onni kicked himself. *Of course! Reino knew the way down to Union Station from the time we went together for the send-off of the volunteers for the Finnish army. Why hadn't I thought of looking for him there earlier? Damn!"*

"He wasn't in very good shape, I'm afraid to report to you, Ma'am. He'd been out in the cold without a coat. All he had on was a thin sweater. He was barely conscious. We took him over the emergency at St. Michael's to be checked out and for rest."

"Oh, dearest God in heaven!" Mrs. Pyykkönen cried.

"He wasn't like the ones we usually find at Union Station, though," the policeman continued. "We did the customary sobriety test on him, but it was clear he hadn't taken a drop of liquor, even though he was totally disoriented and very weak. He could hardly stand if we hadn't been holding him up."

Whenever the officer paused, Mrs. Pyykkönen provided a running translation into Finnish for Onni.

"At what time did he leave the house, Ma'am?"

Mrs. Pyykkönen said that she hadn't noticed since she had been fully engrossed with the bedbug crisis. She looked at Onni.

"Tell him about 3:00 pm or so," Onni said to her.

"We found him at about 21:30, Ma'am. We don't know how long he had been cowering in Union Station, but judging from the possible frostbite on his fingers, feet and arms, he'd been out in the cold a long time, a very long time."

Mrs. Pyykkönen placed her hand over her mouth. "Oh, Jesus," she exclaimed.

"I'm sorry I don't have a more positive report, Ma'am. If we hear from the folks at St. Mike's, we'll give you a call right away. Good night, Ma'am."

The call from the police department came first thing the next morning. Neither Onni nor Mrs. Pyykkönen had slept much at all during the night. As he tossed and turned in his sheets and blanket, Onni prayed feverishly that the call would not come, and that Reino would be beginning his recovery from the frostbite. Mrs. Pyykkönen, on the other hand, couldn't fall asleep because she was sure the call would come, and that the news would not be good.

Turns out the wise landlady was right. Reino had died during the night of acute hypothermia. He had frozen to death.

The news cast a pall of sadness over the occupants of 31 Beverley Street. Onni was repeating his ritual of sorrow by himself in his room from the previous morning.

It seems I'm hit harder by Reino's death than Väinö's. How can that be? Perhaps it's because I feel we had a chance

208

to save Reino if we had been sharper in our efforts to find him. If only I had remembered about Union Station and gone there right away to look for him. Perhaps my grief over Reino's death seems more acute because I feel such anger towards Pellonpää for his thoughtlessness and careless tongue. Or maybe it's just the accumulated grief of two deaths in such a short time.

Mrs. Pyykkönen cleared Reino's small room of his belongings, placing the paltry collection of Reino's possessions into a paper bag. She held another bag in her hands as she emerged from the room with a look bordering on disgust on her face. She took the bag and tossed into the tin garbage can in the rear mud room at the back of the house

Mrs. Pyykkönen requested Pastor Hepola to conduct the funeral. Hepola didn't know Reino very well, but he had noticed him when he attended worship.

~~~~~~~~~~~~~~~~~~~~~~~~~~~~~~~~~~~~~

The chairs in the living room converted into a worship space in church house on Huron Street were vacant two afternoons later, save those occupied by Mrs. Pyykkönen, Kalle, Dmytro, Aune Kyllönen and Onni. The three men had gone to a thrift store on Bathurst Street the previous day to purchase dark second-hand suits which they wore for the service. Mrs. Pyykkönen wore a black flower-pot hat that had a mesh veil to cover part of her face. Aune wore one like it, but it sat on her head at an awkward crooked angle, looking as if it might fall off at the slightest tilt of her head.

After the small assemblage sang some painfully slow-paced hymns self-consciously and without much audible volume at all, and heard a couple of selections from the Bible, Pastor Hepola stood before them and began his homily in an earnest tone.

Hepola wasn't more than two sentences into his homily when the small group's attention was diverted by the sound of the front door opening. They heard someone stamping his or her feet to shake off the snow. Then the latecomer entered the worship space. Because of the awkward way the room had been reconfigured in the conversion from a living room, the entrance was in the front of the room, behind the plain wooden casket which lay before the mourners.

The new entrant was Pellonpää. He moved past the row of chairs on which the others sat listening to Hepola's homily, and sat in a chair two rows behind them.

Hepola had paused when he had heard the sound of someone entering the front door as well. He made a conscious effort, it seemed, not to look the least bit surprised when he saw that it was Pellonpää.

But Pellonpää's sudden, unannounced appearance at the service caused Onni to lose his focus on Hepola's homily.

What is he doing here? How can he show his face at Reino's funeral? Shit, if he had kept his big mouth shut the other day, or at least thought before he blurted out his remark about Reino and his mother, none of us would be here at a funeral today. Our lives, Reino's life, would have gone on as before. The stupid shithead!

What does Pellonpää's being here mean? Is he feeling remorse at what he said and caused? Not likely. Not the kind of thing I can imagine Pellonpää feeling. Why, then, is he here?

Onni realized near the end of the homily that he hadn't heard it at all. He shook his head almost imperceptibly to shake off his thoughts about Pellonpää, and try to concentrate on the pastor's words.

"Reino was usually quiet, even in the midst of company. Yet one got the impressions sometimes that there were thoughts within him that he longed to share with others if only he could form the words and shape the phrases to do so."

What had Reino been trying to communicate to me, especially after the night we went to Union Station together? What did his hand inserted in mine really mean? Why did he say he wouldn't want me volunteer for the Finnish war effort like the men we were seeing off? Had he wanted to start a

210

conversation with me when he mentioned that his mother had died years ago? Was I just so preoccupied with my grief over Väinö's death to even ask myself this question at the time?

Hepola was still speaking.

"To be heard by another: is there anything that a child of God longs for more deeply than that? Thereby to be received and accepted and loved by them? Good Christian fiends, let me assure you that Reino is being ushered by his Lord into a realm of glory where his precious voice will be heard in the heart of God the Father, and he will be received, accepted and loved eternally by the One who created him.

"In the meantime, friends, let our short time with Reino Aleksanteri Hutari teach us to listen to one another with our hearts as well as our ears. Amen."

Chapter Twenty-Nine:
Toronto
March 10, 1940

The routine at 31 Beverley Street resumed and appeared much the same as before. But since Reino's death, the mood felt more subdued. Pellonpää seldom provided his unsolicited editorials on developments in the war back home, and when he did, the editorials seemed more restrained. Residents spoke to one another at meals in muted tones, as though they were anxious about offending the others in some way by saying the wrong thing or in an inappropriate manner.

Onni spent more time reading. Twice a week, he'd return from an English lesson at the church house, carrying a book or two from the library there. He was approaching the point of running out of Finnish books on the shelves that he had not read, and the number of books in English he was capable of reading was still limited.

On this Saturday, Onni entered a nearly silent house upon his walk back from the church house. The only sound he could hear was a crackly Finnish voice emanating from the radio in Mrs. Pyykkönen's private living quarters. Onni made a mental vow to join the others by the radio. But he had an urgent need to void his bladder first, and so he ascended the stairs towards the third floor.

As he was making his way between the first and second floors, he heard a throaty yowling, like that of a wounded animal, coming from the second floor. After he completed his errand on the third floor, he came back down, stopping this time at the head of the stairs on the second floor where the strange wailing sound continued.

It seemed to be coming from Aune Kyllönen's room. Was she ailing in some way? Had she fallen and injured herself in her room?

Onni thought he'd better go knock on her door and ask if she's alright, and if there's anything he could do, even though he was hesitant about doing so. But when he got to the door, it was open. Aune was tossing to and fro on her back on top of the cover on her bed, he right arm covering her eyes.

"Mrs. Kyllönen, is everything alright?"

Without lifting her arm from her face or looking up, Aune moaned in a voice both haunted and haunting, "They've taken our home. Oh dear Jesus, what will we do? They've taken our home."

"Mrs. Kyllönen, I'd like to help you. But I don't understand what you mean? Your home? You've lost your home? But this is our home.".

"Our home . . . in Viipuri . . . gone . . . destroyed."

Not knowing what she meant, and not knowing what he could say, he said nothing, retreated from her room, and went down the stairs and knocked on the door of Mrs. Pyykkönen's quarters.

After he was invited in by Mrs. Pyykkönen's voice, Onni told the group assembled about Aune's wailing.

"Does anybody know what she means? That she's lost her home?"

"The Finnish soldiers have retreated from Viipuri," Mrs. Pyykkönen said, shaking her head. "Viipuri is where poor Aune and her late husband left to come to Canada. The Russians came in an irresistible wave through the Mannerheim Line this past week. The war is lost, Onni, the war is lost. All those boys killed, and now the war is lost."

Onni did not argue with her assessment, even though in his mind, he hoped that Soviet infiltration through the Mannerheim Line might just be a temporary setback, like Suomussalmi in December. Didn't the Finns counterattack and repel the Russians there? Couldn't they do it again?

Like the others, Onni felt this had been his war, too. Väinö had been one of those boys sacrificed at the altar of the victor. Since Väinö's death, it was as though it were up to Onni now to pick up his brother's rifle off the frozen lake and, even though he was thousands of kilometers away, continue Väinö's march from the ruins of Suomussalmi onto the heaths and into the woods of Karelia.

For four months, the residents of 31 Beverley Street had been gathering around Mrs. Pyykkönen's radio console like moths drawn to a porch light, hoping to hear word of another Finnish advance or success in defending a strategic Finnish position. They had been encouraged by every skirmish won by his countrymen.

By February, however, the residents' hopes were disappointed day by day as it became apparent that with each single Russian casualty, three or four men were dispatched to the front to replace him. The Russian supply of human manpower and new materiel seemed inexhaustible. The Finns were losing their grasp of their hard-won independence with each passing day.

The residents sat quietly during the Finnish radio broadcasts, and left unspoken whatever fears they might have had about an ominous ending to the conflict. No one wanted to be the one to burst the fragile bubble of hope that they had built around themselves to protect them from the unthinkable.

Finally, on March 13, they received the news they were all fearing. At the end of February, Molotov's earlier peace proposal had been upgraded into an ultimatum. The price exacted from the Finns for the cessation of the relentless Russian attacks on Finnish positons would be all of Finnish Karelia, the ice-free port of Petsamo on the Arctic, unlimited use by the Russians of the port of Hanko, and delivery to the Russians of a third of Finland's hydro-electric output. The Finnish leadership was given forty-eight hours to respond.

On March 13, reluctantly, but probably prudently, the Finns signed the Treaty of Moscow, and the winter war came to an inglorious end.

Pellonpää burst unabashedly into tears when the broadcast was over. He whimpered something unintelligible, but the others could not raise their gaze from the floor to look at him. Mrs. Pyykkönen's eyes were tear-filled, but she remained silent. Kalle and Dmytro sat shaking their heads and gritting their teeth in anger, perhaps reliving the loss of their own native lands to these same Russians. Aune Kyllönen was impassive and stoical, as though the final announcement of defeat and surrender was just a formality acknowledging that the war had been lost when her home in Viipuri was lost.

Onni's silent tears were for Väinö. For him, Väinö represented everything that was essentially and fundamentally Finnish. He felt that somehow, by pulling up roots from the Peurajoki soil and emigrating to Canada, he had let Väinö and his father and Finland down at their time of need. What would Väinö be thinking now as his younger brother mourned in the wake of the news of Finland's demise at a safe distance in faraway Canada? Onni grieved his brother's soldierly death, to be sure. But also the loss of the country that he had left willingly, cavalierly even, just to pursue some dream that Väinö would undoubtedly have trouble understanding and would consider ethereal and patently impractical.

Chapter Thirty:
Toronto
June-July 1940

The fog of defeat that had fallen over 31 Beverley Street evaporated gradually over the course of the spring. They had shed tears and the numbness eased. The residents grew more aware day by day of the fact that unlike Kalle's Estonia, all of Finland had not been swallowed whole by the snarling Soviet empire. Because of some shred of reluctant admiration by Stalin and Molotov for the valiant resistance of the outnumbered Finns, or by some stroke of divine grace, Finland would retain most of its territory and exercise at least some semblance of autonomy and independence.

They were cheered by the miracle. Even though each Finnish immigrant in the house had endured hardships of various kinds, expended precious resources, and traveled many miles to come to a new country, each had clung to the possibility that, should conditions in Canada worsen, or the prospects of their own future in Canada deteriorate, they could return to Finland. Oh, the journey back was prohibitively expensive for a poor immigrant, and therefore impractical. Nonetheless, each secretly hatched at least one imaginary plot to return, even if they would never dare to confide in anyone else about it.

Onni dove into English lessons with Pastor Hepola with new urgency as his realization grew that hand-delivering advertising fliers was not part of his dream. He needed an income, to be sure. But his intellect was not challenged sufficiently. He tried to converse occasionally with his fellow day laborers to little avail since language proved to be an insurmountable. The others were Italians, Greeks, Ukrainians or Armenians. He had picked up some phrases of Ukrainian from Dmytro, but Onni suspected, the wrong ones for polite conversation with strangers. A few of his fellow laborers spoke a smidgeon of English. Onni was determined to do better than that.

One day after English class, Hepola asked Onni to remain behind once again.

When the others had left, he asked, "How are you doing with your job, Onni?"

"Now that the cold weather has passed, it's a little more pleasant. I enjoy getting into the various neighborhoods around the city. But still, I'm not sure pleasant is the right word to describe it."

"Getting a little bored with it, are you?"

"I've got work, so I try not to complain about it. But yes, I feel ready for something more challenging."

"I've noticed your English improving."

"Isn't it about time?"

"Surely. Here's something for you to think about. My physician's brother is the home delivery manager at the *Evening Telegram*. We got to talking about things, and your situation came up. He said the paper's circulation is climbing sky-high, now that the worst of the depression seems to be behind us. People have a little more money now for things like a subscription to the newspaper."

"I imagine people want to read about the war in Europe, too."

"I suppose some of the more internationally-minded do. But the reason I bring up the subject of the increase in newspaper circulation with you is that the *Tely* has an increasing need for those newspapers to be delivered to those new subscribers."

Onni felt slightly deflated. Was the pastor leading up to an effort to convince him to apply for a newspaper delivery boy? That's not much different from delivering advertising fliers.

"My doctor's brother has mentioned to him that with so many men being called up to the forces, there's a dire shortage of people to drive the trucks that delver bundles of newspapers to street corners, where the paperboys pick them up to deliver on foot or on their bicycle to people's homes. I thought perhaps you might like to consider doing that."

"Driving a truck? All we had in Peurajoki was a horse and wagon. But I think could learn to do that fairly quickly. But I've just turned eighteen. Do you think they'd be interested in someone so young?"

"With all the call-ups, they can't afford to be picky. The job would entail some physical strength, so perhaps the younger, the better."

"I'd need a driver's license, wouldn't I? I don't have one of those, never have."

"Not just a driver's license, but what's called a commercial driver's license. That's a little harder to get. There's a written test as well as the road test. You'd have to be more fluent in English."

Onni was growing simultaneously both more excited and apprehensive. Driving a truck for the *Evening Telegram* would constitute one step closer to working for the paper as a reporter. But he didn't feel very confident at all about passing a written test in English.

"I could help you, Onni. If you are interested, I'll get the name and telephone number of the doctor's brother. We could make an appointment for an interview, and I'd be willing to come along as an interpreter. I've done that for plenty of other Finns in Toronto."

Onni felt a little more reassured, though just a little.

"I could see if I could get a copy of the written test from my doctor's brother. If you'd like, I could help you learn the English you'd need to understand and answer the questions."

Onni's day brightened. He walked back to the boarding house that Saturday afternoon with a decided spring in his step.

Over the summer, Onni worked diligently with Hepola's help to prepare for the written portion of the commercial license. In the evenings, Esko Tuuri from the church took him in his pick-up truck to a vacant lot in the east end near the Don River where Onni could practice driving it. The hard work of the three of them resulted in his receiving the license.

The next Monday, he reported to the distribution manager at the *Evening Telegram*. He was given the Forest Hill route.

~~~~~~

Each Sunday, Onni had heard Hepola in his announcements invite any and all to the brief Bible study and prayer service on Wednesday evenings, followed by a meal prepared and served by the women of the congregation. It might have been after the seventh time Onni had heard the announcement that he finally realized that the invitation included him, that he was welcome to come to the church house on Wednesday evenings for a dose of spiritual devotion and a meal that would cost him no more than whatever he wanted to place as a free-will offering in a crystal bowl placed on the serving table.

On his very first Wednesday evening, the sweet Mrs. Aalto filled his plate with two huge dollops of mashed potatoes and a tall pile of meatballs. The fresh rye bread was plentiful as was the beloved sweet and lemony home-brew *sima*.

Onni was joined at his table by two calloused middle-aged men in ill-fitting grey suits who nodded politely at Onni when they sat down. Onni nodded in return to indicate that they were welcome to join him. The men seemed to know each other but didn't speak a word to the other. They were serious about downing their helping of potatoes and meatballs and didn't speak to Onni either.

Finally, Onni broke the silence by introducing himself. He thought as he did so that he would never have been the one to initiate conversation had he not had the experience on the *S.S. Arcturus*. There the unwritten rule was that unless you wanted absolute privacy and time alone the whole journey, it was up to you to reach out from your solitude for company.

Besides, if he was ever to be a successful journalist, he knew he had to transcend his native reticence and preference to be an observer of things rather than participant.

Having introduced himself, Onni waited in silence for the men to offer their names. They were slow in doing so, and mumbled their names in a dialect to which Onni was not accustomed.

Onni discovered that the men had immigrated at the very beginning of the previous decade, having gone first to northern Ontario where work was more than plentiful at the time, and then settling in Toronto at the end of the decade when the mining companies laid them off.

"That's pretty well the story of a lot of us," said the more open one of the close-lipped pair. "We're not in this filthy and hot city because we want to be here. A Finn needs to be in the woods or on a lake, don't you think?"

Onni couldn't remember, in fact, the last time he'd been in the woods or on a lake. He'd learned from other conversations he'd had that a walk on Sunnyside beach on Lake Ontario didn't count.

The pastor had taken off his robe and assumed a position at the serving table beside the industrious women. The sleeves of his black clerical shirt were rolled up, an indication of his desire to help serve the meal.

"The pastor here has been a big help," the man continued unprompted. "Hepola's a man of the people."

Onni related his own experience with Hepola, how the pastor has been sacrificing his time to teach English to him and a few other recent immigrants, and how invaluable the pastor had been in his getting his commercial license and his new job at the newspaper.

The other man spoke up for the first time. "I find it hard to believe some of the rumors I hear bandied about by some that Hepola is actually a family man, even though he pretends to be a bachelor."

This was new to Onni. "I don't think I know what you mean," he said to the second man.

"Oh, some say he applied to the church to come here and then left a wife and small child back in the old country."

"Ilmari, consider the source of those rumors, for heaven's sake."

Onni looked towards Ilmari for his response.

"I don't think all the reds are dishonest, Severi."

"You can't count on them. They're still fighting the civil war almost twenty-five years after the fact. If they can drag the name of a white through the mud, they'll do it, especially the church."

Onni was surprised and pleased that these taciturn dining partners weren't men of such few words after all.

"Severi, look who's still fighting the civil war now? You automatically suspect the hall people of being dishonest just because they're reds," Ilmari protested.

Onni had been warned by Mrs. Pyykkönen of the "hall people". These were the hardened Finnish immigrants who had fled Finland to escape the potential retribution by the victorious whites after the civil war of 1917-1920. Mrs. Pyykkönen, and apparently Severi, were suspicious of the motives of the reds that formed their labor unions and built their halls in opposition to the church. For all practical purposes, even though they were fellow countrymen, she considered them to be virtual enemies.

"Anyway," Ilmari continued, "I'm just reporting what I've heard. I'm not saying it's the 100% truth. But some people are convinced that Hepola is hiding something, and that something is a family that he abandoned back in Finland. Some also wonder if he doesn't have new secret woman here in Canada."

As the evening progressed, Onni chased the rumor about Hepola out of his thoughts. Yet, as Hepola worked the room greeting the dining guests, Onni caught himself paying special attention whenever Hepola was in the vicinity of un-accompanied women.

Chapter Thirty-One:
Toronto
January 1941

Onni's eighteenth year ended with a blowing snow-storm on New Year's Eve 1940. The year had given him a new job, a growing fluency with the language of his newly-adopted country, and an increasing comfort in his new sur-roundings. He had a new job and renewed hopes for his fu-ture.

That year had also dawned with the death of his older brother. Barely had the wound in his heart begun to heal when the mysterious Reino Hutari disappeared and then died of exposure to the cold. As a new year began, Onni felt in many ways that he was a different man. The smooth skin and complexion of youth had been toughened by independence and loss.

Onni had settled into the routine of his job with the *Evening Telegram.* He was thankful that it was the late after-noon edition which the paper boys expected at various stra-tegic intersections throughout Forest Hill because he didn't need to load the bundles of newspapers on the truck until early afternoon. He could sleep in a little later than his col-leagues at the morning *Globe and Mail.*

Once he grew accustomed to the idiosyncrasies of the individual delivery trucks of the fleet, he didn't experience difficulty driving the truck or navigating the streets. He felt fortunate to be able to be part of the energy of the city which was coming back to life, it seemed, after a decade's deep sleep. He could tell whether or not he was on schedule by the move-ments of various individuals on their way home from work. The man who had a copy of the *Globe* tucked underneath his arm every morning caught the St. Clair street car at the cor-ner of Avenue Road at 2:47 each day. If the man wasn't stand-ing at the street car stop on the curb, Onni knew that the man had already boarded the street car, and that therefore, he was a minute or two behind in his delivery schedule.

He was at the church most Sunday mornings to hear Hepola, and back on Wednesday evenings for Bible study and most importantly, an inexpensive supper and perhaps conversation with one or two other men.

On the second Wednesday of the new year, Onni noticed a youngish woman assisting the older women in laying out and serving the food to the twenty or so men who had arrived. Onni didn't recall ever having seen this woman at the church either on Sunday mornings or Wednesday evenings. She was probably a couple of years older than him, of average height. She was dressed that first evening in a skirt and blouse that were distinctively Old World rather than components of a wardrobe purchased in Canada. Onni deduced that she must be a recent arrival.

Onni made a point of greeting her with a "Good evening" when it was his turn in line to be handed his bowl of *mojakka* stew. He flashed an eager smile at her, which she returned very diffidently, quickly lowering her eyes back to the other bowls of stew on the table.

Onni carried his bowl and glass of water to a table. He detoured around to the back of the table beside another man where he could get a good view of the serving table. He put down the bowl and glass, but did not dig into the stew immediately as had the man beside him who had pretty well emptied his bowl by the time Onni sat down. Instead, he kept his gaze on the young new server behind the serving table performing the same tasks as the other women, yet looking altogether different. She smiled sweetly and cordially greeted every man who came to her for the bowl of stew. She glanced very now and then towards a middle-aged woman in charge of the meal that evening as though awaiting a signal from her as to what task to address next.

Her clear blue eyes and thick silky blond hair attracted Onni's attention and admiration. Her face, with its soft pink skin, pleased him. Even when she smiled, though, Onni could detect a slight element of melancholy on her face. It indicated to Onni that she hadn't ever expected to be there

224

or in that circumstance. That hint of sadness in her appearance and bearing seemed to reach out and gently touch a similar strain of sadness within himself.

Perhaps it was his suspicion that she was a newcomer to Toronto that served to attract him as well. Looking at her performing her service, Onni recognized the signs of uncertainty that he remembered having in his own first weeks in the city and at 31 Beverley Street, the sense of being overwhelmed by the newness and unfamiliarity of just about every new experience. He did not know for certain, of course, if that's what she was feeling. But his thinking that it was formed an instant bond of empathy between Onni and her.

"I can't help but notice, friend, that you haven't lifted a spoon to eat your stew, and that you haven't taken your eyes off that young woman since you sat down," the man beside him said.

Onni was taken aback by the man's candidness and directness, so unlike the way conversations usually opened at these Wednesday evening affairs. He could feel his face turning red.

"The name is Paavo," the man said very casually and held out his right hand to Onni. "And her name, in case you're interested, is Helina Mäki."

"A pleasure to meet you, Paavo. How is it you know the young lady's name. I think this is her first time here."

"The first time for Wednesday evening supper, perhaps. But she and I are volunteers for Canada-Finland Aid, and I have come to know her there. We pack small boxes of supplies to be sent back home to the war veterans' home in Järvenpää. You know, bandages, cigarettes, chocolate bars, that kind of thing. We do that here at the church every Wednesday afternoon."

"I hadn't heard about that," Onni said.

"We could use your help. The damn war left so many of our boys wounded and maimed for life."

225

"I work during the days, which is why I can come in the evening for this meal."

"Helina has her own sad war story to tell. But why don't you come with me and I'll introduce you to her?"

Paavo was already up from his folding chair when he finished his sentence. Onni was close to practically freezing in his chair, so sudden was Paavo's suggestion, and so unexpected his opportunity to meet this beautiful Helina Mäki. Onni rose from his chair as well, trying to reason his nervousness away.

"Helina," Paavo started. "I just met my friend here this evening . . ." And then looking at Onni, asked, "I'm sorry, what did you say your name is?"

"Onni Syrjälä."

"Helina, I'd like you to meet a new friend, Onni Syrjälä. Onni, meet Helina Mäki."

Onni felt embarrassed but grateful for Paavo's assistance. He smiled at Helina, and bowed his head chivalrously in her direction and snapped the heels of his shoes together in an almost military manner that surprised him. He waited for her to reach out her hand for him to shake it.

The corners of her mouth curled up slowly into a charming, innocent smile. Onni was so enchanted by it that in his aroused imagination, he pictured kissing her lips, an impulse that almost startled him.

"I'm pleased to meet you," Onni said to her.

"Likewise, Mr. Syrjälä.

"Oh, just plain old Onni, please."

"A nice name that, Onni. Something I could use more of," Helina said in reply.

Onni raised his eyebrows slightly in surprise at her cryptic comment.

"Oh, I'm sorry, Onni. I shouldn't be so personal. This is just our first meeting, for land's sake. I apologize. Please forgive me."

Wisely and generously, Paavo stepped away quietly.

"It seems that these recent years have been a time for us all to be more personal," Onni remarked. "The war has kind of stripped the veneer off and we're more naked than usual."

As soon as the sentence was out of his mouth, Onni regretted this choice of words. Again, he felt is face turning red with embarrassment.

"Oh, now the one who's sorry. I didn't mean 'naked' in the usual sense, of course." He let out a nervous, embarrassed chuckle.

"Oh, I understood what you meant, Onni. This war has made us all feel more vulnerable, so much more exposed to one another."

"Yes, thank you for rescuing me from my embarrassment. That's what I intended to say."

"It's so true," she added, and then stopped as though she was trying to think of what to say or do next, or else she wanted to steer the conversation in another direction.

"Helina – may I call you that? – you mentioned that this is our first meeting. Is there possibly a chance that there might be at least a second meeting? I'm off work on Saturdays. Would you like to have a cup of coffee with me then?"

Onni surprised himself with how smoothly he had made the transition from conversation to invitation to a date.

"Well, you can never go wrong with a Finn if you suggest coffee. That sounds pleasant. I am boarding at the house where I work as a domestic. In Forest Hill."

"Small world. My delivery truck route is Forest Hill. If it's not too cold and windy on Saturday, what if I pick you up at your residence at 3:00 pm and we can walk on St. Clair over to Fran's Restaurant near Yonge Street?"

"I'm new to the city and haven't wandered much off my street, Russell Hill Road. But I think I can get myself to the restaurant and meet you there. A Finnish farm girl isn't going to let a little snow prevent her from walking."

~~~~~~~~~~~~~~~~~~~~~~~~~~~~~~~~~~~~

Onni arrived at Fran's restaurant at least a half-hour before the agreed time. Since the previous Wednesday evening at the church, Onni hadn't been able to stop thinking about Helina. He smiled approvingly as he recalled her soft blond hair parted so neatly in the center of her scalp. He reviewed her face in his mind: the full lips with just a touch of color, her alert blue eyes that betrayed that hint of melancholy that he found so fascinating and alluring.

He was still surprised three days later by how seemingly self-assured, bold even, he had been when he invited her for coffee. How presumptuous, really. He had dared to be to assume that she didn't already have a male friend to whom she was committed, and would therefore be free to accept his invitation upon just having met him.

He had observed other young women, of course, some at the church, and some crossing the street as pedestrians in front of his truck when he was waiting at a traffic light. But the available young women at the church had been little girls when they immigrated to Toronto with their families in the 1920s. They had adapted almost completely to English Canadian culture. They were not particularly interested in a relationship with a man from the "old country" like him.

And the pretty female pedestrians he observed were inaccessible to him because of his rudimentary English. They were to him no more real than the female mannequins in Eaton's and Simpson's windows, all dressed up in the latest fashions.

As he sat in a booth at Fran's, from time to time, in intervals that got shorter with the passing time, he pulled out from his vest pocket the pocket watch that Aukusti had given him as he was leaving Peurajoki, a small timepiece set in brass. The agreed-upon time for meeting came and went without a sign of Helina at the front door to which Onni's attention was riveted whenever he wasn't looking down at his watch.

She didn't seem like the kind of woman who would promise to come and then not show up. It's a bit of a walk from Russell Hill Road, after all. Stop worrying. And stop watching the front door as though you are some kind of detective. You look too anxious, too eager.

At about fifteen minutes after the time set for the visit over coffee, Helina came through the door and scanned the room until her eyes spotted Onni sipping from a cup.

"I'm so sorry, Mr. Syrjälä - I mean Onni - for being so late. Please forgive me."

"That's no problem. I had a warm place in which to wait. Here, let me take your coat."

She smiled and turned her back towards him to allow him to take her coat by the collar and help her slide her arms from the coat. Onni walked over to a coat rack a few booths away. When he returned to his seat, she thanked him.

Sitting back down in the booth, he said, "I took the liberty of ordering myself a cup of coffee before you arrived. I am sorry if that is rude. Here, I will flag down the waiter and order you a cup. What do you take with it, cream and sugar?"

Onni refrained from sipping from his cup until the waiter brought her cup and saucer. Spontaneously and without any forethought, Onni raised his cup as though it were a flute of champagne and proposed a toast.

"To our adopted country, Canada, and the one we left behind, Finland. May God grant them both peace and freedom."

She raised her cup. They clicked their cups together and proceeded to take a sip and giggled afterward.

"Have you been in Toronto very long, Onni?"

"No, not long. I think this is my seventeenth month."

"I'm impressed that you know so precisely. I can't do such mental arithmetic on the spot like that. Where are you from?"

"A little farming village in far northern Oulu province named Peurajoki. My mother and father and two older sisters are still there. I came alone."

"That's very brave of you, to come all that way to a strange country all alone."

"I didn't think I had much of a future as a farmer. Or the inclination, for that matter. Besides, my older brother would have been the one to take over the farm when the time comes."

"*Would* have?"

"He was called up into the army in 1938. But as the rumblings of war with Russia grew louder, he was not discharged. Unfortunately, he was killed very early in the war."

Helina appeared to blanche for a second or two. She looked up at the large plate glass window to their right but not as though she were looking for anything in particular;

230

more that she didn't want to look directly at Onni. Or perhaps the other way around, that she didn't want him to be looking at her. Onni wondered, but didn't think he had said anything offensive.

The ensuing silence was awkward. To break the silence, Onni continued.

"He was barely over twenty when he was shot a year ago in January."

"I'm so sorry for your loss. There wasn't much active conflict yet in January. Where was he shot?"

"Near Suomussalmi."

Suddenly, Helina's face grew pale again as if life were being drained from it. Her eyes grew bigger and they began welling up with tears. Onni was grateful, although he hadn't expected such an unusually open display of empathy so soon. They had barely met, but she appeared to be so deeply affected by his brother's death.

"I'm sorry, Onni. It's not anything that you said. Nothing like that. It's just that . . ."

She paused to try to gather herself. Onni could tell that she was on the cusp of saying more, but perhaps was forming a sentence in her mind.

When the pause grew longer, he asked, "It's just that . . . what?"

Her face looked conflicted as though she was considering whether or not to say whatever was on her mind.

Then the crease in her brow relaxed as though she had come to a decision, and said, "Oh, sorry, Onni. It's nothing. I'm sorry to interrupt your story."

"No, I think I've said all I want to about Väinö's death. We weren't terribly close, but still, he was my only brother."

231

Spontaneously, Helina reached one hand across the table and took hold of one of Onni's. Initially, he almost pulled back his hand, but then eased the muscles in his forearm and allowed her to hold his hand in his. Her gesture seemed so natural and genuine that it cancelled out any surprise and confusion Onni was feeling.

At her touch, Onni lowered his head and closed his eyes. He relaxed his shoulders so that he slumped slightly in his seat the direction of the table. He renounced any valiant effort to appear manly, and began to weep.

Helina continued to hold his hand in silence. But she wasn't made uncomfortable at all by a man crying in front of her on their first date.

"It's good that you're crying, Onni. I'm glad you feel free to cry. My grandmother used to say to me whenever I cried as a girl that unhappiness can't stick in a person's soul when it's slick with tears."

Onni looked up at her, his eyes wet with tears, and nodded his gratitude.

The two sat in the restaurant booth in silence for a time that couldn't be measured. Her eyes started welling up with tears as well. She turned her head and looked out the window again.

When she was sure that he had no more to say for the time being about his brother's death, she said, almost in an inaudible whisper, "Onni, I think I know how you feel. I have just lost someone, too."

It was as though Onni was awakened from a sleep.

"I'm sorry," he said almost instinctively. It was time to move from his loss to hers. "Tell me about it."

"It was my husband, Aulis. He died suddenly last January as well."

232

Onni placed his other hand over their joined hands on the table, enveloping her hand in both of his. It occurred to him just then that though he had imagined holding the hand of a beautiful woman, he never pictured it as happening in this kind of situation. He pushed the thought from his mind in order to be attentive to her sorrow.

"Thank you, Onni. But please don't ask me to say more about it just now. It's still very painful to talk about it."

As they returned to a respectful and not uncomfortable silence, Onni thought how bizarre the scene would seem to an onlooker. Two young people on their first date, hardly having touched their coffee, holding hands and weeping. Someone could conclude from the tears that the couple had just had a bitter row. But if anyone else at Fran's noticed them, he didn't care just then what they might have been thinking about the situation.

"You are so right," Helina said through her tears. "Would a man and woman be so exposed to each other so quickly were it not for this war? It has made us so vulnerable, our wounds so raw."

Väinö winced internally as he recalled his use of the word "naked" earlier. He was thankful that she hadn't repeated it.

"I usually wallow in my grief alone, privately," Onni confessed. "Isn't that how we Finns are supposed to do it? But sitting here with you makes me feel as if Väinö isn't totally gone, that in a way he continues to live because I still feel the pain, and have shared it with someone else who is also grieving."

"Yes, that's it, isn't it?" Helina responded. "I'm sorry, I didn't intend to open up about Aulis' death like this. Not so soon. I haven't mentioned Aulis to anyone for a long time. But after you told me your brother was shot at Suomussalmi, it's as if I felt a compulsion to speak about it. I didn't mean to divert us from talking about your brother. I'm sorry, Onni."

"There's no reason to be sorry. Really, I'm honored it that you think enough of me to talk about it with me."

They rested in the silence for a few moments. They experienced no discomfort, no sense of urgency to fill the silence. They were together, but each one alone with his or her own thoughts of the lost loved one."

Finally, having gained control of her weeping, and feeling stronger, she said, "Each person's loss is their own unique loss. Aulis' family suffered the same loss, but it was of a son, a brother. Mine was of a husband."

"How long had you and Aulis been married?"

"We got married on All Saints' Day in November '39.

"That soon before the war broke out? That must have hurt," Onni offered as an attempt to lend comfort. He paused, and then continued, "That's such a clumsy thing for me to say. Of course it hurt."

"Onni, there are no right words to say. I appreciate your consolation. You know as well that no word in our, or any language, can bring out loved one back."

They were content to sit holding hands across the table in silence for a time that felt eternal to them.

"You were probably looking for more fun when you invited me to coffee, weren't you, Onni? she said, and chuckled. "I'm sorry our date became a mutual consoling society instead."

"There will be occasion for having fun some other time" Onni replied. "Perhaps a mutual consoling society is what each of us really needed today."

234

Chapter Thirty-Two:
Toronto
June 1941

Onni and Helina continued to see each other, from a distance anyway, at the Wednesday evening meals at the church house. Helina had Wednesday afternoons off from her job as a domestic with the Fishers on Russell Hill Road. Some weeks, she was part of the team preparing and serving the meal. At other times, she would sit and eat at a table with Onni. Every now and then, she would bring her friend Helvi along to join them.

Onni invited Helina on dates for just the two of them every few weeks. Onni suggested seeing *Gone with the Wind,* which by popular demand had been held over at the Imperial Theatre for a historic third year. Helina was open to the suggestion, but proposed they go see *The Wizard of Oz* at the Eglinton Theatre closer to Forest Hill. *The Wizard of Oz* was competing with *Gone with the Wind* for the longest continuous run of a moving picture in Toronto's history. Liberated from the grimness of the Depression, and finally enjoying the security of steady employment for the first time in over a decade, Torontonians immersed themselves in the big screen.

Onni was happy just to have Helina as a companion with whom to go to the movies, so he didn't insist on *Gone with the Wind.* In Finland, he had read about such things as movies, but he would have had to go all the way to Oulu if he had the inclination to go see one, and then on only the few nights in the week that they showed movies. He was looking forward to seeing one now.

They met at the intersection of Yonge Street and Eglinton on a June evening when the city was experiencing an unusual heat wave so early in the season. The Eglinton Theatre had recently installed an air conditioning system, so the line to purchase tickets and to enter the theatre was long. Onni was concerned that they'd run out of tickets by the time he and Helina got to the box office.

He needn't have worried, because there were still several rows of vacant seats hen Onni and Helina entered the slightly darkened auditorium.

When they sat down in their seats, Onni knew better than to park his extended arm on the back of Helina's seat as so many of the other young men in the theatre were doing. Helina was still mourning Aulis' death and might not be prepared of a romantic relationship with him. Would she even be desirous of one? She seemed more than content, outwardly pleased in fact, to have a male companion who was patient with her progress, and who seemed to understand her feelings because he himself was still grieving as well. If Onni was honest with himself, he would admit to himself that since he wasn't mourning the loss of a life partner as she was, he had stirrings of a romantic interest in Helina. He tried to discipline his imagination not to picture him and her in a naked embrace on a bed. He scolded himself not to get ahead of things because she was in no position to allow such a thing happening, much less desire it herself.

The screen at the Eglinton was huge and impressive, covering almost the entire wall of the stage at the front.

When Dorothy and Toto were carried up in the cyclone near the beginning of the movie, Helina took hold of Onni's arm with her two hands, and whispered, "Incredible. Doesn't it feel as though we're caught up in the same tornado?"

Onni lost interest in the story not long after the cyclone deposited Dorothy, Toto, and her aunt's and uncle's farm in Munchkinland, although his attention was recaptured temporarily by the sight of the Wicked Which of the East's being crushed by the farmhouse.

Once the Munchkins begin singing "Follow the Yellow Brick Road", Helina smiled as she heard Onni whispering to himself, repeating the words "follow the yellow brick road . . . follow the yellow brick road."

She laughed inwardly as Onni tried but could not repeat the words of the song that followed:

"You'll find he is a whiz of a Wiz
if ever a Wiz there was.
If ever oh ever a Wiz there was
the Wizard of Oz."

She knew those lines are ones that would get a native English speaker to be absolutely tongue-tied, much less a relatively newly-arrived immigrant from a country whose language bore precious little resemblance to English.

A few minutes later, his voice was more audible as he repeated, "Scarecrow . . . scarecrow . . ."

"Shh! Onni, keep your voice down," Helina whispered. "You're bothering the others. What are you doing?"

"I'm learning English. Pastor Hepola told us to repeat words we hear in the movies to learn the proper pronunciation."

"Well, do it quietly. I'd like to follow the story."

There were subsequent dates – to the Toronto islands; walking through the St. Lawrence Market; enjoying the flowers at Allan Gardens.

One Saturday, they went with others from the church to a congregational picnic at the Viitanen family farm near King City. It struck him that this was the first time since he left Peurajoki that he was in the countryside. His heart felt a warm wash of familiarity and nostalgia as he regarded the scenery from Sulo and Aino Häkkinen's automobile. He hadn't ever wanted to become a farmer, but the farm was where he was born and raised. He knew that many city-dwellers in Finland still felt an attraction to the rural districts even after generations in the city.

Conversation in the car on the way to the farm, and at the picnic itself, was focused almost completely on recent developments in Finland. The Moscow Treaty may have ended what was beginning to be called the Winter War in March of the previous year, but it didn't cause tensions between the neighboring countries to abate. Finnish leaders waited for an opportune time to try to wrest back from Russia the lands Finns were forced to cede. Forces to defend further losses of territory were strengthened in the time since the treaty.

Axel Helenius, an active member of the congregation, an attorney who served as Toronto Vice-Consul for Finland had just arrived back from Finland the previous week. The table where he ate the lunch of traditional country soup made with freshly-caught fish after the brief devotional service attracted a small bevy of other picnickers who wanted geo-political updates from one in the know.

"Are the rumors that I hear from some of the hall gang true that Finland will soon re-open diplomatic relations with Germany?" asked Urpo Tenhunen, a plasterer.

"Urpo, are you asking me if that's just more fabrication of the truth by those aging leftists? Well, I'll tell you: no it isn't. Finland has been trying to do so with France and Great Britain, too, but we've been rebuffed because we fought the Russians. But Germany seems more interested."

"Why in heaven's name would we want to go to bed with Hitler?" Urpo protested.

"In war time, Urpo, it's prudent to cover all your bases. If you can't find a partner for the dance among the pretty girls, you lick your wounds and ask the wallflowers."

"But Hitler and Stalin signed the Molotov-Ribbentropp pact a couple of years ago," inserted Jouni Siitonen, a young, studious-looking man. "That makes them allies. Should we really be getting cozy with an ally of Stalin?"

Helenius looked as though he were conducting a press conference, and enjoying it."

238

"I can see you're a bright young man, Jouni. But the pact is just a piece of paper. Does anyone really expect Stalin or Hitler to be dissuaded from their ambitions by a piece of paper?"

Helenius' response got the picnickers around the table thinking.

Oskari Numminen, sitting beside Onni and Helina, made a contribution, too.

"The Nazi's invaded Norway a couple of months ago. I don't suppose they're there just because they want to see the fjords. That's getting close to home."

"Yes, it's a short distance, relatively speaking," Helenius added, "from Norway to Russia."

"Next thing you know, the Germans will be tramping over Finnish Lapland on their way to the Russian border," conjectured Eetu Sallinen, known to the rest of the church folk as the resident cynic.

Later, Helina pulled Onni aside and asked, "Do you think we will have yet another war, with the Russians, or the Germans, or both?" Her tone of voice indicated she preferred that he answer in the negative,

"I really don't know, Helina. I can't keep all the pieces of this chess game straight in my head. But I hope not."

After the men and women had been in the sauna in separate shifts, Onni and Helina were standing near the Ollikainens, a couple perhaps three decades or so older than them.

"We've met Onni previously," the husband said. "We've seen the young lady at the church, but we haven't met. We are Henry and Elma Ollikainen."

Onni introduced Helina to the couple.

"We came from Helsinki to Canada a couple of decades ago. Am I to presume, Helina, that not only were you not born at that time, but also that you have arrived much more recently?"

All the talk about growing tensions with Russia had made Helina uneasy. She didn't appear to be in the mood for this interview. But she was courteous and smiled throughout.

"Yes, I arrived just this past January."

"That recently?" Elma exclaimed. "We don't get to meet many newcomer Finns anymore."

"From where in Finland did you come?" asked her husband.

"From Vaala, a little village near Oulujärvi." Her reply was terse but not brusque. Onni sensed that she didn't want the conversation to proceed much further.

"Will you excuse us, please?" he said to the Ollikainens cordially, and then took Helina gently by the elbow and led her to the table that held the refreshments.

When the Häkkinens' automobile arrived in front of Helina's residence on Russell Hill Road after the picnic, Onni exited as well, which surprised Helina. While she may have wished to invite Onni up to her two-room efficiency flat on the third floor, she also knew this was not her house.

They stepped up to a grand porch that traveled almost half the width of the stately house. Helina asked if he'd like to sit on the porch for a while since it as such a warm night.

"Yes, I'd like that. I want to hear more of your immigration story. I know you didn't want to get into it with the Ollikainens since you just met them today. But I'm really interested to hear more."

She gave him a soft playful jab in the ribs. "You really are an incorrigible newspaper reporter, aren't you?" She laughed in a way that told Onni she was giving permission to hear her tale.

"I'm not going to write an article. I'm just interested in you."

Helina blushed at Onni's statement of interest, in her story, but also in her.

"You said today your home town is Vaala. Didn't you tell me when we met that you came from Kalajoki?" Onni asked.

"Yes, that was the truth. Or part of it. Kalajoki was Aulis' home. He had inherited a general store from his uncle who had no other heirs. Aulis and I operated the store before he had to go away. I continued to run it after he left, even after we got news that he had died while he was away. His parents lent a hand, as well – reluctantly, to tell the truth."

"Reluctantly? But they were Aulis' parents."

"Yes, and that's the only reason, I believe, why they helped. They wanted their son's business to succeed in his absence. But they didn't trust that I could make a go of it without Aulis."

She paused as if she were searching for the words to continue.

"I was the outsider, the woman from Vaala that Aulis found at school. I was never going to be good enough for their precious only son. They made it clear that I was no longer welcome, if I ever had been in the first place."

"They were making a mistake."

"I felt their judgmental gaze on me all the time. They had badmouthed me to half the village, even before our wedding. There was another small store in the village.

The people took their business there. I knew it would be hard for me to make the business go. So I found buyers in Liminka for the store."

"Where did you go from there?"

"I thought I'd give Vaala a try again. I moved back to my parents' farm. But deep down I knew even before I went that it would never work out."

She shook her head as though she were reliving a sorry episode.

"Sadly, my father is a slave to whiskey. Before I left for Kalajoki, he managed to keep the heavy drinking to the weekends. But when I went back after Aulis died, I couldn't believe how bad things had gotten. He was drunk from morning to night. He berated mother. One morning I found bruises on her face that she was trying to hide from me. That was it. I asked her to come with me. But she said that a wife's place is beside her husband, for better, for worse. I felt awful about leaving her there. But I knew I had to get out of there"

"All the way to Canada?"

"Helvi had been a friend in Vaala when we were little girls. You remember Helvi, don't you?"

Not waiting for Onni to nod his head, she went on.

"Helvi came to Port Arthur with her family when she was a little girl. We would exchange girlish letters over the years. I loved having a pen pal in a faraway country. It took me away from my life in Vaala. When she left Port Arthur at age eighteen, she came to Toronto. In spite of the hard times, she got work almost the next day as a domestic with a family in Forest Hill. Finns were in great demand as domestics then. After I wrote her about Aulis and my unhappiness at my parents' home, she urged me to come to Canada. She arranged a job for me with the Fishers here on Russell Hill Road. The Fishers were friends of her boss' family."

She stopped. Onni remained silent in a meditative mode.

"And so, that's my story."

Onni fished for the appropriate words.

"Your story includes a lot of pain."

"Don't all immigrant stories? Like yours, for instance."

Onni had told her previously about the fire at Peurajoki.

"But you know. I had the notion of coming to Canada in my head long before the fire. Ever since I was a little boy and I learned that my mother's father had spent time in northern Ontario before he went back to Finland and started a family. I liked the idea of a life in a faraway country, too"

Helina smiled at this. "I can just imagine this cute toe-headed little farm boy going on and on and driving his parents crazy about his plan to go across the ocean to Canada."

"So the pain is just a part, a small part, really, of my story. The pain came later when I heard that Väinö died. How is it possible that I knew he was in the war, but I never imagined that he'd be shot? I always assumed Väinö was invincible."

"Do we ever want to think about the death of loved ones?"

After they'd said goodnight and parted for the night, Onni decided to walk all the way back to 31 Beverley Street. He wanted to reflect on the day, and more specifically on what he felt in Helvi's presence.

This was a good day, a very good one, he judged. He felt an unexpected kind of self-confidence and comfort in Helina's presence. It wasn't that he thought he was in some way more competent in the world than she, which is what he had always thought the man in a relationship should feel. This evening, she calmed him, soothed him, just by being herself, by listening to him, but also by sharing what was on her mind and heart.

Onni wondered if he was in love with her. What he was feeling towards her was more than the surface attraction to her classic Finnish beauty, her blond hair, her exquisite lips that were lightly highlighted by subtle red lipstick on this day. Being in love, he reckoned, must be different from falling *into* love. On the first night they met at the church, he recalls that he was overcome instantly by the kind of infatuation that had felt long ago for Anna-Liisa. He recalled how much better the food tasted that evening, how he woke up the next morning with joyful anticipation of the day, how even the most ordinary things in the next few days felt extraordinary.

But by their second meeting, the one at Fran's Restaurant, the infatuation had evolved happily into a profound respect for her uniqueness and the inimitability of her experience of losing her husband at such a young age, and her being unwelcome in Kalajoki and unhappy in Vaala.

He marveled that they had both come from places in Finland separated by less than a couple hundred kilometers, and had come separately such a long distance to a new land and then met each other. He had heard similar tales from married Finnish immigrant couples at the church. There's something miraculous, Onni thought, something that can only be attributed to some invisible hand, that disparate paths from common roots should lead to such serendipitous encounters so far away.

When did he first feel what he'd now call love for her, he asked himself as he walked down Spadina Avenue towards home without in any way noticing the distance he'd walked. Onni guessed that it was at Fran's as she and he were sharing their immigrant stories. They found such happy commonality in their experience of loss and ongoing grief.

Is that, perhaps, what real love consists of?

Chapter Thirty-Three:
Toronto
September 1941

The Wednesday evening devotions and suppers resumed after a hiatus for the very hot summer. Onni had been
looking forward towards the end of the summer to the conversations over rye bread and *mojakka*.

The Continuation War, as it came to be called, hadn't
broken out officially yet the last time the congregants gathered on a Wednesday evening in May. But things had deteri-
orated at a rapid pace over the early summer to result in what
Helina had been afraid of: a second phase in the war with the
Soviet Union.

In early June, selected leaders of Germany and Finland met in secret in Helsinki to discuss Finland's role in Hitler's Operation Barbarossa – his plan to invade the Soviet Union. In mid-June, Finland called up all its reservists to try to
ensure that the Finnish forces would not be as badly outnumbered by the Soviets this time

When Onni learned of the call-up and deployment,
he remembered that he was nineteen years-old now. He presumed old friends from Peurajoki like Asikainen and Launikari, and other boys who were confirmed with him, had
been called up. It was their war now. If Onni weren't in Canada, it would be his war, too.

Eetu Sallinen had been right in his assumption at the
picnic back in June that Germany would indeed request permission for its troops to be transported without hindrance
from Norway to the northern Soviet border through Finnish
territory in Lapland. In return, Finland asked that no German
attack on the Soviet Union be made from Finnish soil.

After the Germans infiltrated onto Russian soil, the
surprised Russians retaliated with bombing run after run on
airfields in Finland leased to the Germans. They took advantage and bombed a few Finnish cities on their way back

from their bombing runs at the airfields, particularly the capital.

While the Germans were mobilizing thus on the north and south, Finnish infantry surrounded Viipuri and claimed much materiel and supplies left by the retreating Russians. At the beginning of September, the Finns reached the border that existed between the two countries in 1939 at the outset of the Winter War. They were then ordered to halt.

These events formed the topic of conversation at the Wednesday evening suppers. Onni took the stance of an invested listener for the most part. Some of his older fellow congregants were veterans of the Great War and civil war, so he listened intently to their perspective on this new war. With each fascinating detail in the stories they related about their experiences, Onni composed a mental newspaper article.

However, he was acutely cognizant that he was the sole nineteen-year-old sitting at the tables. No one else pointed out that fact in conversation. But Onni couldn't help but think that the older men might be wondering why a fit young man like him was sitting in a safe and comfortable church fellowship room when his contemporaries back home were taking shelter in trenches in the swampy Karelian woods.

He had warm memories of his dates with Helina. They had laughed and frolicked at the Canadian National Exhibition in August. They hadn't been able to see each other since that pleasant day.

One late Wednesday afternoon, he walked with the lightness of happy anticipation up to Huron Street and into the church house. The fellowship room was abuzz with animated conversation and laughter. His eyes scanned the tables. Finally, they landed on one table which was lit by Helina's gay smile. Alone with her at the table, leaning his body in her direction, smiling broadly and listening intently to her, was none other than Pastor Hepola.

Performing his pastoral duties, was he?

Chapter Thirty-Four:
Toronto
December 6, 1941

The celebration of the twenty-fourth anniversary of Finland's independence on December 6 was a muted one among the Toronto Finns. In the dining room, Mrs. Pyykkönen had hung every small blue and white Finnish flag she owned. As if on cue at supper, Pellonpää rose from his table to propose a toast to the land of the fathers and mothers, and to the sons who were now fighting ferociously to repatriate the land that had been demanded from Finland in 1940. But even the blow-hard Pellonpää couldn't work up a head of steam for his oration, and his listeners couldn't summon the willingness to listen to him.

The news had been broadcast from London that morning that England was declaring war on Finland because of the Finns' association with Germany. In the Winter War, Finland had petitioned England for materiel assistance against the Russians. But Britain had been cautious about angering Stalin, and thus declined despite initially vowing its moral support for the Finnish effort. Now she was declaring its active opposition to it.

The broadcast also included a call for all the nations of the British Commonwealth to follow suit and treat Finland as an enemy combatant. So, as the surviving residents of 31 Beverley Street tried to summon celebratory joy on Independence Day, they knew that any day now, as a dominion of the Commonwealth, Canada would most likely declare war on their homeland as well.

That's not all that was dragging Onni's spirits down. It had been weeks, almost a month and a half, since he had seen Helina at the Wednesday evening suppers at the church house. She had sent him no word of explanation for her sudden absence. He dared not telephone her at the Fishers' residence, not knowing the house rules there for telephone use by the domestic staff. Helina had mentioned once that the

Fishers were rather strict and unbending about restricting telephone calls to and by the staff. Even less did he consider venturing to the front door of the Fishers' residence to ask to see Helina.

More than once, Onni did walk up to Russell Hill Road in the hopes that by chance, she would might be coming out of the house on some errand, or that she might just happen to catch sight of him out on the sidewalk when she was cleaning one of the front windows, though it's unlikely she would be washing them in November or December.

Despite his hesitation, he finally asked Hepola if he had any idea why she was absenting herself from the church, or any knowledge of her whereabouts. Had she reported to her pastor that she was ill? Or that she had to return to Finland, God forbid? Hepola merely responded that he was wondering the very same things.

Onni had suspicions that Hepola might, in fact, be the very cause of her disappearance. Had Hepola been coming on to her in a way that was unwelcome that Wednesday evening when Onni spied them together by themselves at a table? Had that encounter now caused Helina to feel such discomfort in Hepola's presence that she elected to stay away? Or, worse still, had she responded positively to Hepola's advances, and welcomed them, if indeed he had made any. Was dhe now regretting it, or feeling embarrassed about it? Good Lord, she wasn't staying with him secretly in his bachelor apartment on McCaul Street, was she?

With each passing Wednesday that she was not at the supper, Onni's mind raced faster and faster, and he was more besieged by suspicion. His apprehensions began to have an independent power of their own that he was increasingly impotent to counter with rationalizations. If she were to come through the door of the church house that very moment, he knew he would welcome her with open arms and forgive her, if forgiveness was warranted, for putting him through such uncertainty and fretfulness. But week by week, he sensed his store of patience and willingness to overlook her failure to contact him was diminishing. Onni was growing bitter and losing hope.

On Russell Hill Drive, Helina checked with Mrs. Fisher to make sure it as alright to clean the second-floor rooms once she had finished cleaning the rooms on the first floor of the Fishers' home. Mrs. Fisher informed Helina that she and Mr. Fisher would be engaged in activities on the ground floor for the next hour or so. The second floor space was vacated so that Helina clean the bedrooms unimpeded.

She always began with the master bedroom and bath since they were the most used rooms on that floor and thus required the most time and effort to clean. She liked to address the situation in the master bathroom first. It was smaller than the bedroom, of course, and it gave her a feeling of accomplishment to check that room off her mental to-do list before attacking the bedroom itself.

In a matter of thirty minutes she surveyed the bathroom and pronounced it cleaned. She headed through the door and launched into vacuuming the Turkish rug in the master bedroom with the new Hoover which Mr. Fisher had purchased recently. Helina had reported several times that the old Kirby was no longer sucking up dust and dirt as efficiently as before.

She tried to vacuum clean the bare hardwood floor underneath the wooden dressers that stood raised on six-inch legs. She could maneuver the nozzle of the vacuum part of the way into the space between the floor and the bottom of the dresser, but not all the way.

She went into the bathroom and filled her metal bucket with warm water, added a small dose of powdered soap, and wet a clean rag in the water. She rung out the excess water from the rag into the bucket and took it into her right hand. She knelt on all fours before the dresser and stretched her arm in order to reach the farthest area of the hardwood floor beneath the dressed. Any dust there would be invisible to a person standing or sitting in the bedroom. A person prone on the bed wouldn't be able to see that far underneath the dressed. But Helina would know that there is a thin

250

layer of dust there, and her mind would not rest comfortably knowing that she left it there.

She continued to stretch her short right arm as far as it would go. She knew from all the other times she'd cleaned the master bedroom that she would eventually be able to reach far enough and wipe the dust away with the wet cloth.

The room had been silent except for her sighs of straining as she knelt and stretched. But suddenly, unexpectedly, there was the quiet shuffle of feet behind her. Since she was stationery in her kneeling posture, she couldn't look up to see whose feet they were.

She let out a startled shriek when she felt a hand rubbing her backside which was pointing upwards as she knelt.

"Shhh," whispered a male voice. "Everything's going to be alright."

Reflexively, Helina pulled her body out from under the dressed and tried to stand. But before she could get up to her feet, the man was on his knees as well behind her. He lowered his body onto her back. His groin pushed against her buttocks. He grabbed her breasts from behind as he took her into his embrace. Helina tried to pull her body away from him, but the man merely squeezed her breasts more tightly until he began to hurt her.

"There, there," the man said. "No need to resist. We both know you have been wanting this since your husband died. Every woman likes to be embraced and held."

Helina could turn her head now. She saw who the man fondling her breasts was.

"Mr. Fisher! What you do?"

"I'm just giving you what you want. I'm just having a little fun."

"Stop! I no like this."

251

"You wouldn't be the first Finnish woman who has played games with me in this room. Come on and play."

"I no play, Mr. Fisher. Let me go."

She rammed her two elbows into Fisher's ribs.

Fisher let out a cry of pain that he tried to muffle. He let go of her breasts and put his hands on his sore ribs. Helina took two steps back to create as much safe space between him and her as she could.

"What did you do that for? I was only trying to express affection for you. You Finnish broads are all the same. Your country is being awfully hospitable to the Germans just now. Your Finnish women are fucking them."

Helina didn't comprehend most of what he was saying. But she could see how angry he was.

"John? Is that you in there?" It was Mrs. Fisher's voice from behind the bedroom door.

Before he could answer, she opened the door and stepped into the bedroom. She held the door knob with one hand. Her face was as stern as the face of a craggy mountain.

"Helina what is going on in here? Why have you let John into the bedroom while you are cleaning it?"

"I no let him in. He come in by self."

"John knows that he is not to interrupt you when you are cleaning in this room. You must have given him permission to come in."

Helina was straightening her maid's uniform back into its proper position. She was shaking her head in disbelief.

"I took a chance on a young widow because I felt genuinely sorry for you," Mrs. Fisher said. "But I can see now that no matter how nice they seem, young widows miss the affection of their late husbands and will take advantage of other

252

men, if they have to in order to get the affection they don't get from their husbands any longer. Even if those men are already married. I can't express how disgusted and disappointed I am, Helina."

Mrs. Fisher could have saved herself the trouble of expounding her elaborate theory because Helina was not able to understand a word of it. All she could comprehend was the word "disappointed".

All the while, Fisher took a few steps back from Helina towards his wife. He was perfectly content to let the two women do all the talking.

"I'm disappointed in you, Helina. I trusted you with this house. I trusted you with my husband. You have betrayed my trust. I'll have to let you go, I'm afraid."

Halina's face was still uncomprehending.

"Do you understand what I am saying, Helina? You are being *fired*. You must leave this house immediately and not come back to work here any longer."

Helina appealed silently to Mr. Fisher, as though he could interpret for her what his wife was saying.

"It means no more work here, Helina," Mr. Fisher said to her. "No more work."

Helina understood his words. But she had no comprehension of what was happening. *No more work here? But he's the one who initiated this dirty affair. Why am I being blamed?*

She was too confused, to bewildered by this turn of events, to feel any anger towards him. And she didn't have the fluency, not even the ability to think clearly at the moment, to defend herself and explain to the angry woman what had really happened.

Mrs. Fisher held the door open wide.

253

"It's time you gathered your things, Helina, and left this house. I would hope that if you find work again, you learn to be more dependable and trustworthy than you proved to be here with us."

Chapter Thirty-Five:
Toronto
December 12, 1941

Onni was the last one to get up from the breakfast table. He wasn't due at the *Evening Telegram* plant until shortly after noon. When he carried his dirty dishes into the kitchen, Mrs. Pyykkönen asked him if he had registered yet. Onni had not.

When Canada followed the lead of Mother England and declared war on Finland, the federal government passed emergency wartime legislation that required all Finns within Canad, citizens or not, to report to the Royal Canadian Mounted Police headquarters and register as enemy aliens. Registration brought with it restrictions on sending money back from Canada to relatives in Finland, which had become a common practice for the Finns in Toronto. The Finnish consulate in Toronto and in other Canadian cities were suspended and closed for the time being.

"I find it hard to think of myself as an enemy alien," Onni remarked to Mrs. Pyykkönen.

"It breaks my heart to have my adopted country single us out in this way. We've tried to be good peace-loving citizens and to make positive contributions to Canadian society," she lamented.

"We can thank God, though, that the government isn't treating us the way they do the Japanese and Germans. I don't think we'd like to be shipped to those camps in British Columbia and Manitoba like them."

Onni went upstairs to write a letter to his parents and to study his English before lunch. He had hardly completed the first paragraph of his letter when Mrs. Pyykkönen knocked on his door, a little breathless from climbing two flights of stairs, to tell him that he had a visitor waiting for him downstairs in the foyer.

255

Onni looked surprised.

"She's Finnish, and it's a woman."

Onni's heart was racing. Who could it be? Was in Helina, reappearing after several months of being AWOL? She had never come to 31 Beverley Street on her own before. If this was she, it would be highly uncharacteristic. But then again, her sudden disappearance from their familiar haunts was itself already uncharacteristic of her. What other female even knew where he lived? Who else could possibly come looking for him.

He descended the stairs to the first-floor foyer feeling palpable anxiety. Not knowing whom to expect to see when he arrived in the foyer made him impossibly uncomfortable. The prospect that it might be Helina made him oddly discomfited as well, which he wouldn't have expected. He'd thought he would have been filled with joyful anticipation of their reunion. But he was fearful of his reactions if he saw her, of what mean things he might say, of the bitter tone of voice in which he might say them.

The woman's back was turned to him as he landed in the foyer. At the sound of his feet on the foyer floor, she turned around to greet him.

It was Helina's longtime friend, Helvi.

"Helvi, this is a surprise."

"I'm sorry to come unannounced like this."

She looked as anxious as Onni was feeling.

She continued, "Helina asked me to come."

"Oh?"

"She wanted me to bring a message to you, to tell you that she is safe, and that she is sorry if she has caused you any worry or concern."

"I appreciate the news, Helvi. But couldn't she have come herself to say these things?"

"It's complicated, Onni. Can we sit somewhere private?"

The parlor adjacent to the foyer was empty, as it usually was.

"We can sit in here. Mrs. Pyykkönen, the landlady, is in the kitchen cleaning up after breakfast. The only another person in the house is Aune, but it's highly unlikely she would come down."

They sat in Victorian armchairs opposite each other.

"I don't know how to begin," Helvi said when she was convinced that they had absolute privacy. "This topic is not something I'm accustomed to discussing with a man."

She couldn't look directly at Onni.

"It's because it's awkward that Helina sent me. It's just too overwhelming and shameful for her to tell you directly."

"Helina and I have been pretty honest with each other up to now. What can be so awkward that she can't face me?"

"Onni. . ."

She paused as if to reconsider if she should bring up the subject or not.

"Onni. . . Helina lost her job at the Fishers'."

"What? Lost her job? I can't believe that. What will she do now?"

"But losing the job is not really the main thing. You see, she was molested by Mr. Fisher. . . Sexually molested."

There was fear in Onni's eyes, and sudden anger.

"Molested? God damn!"

"Mr. Fisher didn't get very far, just fondled her when she was quite defenseless doing her job. Mrs. Fisher, thank God . . . I guess . . . interrupted him by storming into the room before he could go on."

"My God! Is Helina hurt?"

"Not hurt if you mean physically. She was fully clothed, and so was he. He didn't hit her."

"But otherwise?"

"Emotionally, she has been devastated. Mrs. Fisher fired her in the spot because she thought that somehow Helina had brought this on herself, had seduced Mr. Fisher."

"That being molested was *her* fault?"

"It never even seemed to occur to the stupid woman that own husband might have been the aggressor."

"Jesus! The bastard!"

"Helina had to leave the house right away. She came to my flat on Bernard Avenue. She was a mess emotionally."

Onni's face was a bright red. His heart was pounding in his chest.

"Do we know what happened to that bastard, Fisher?"

"We don't know a thing. Helina doesn't dare to go back and fetch a few personal items she failed to pack in her haste to leave."

"By God, the man will have to pay! I'll make sure of it."

"Onni, Helina doesn't want you to be involved in this sordid mess at all. You mustn't do anything to make matters worse."

She continued, "I tried to persuade Helina to go to the police when she came to my flat, but she said that since she didn't have a scratch on her, what would they possibly do? Investigate a lion of Canadian industry because of the word of a Finnish immigrant domestic?"

"But there's *got* to be retribution. Does the man think that Helina is some kind of plaything for him? Some cheap brazen hussy? There *have* to be consequences for his boorish behavior."

Helvi allowed him to baste in his own vitriol for a moment.

After he had calmed down some, he asked, "What will she do for work now?"

"Well, she's not willing to go the domestic worker route, that's for sure."

"I would hope not. I wouldn't *let* her."

"She's out in Scarborough with me, at General Engineering. It's almost ironic. We're helping make munitions for Canada to use on her enemies. Onni, Finland is now one of them!'"

"Scarborough? That's the edge of the earth."

"The company is so eager for workers right now that they offer to provide transportation in a school bus from the Luttrell Avenue terminal of the Bloor street car. It's easy enough for Helina and me to ride the street car there to be picked up."

"Helvi, I'm grateful for your visit. I know this wasn't easy for you. You're a good friend to Helina. I've been a bundle of nerves wondering where she was, or whether she was angry at me for some reason I don't understand; or gone with some other man; or even gone back to Finland without telling me. Even if I don't at all like what happened to her, it feels good to know. Thank you for being there for her."

"I think when I get back and tell her how you feel, and that you don't hold it against her, she will feel more confident and comfortable about seeing you again."

~~~~~~~~~~~~~~~~~~~~~~~~~~~~~~~~~~~

When Helvi left, Onni was at a loss about what to do with himself and his growing anger. It seemed as if it were bursting the limits of his mind. Once in his room, he paced the floor, trying to channel the white-hot anger into some kind of constructive plan to make Fisher pay for his violation of sweet Helina.

He considered seriously maiming Fisher with a gunshot – not killing him, just wounding him so that for the rest of his cursed life, Fisher would regret his attempted exploitation of Helina.

His fury expanded to include all of Fisher's social class, the privileged Anglo-Saxon Toronto aristocracy in their elegant Forest Hill and Rosedale mansions. They provided work out of their *noblesse oblige* to Finnish men as chauffeurs and women as domestics and cleaning women. But they assumed a self-congratulatory superiority. The gall of Fisher to presume that as her employer, he had some kind of implicit right to her body and virtue.

As a farm boy, Onni had handled a weapon before, so he was confident he could aim a gun just right so that the bullet would not be fatal. He would hit Fisher in a part of his body that would be wounded and disabled as a reminder to him for all eternity.

The problem was, now that he had registered with the RCMP, he was not allowed to purchase a firearm. If he was to get his hands on one, he would have to buy it on the black market. He had heard about such a market among the Italian immigrants. Perhaps he could secure one by walking over to College and Bathurst and keeping his ears open.

Then he remembered the tire iron on the back of his *Evening Telegram* truck, put there in case he ever had to fix a flat tire. He imagined himself ringing the Fishers' doorbell and then swinging the tire iron at Fisher when he came to open the door. He would hit Fisher just hard enough to leave a permanent mark, perhaps even inflict some kind of brain damage, but not hard enough to kill him.

In his fevered creation of a workable plan, he wished dearly that he had Väinö at his side to advise him, to vet Onni's plan for obvious errors of judgment, and iron out the difficulties. Väinö would encourage him to proceed with his plan for retribution, Onni was sure of it. If Onni were to overlook Fisher's offense, in fact, Väinö would surely be disgusted in Onni's lack of courage or manliness.

Onni went to pick up his loaded truck at the *Evening Telegram* with the peace of mind that comes from having made a decision after wrestling with it. He would drop off the bundles of newspapers at all the normal street corners for the route boys to pick up and deliver to home on their route. The exception was that he would make the drop-off in front of Upper Canada College on Lonsdale before the one at St. Clair and Spadina, thus reversing the normal order. From his last drop-off, before he took the truck back to the plant, he would make a detour a few blocks to Russell Hill Road and pay a little visit to the Fishers.

Onni grew increasingly anxious with each drop-off. After the Upper Canada College drop-off, he took a deep breath to try to quell the anxiety in his chest. He looked with contempt at the grand brick edifice of the college on its treed and manicured grounds. The college represented all the revulsion Onni was feeling towards the privilege and self-importance of the Fishers' and their Forest Hill crowd. The sight of the gilded college pushed his anxiety out to the periphery of his mind and reinforced his sense of the rightness of his plan.

He made the last drop-off at Spadina and St. Clair. The delivery boy looked at Onni with annoyance that his papers were being delivered a quarter hour later than usual.

Onni felt his heart beating more quickly. He was aware that the moment was at hand. He pulled the truck away from the curb. Not until he had driven through the intersection did he realize that he had gone through a red light. He was fortunate not have been hit by another vehicle.

Onni turned the truck east off Spadina onto Heath Street. His heart was thumping almost audibly. His palms were slippery with sweat. His shirt stuck to the skin on his back.

He drove through the intersection at Parkwood Avenue. Russell Hill Road was next. He pictured the tire iron in his mind.

He came to a stop at the stop sign at Russell Hill Road. He looked to his right at the Fishers' home which was on the southwest corner. It was dark already, but from the wheel of the truck he couldn't see any lights on in the house.

He parked the truck at the next block between Russell Hill Road and Warren Road. He took the tire iron from the back of the truck. He placed it into an A & P grocery store shopping bag so that it was not conspicuous to any pedestrians or drivers in passing cars.

He took another deep breath to shove the anxiety further down his throat. He noticed from the sidewalk that there was no light in the windows on either the first or second floor.

He raised his right hand to ring the doorbell. He held his hand just an inch away from the knob for a moment, as though reconsidering. He glanced behind him one last time to make sure that no can was passing to witness what he was about to do. Then he pushed the doorbell. He heard the sound of the bell somewhere in the house.

There was no response. Onni took a quick look at the tire iron in the shopping bag as though he were double-checking that it hadn't dropped out the bottom of the bag.

After almost two minutes of waiting, the front door opened slightly. The head of a female, probably twenty-five years old, Onni figured, peered out for behind the door.

"Yes, may I help you?" she asked in broken English. It was not a Finnish accent however, possibly Latvian or Lithuanian.

"From the *Evening Telegram*, Ma'am, looking for Mr. Fisher," Onni said, trying to sound as authoritative as he could. He was surprised at how easily the English sentence flowed from his mouth.

"Sorry, sir. Mr. and Mrs. Fisher go to Jamaica for Christmas. No at home."

For a moment, Onni was at a loss. He didn't have an alternative plan. He felt empty-handed. His fury had nowhere to go. He tried to hide his disappointment. He thanked the woman, said goodnight, and walked back to the truck.

Before he turned on the ignition, Onni let out a deep, windy, audible breath. He recognized it as a sigh of relief as much as of disappointment that Fisher was not at home. He hadn't noticed how damp his armpits were from sweat.

Only now did he begin to consider the consequences if his plan to batter Fisher for revenge had been successful. Did he really think that the police wouldn't trace a trail from the Fishers' home to Onni somehow? Surely they'd interview Helina as a former employee of the Fishers and ask if she had any male friends who knew of the Fishers. The police would assume right away that a crime like that one would be committed by an immigrant.

Was facing charges and spending time in the Don Jail some way to make progress towards becoming fluent in English and a career in journalism? Would Helina really be proud of him for exacting revenge on her behalf by violence? Hardly.

263

As he pulled the truck away from the curb on Heath Dtreet and headed back to the *Telegram* plant, he was grateful he had been saved from a terrible mistake.

Chapter Thirty-Six
Toronto
March 1942

Helina had been behind the serving table once again on the first Wednesday evening of the new year. Onni didn't suppress his happiness in seeing her again. But Helina lowered her eyes so as not to meet his.

"I'm so very glad to see you, Helina," he told her as he took one of the plates of mashed potatoes and meat loaf she was distributing. "You can't imagine how I have missed seeing you."

"I can't stop and talk right now, Onni," she said quietly, although not in a way that felt to Onni as though she were pushing him away. "Later, after supper, okay?"

When they retreated to the church house parlor after the evening program and supper, Onni was careful not to bring up the subject of her sexual assault.

"I'm sorry I caused you worry, Onni," she began. "Helvi explained the situation to you?"

"Yes, she did. I was very sorry to hear what happened. But at the same time, I was grateful to hear from her where you had been, and that in spite of everything you were well."

"I don't know if I will ever be able to put it behind me, but I have to try. Please keep it between you and me."

"Of course. I wouldn't dream of talking about it with anyone. You know that."

They went on a few outings together or with other couples from the congregation in the winter: sledding and tobogganing at Riverdale Park and ice-skating at the Mutual Street Arena. Helina tried her best to be worry-free on those occasions. She was grateful for Onni's attempts to be solicitous of her. He was trying to be less inhibited and more fun-loving than usual.

Onni had just turned twenty years of age. He knew that by this age, his father Martti had already proposed to Tyyne. Onni went back to 31 Beverley Street after each outing with Helina with feverish thoughts about the prospect of marriage with Helina. He felt such a sense of ease in her presence, such a surge of confidence in himself as though she had an invisible hand that dug into the deepest part of him and brought forth all the good in him.

His feelings of loneliness and longing during her absence the previous months were still fresh in his mind. Ironically, it was those feelings precisely that convinced him that marrying her was the right thing for him.

Nnot knowing for sure how she would react, after the ice-skating outing, he had gently embraced her and then carefully kissed her on the lips. The cool tip of her nose rubbed against his cheek. She didn't pull back from his embrace or turn her head when he bent to kiss her again.

He understood why she didn't bring up the episode with Fisher. But he was disappointed all the same because before then, they had been able to talk about just about anything. It was as though the assault by Fisher had caused them to take a step backwards in their intimacy.

He would propose to her tomorrow if he could be sure that she was feeling anything approximating the same way towards him. Women were difficult to read in any circumstance, Onni thought, so different from men in their way of looking at life. But to read the feelings of a woman still grieving the death of her husband barely two years' prior was challenging, to say the least.

He wished Eino were closer so that he could discuss the matter with someone older who had been married. A few months earlier he might have sought Hepola's counsel, but he was less than sure now of Hepola's intentions towards Helina.

Perhaps he had better bide his time, he concluded.

But then he saw her again the next Wednesday evening. Forgetting his promise to himself to be patient and wait, he proposed marriage.

Helina seemed taken aback by the suddenness and directness of his proposal. There was nothing florid or ornate in his proposal. Just, "Do you want to get married?"

It wasn't all that different, she reflected, on how Aulis had proposed to her four or so years' prior. Perhaps that is the way with northern men: straightforward, to the point, and in as few words as possible.

It also wasn't like northern *women,* however, to give an answer immediately to a question that required caution and significant thought. She expressed her gratitude to him that he considered her worthy of being asked, and then requested time to consider the proposal.

Onni didn't seem overly disappointed that she didn't accept on the spot. He knew her cautious, prudent nature, and so he wasn't surprised that she pleaded for time to ponder the idea. All the same, he had to push from his consciousness the idea that her request signaled that she might not be ready yet to commit to a man other than the one who had been her husband. Much worse, there crept into his heart the suspicion that she was holding out for a similar proposal from their handsome, lively pastor who may - or possibly may not - be a bachelor. He forced the distrust out of his mind.

Helina felt both delighted and, in a way, burdened by his proposal.

He is such a kind, patient man, a gentleman. I should feel more grateful that he wants to spend a lifetime with me. I didn't think a man other than Aulis would ever really want a shy and reticent woman like me. Now Onni says he wants me.

I've tried not to lead him on. I've tried not to give even the slightest hint of anything beyond friendship. When Aulis was killed, I vowed that one good, if short, marriage in a life-time is enough for me. I would not allow myself to be hurt again.

But whenever I look at his earnest face when we are together, my resolve seems to melt. I re-draw the boundaries I have set for this relationship. Over that cup of coffee at Fran's Restaurant, he saw the most wounded part of me, and yet he didn't run. He began that night to pave a path to my heart.

But still, I'm not sure I love Onni the way I loved Aulis. Is that fair to Onni? Would it be fair to Aulis if I did? Can a woman love two men in the same way and to the same depth? Is a true marriage possible if it doesn't start with passion and sexual attraction? Could I learn love Onni in a way that he deserves? God, I don't even know what love is any more.

Do I deserve happiness when poor Aulis' life was cut short and we can't share happiness together? Can I allow myself to experience happiness without him as Helvi encourages me to?

Oh, this is downright silly and ridiculous! I'm three years older than him, for goodness sake. In those three years, I was married and lost a husband. In that time, I lived a whole lifetime. He's still just a boy. What can he possibly bring to the marriage?

And yet . . . he's resurrected parts of me that I thought had died with Aulis in those frigid woods: the simple desire for closeness with another human being; for physical touch; for the risky fragility of commitment and intimacy.

How will I answer him?

Chapter Thirty-Seven:
Toronto
Summer 1942

Onni was surprisingly patient with Helina in the three months since he had proposed. The hot summer had come, and still she hadn't given an answer. Mitigating any impatience was a conversation he had had as a young pre-adolescent with Tyyne in which she divulged that her mother had been against the idea of her marrying Martti because of his landless status. She pleaded with Martti for time to try to persuade her mother to agree to the marriage so that she could proceed towards the wedding with her blessing. It had taken her many months to come to the realization that if she were to wait for her mother's blessing, hell itself might freeze over before that. So she simply announced to her mother that the wedding was on, and that was that.

After the Wednesday evening dinners, she started to welcome his offer to walk her to the street car stop at Spadina Avenue and Queen Street. She began weaving her left arm inside his right one. Onni was satisfied that to the public, they were now a couple, if not quite an engaged one.

Attendance at the Wednesday evening suppers at 246 Huron Street diminished slightly as the Finnish immigrants began to relocate to areas of the city removed from the Queen Street – Spadina district that had been their nest since the first Finns arrived early in the century. But conversation at the tables was as heated as ever.

Mauri Hyytiäinen was one of the first of a small group of Canadian-born adult children of the earlier immigrants to be a regular at the suppers. The English language was their preferred vehicle for communication. Their broken Finnish, in fact, was a secret source of comic entertainment for the more recently arrived immigrant Finns. Of the fifteen cases that Finnish nouns could take, they were familiar with possibly two or three at most. Their sentence structure seemed so humorously ragged.

Mauri carried himself with a lot of confidence. As a native-born Canadian, he assumed that the older immigrant generations were slightly backward and needlessly conservative in this country and city that until the outbreak of the war at least, had been forward-looking.

Onni overheard Mauri's voice conversing with a couple of the other second-generation Finns table beside his.

"This whole pact of the Finns with the Germans is craziness, don't you think? The Germans won't win this war despite what it has looked like up to now. To be tied to a sinking ship as the Finns now are is wrongheaded. And even if the Germans could win, do you think they would just pack up their stuff in Finland, say thank you for the hospitality, and let the Finns have their own country back? Preposterous."

Onni had learned enough English by now that he gathered the general gist of what Hyytiäinen was arguing.

"The Russian will throw them out. The Germans will eventually learn their lesson. Finland learned in the Winter War that there are simply too many of the Russkies to handle so far from home, so far from their gasoline and food supplies."

Hyytiäinen's two conversation partners seemed more interested in their food that his military analysis.

"Now Hitler has been photographed being received in Helsinki for Mannerheim's birthday. Don't the Finnish leaders see how this is perceived over here, in the U.S. and by the Allies? They won't take kindly to the Finns lying in bed with Hitler."

Onni couldn't simply eavesdrop on the monologue any longer.

"What other choice has the President Ryti?" he tossed out to Hyytiäinen. His boldness surprised him once the words were out of his mouth.

Hyytiäinen took a forkful of the mashed potatoes from his plate and shoveled it into his mouth. After swallowing it, he said, "None. Absolutely none. There's no way for Finns to win back their lost territory without help. Maybe the Finns would have been wiser just to let things be the way they were after the Winter War. After all, they may have lost a portion of their territory, but they still had the rest of it, unlike our Estonian cousins. They still had their own government."

The conversations at the other tables had ceased. All ears were on Hyytiäinen now.

Esko Vuori, the accountant, who had come to Toronto as a young man early in the 1920s, was much more fluent in English than the other immigrants, and so felt the need to speak up.

"Mauri, just think. What if the Russians or somebody else invaded Canada and conquered, say, Nova Scotia, and decided to keep it for themselves? And then, on top of that, what if they demanded use of the port of Montreal to boot. What should Canada do? Roll out the welcome mat? Accept it as the new *status quo*?"

He inserted a strategic solicitor's pause, then continued, "Or see what other country might share an interest in fighting the trespassing country?"

"OK, OK, you have a point, Esko. But all I'm trying to say is that people at work keep asking me how Finland could attach itself to Germany. People had respect for the Finns. I try to assure them that the Finns are not Nazis, that we don't hate and kill Jews. But they can't get past the symbolism of Hitler in Helsinki, and German planes taking off to bomb Russia from Finnish airfields. Canadians are no fans of the Russians, God knows. But they wonder if it's a greater evil to sidle up to the Nazis."

Neither Onni nor Vuori had an answer. It was as though Hyytiäinen had exhausted the subject. The truth was that both Onni and Vuori knew in their heart of hearts that Hyytiäinen's point was well taken. They, too, were embarrassed to a point by the Finns' association with the Germans, this marriage of convenience, this compromise of principles and values that war has an inevitable way of demanding.

One Wednesday evening, Lempi Hirvonen remarked that she was fed up with Canadian yeast.

"It's nearly impossible to make *pulla* the way we used to back home. I can't find wet yeast anywhere in Toronto. This dry powdery yeast they sell here doesn't work nearly as well.

The other women at the table nodded their heads in agreement. But they were all familiar enough with Lempi's penchant for finding something amiss in Canada just about every time they gathered, and were therefore not inclined to do more to encourage her to continue her complaint.

"Your *pulla* is perfectly fine, Lempi," Esko Vuori said diplomatically. "I suppose there are a lot of things we loved in Finland that we can't find here."

"True," Valtteri Tuhkala agreed. "But still, I don't regret having emigrated to Canada."

"Neither do I," Jalmari Revonlahti said. "Why would anyone regret having left the old country?"

Onni observed the exchange and wondered how he himself would answer. Coming to Canada had not been the altogether positive experience he had imagined. It's not that he was disappointed in the destination at which he'd arrived. It's just that on some days, he was disappointed in the one who had made the journey.

Mauri Hyytiäinen entered the conversation. "I sure am glad that my parents decided to leave the old country when they did. They would have had no chance of coming in the thirties."

On the whole, however, Revonlahti's question seemed to have caught the group unaware, and a spell of silent nostalgia fell over them.

Breaking the silence, however, was the scraping of Helina's metal chair against the floor as she rose suddenly and without a word. Her hand was covering her face to hide her abrupt tears. She
ran out of the room into the empty kitchen.

Chapter Thirty-Eight:
Toronto
Fall 1942

Helina settled on an answer to Onni's proposal. Several years earlier, she had been so overcome by love and affection for Aulis that she had never really considered the risk, the leap of faith, that marriage is. Now, in the six months of mulling over Onni's proposal, she became acutely aware that the mind can never become 100% convinced of the rightness and wisdom of marriage. The mind will always have doubts and questions. She was basing her decision on her heart, her intuition really. Her mind could come up with an endless list of rational reasons to say no to Onni. But her intuition overrode those reasons. She simply had a powerful sense that marrying Onni was the right thing to do.

Onni was overjoyed be her affirmative answer. One afternoon they took the Queen Street streetcar to Nordic Jewelers near Jarvis Street. Vilho Kihlanki had opened the jewelry business in 1940. He carried the simple Finnish-style engagement and wedding rings, two unadorned bands of gold.

Onni was ready to tie the knot immediately, but Helina requested that they wait until the spring of the following year.

"Perhaps this war will be over by then. I'd feel so much better starting married life in peacetime."

"Oh, I doubt the war will be over by then. There's an outside chance, maybe, that the Finnish role in it may be near an end. But Hitler has advanced deep into Russia. His armies are only twenty miles outside Moscow. He seems a long way from being done. And I don't think the Russian are just going to lie down and give up, either."

"If we wait, we'd also be able to take our time finding a house that we could afford. I don't want to rush into that decision either."

Onni deferred to her practical wisdom. But they did make an appointment with Pastor Hepola to discuss plans, however.

"That is wonderful news!" Hepola enthused when they announced their engagement to him. "Congratulations. You have always appeared to me to be a well suited for each other"

Onni tried to read Hepola's facial expressions and body language when he said this. Onni judged that the man either was genuinely delighted for them, or else a very good actor. There didn't seem to be a hint of disappointment in Hepola's voice that he had been beaten to the finish line by the younger man from Peurajoki. Either Onni was misreading him now. Or had he misread him the evening he saw Hepola and Helina sitting face to face at the table at the Wednesday evening supper.

Onni felt a tinge of shame come over him for having suspected his pastor, of all people, of having intentions towards his girl.

The couple and Hepola scheduled the small wedding for the first of April, 1943.

~~~~~~~~~~~~~~~~~~~~~~~~~~~~~~~~

The couple was busy over the winter. They found a good deal on a house – 92 Kendal Avenue – in a district north of Bloor Street that was beginning to be attractive to the younger Finnish immigrants. It was a whole new environment for them in which to begin a new life together.

Helina had more work than she could handle at General Engineering. Now that Canada had joined the Allied war effort in Europe, the demand for arms and weapons was high.

Young men of Finnish lineage who were Canadian citizens volunteered for the armed forces. In fact, Hyytiäinen was one of those, deployed with the Second Division to raid Dieppe on the northern French coast. Before he left, he expressed to anyone at the Wednesday supper who cared to listen his sincere hope that he not be assigned to a unit fighting alongside the Russians against the Finns. Esko Vuori admitted that it was theoretically possible, but highly unlikely, since to his knowledge no Canadian unit had been deployed to Karelia.

Hyytiäinen's volunteering, however, did remind the young couple that Onni would be eligible to apply for Canadian citizenship in a little over a year.

"Good Lord, Onni," Helina told him. "Don't you even mention the possibility of your volunteering. Remember, you'll have a wife to support soon."

She said this despite the fact that with all her extra hours at the munitions works at General Engineering, she brought home a bigger paycheck than he did.

As for Onni, he had been invited inside from the cold at the *Evening Telegram*. The circulation department was pleased with his work in delivering the bundles of papers to street corners, and offered him a position as a single copy sales manager. Torontonians' trust in the improvement of the economy still hadn't recovered fully after the trauma of the depression. Some households were still wary of committing to a daily subscription to the newspaper, and the weekly cost of it. They preferred to purchase a single copy of the paper at their neighborhood corner store on days when the headlines tempted them to buy one.

Onni was proud of his promotion. To be given the title of manager gave him a feeling of having achieved a respectable status. He had gone to Simpson's basement to buy a couple of new suits to wear on the job instead of the shirt and wool slacks he wore on the delivery truck. That his superiors offered him a job that involved developing relationships with the store owners and operators whom he supplied with a pile of single copies of the *Telegram* gave him confidence that his English had improved tremendously.

Besides, the office he shared with other single copy managers was just down the hall from the news department, near enough that Onni could practically smell it.

The wedding was a small private one performed in front of the altar at the church house. Hepola officiated, of course. Helvi was Helina's only attendant, and Onni invited Kalle to be his best man. A few members of the church and the residents of 31 Beverley Street – even Pellonpää – comprised the congregation.

Kalle proposed a toast in Estonian with a glass of ginger ale in the fellowship room after the service. *"Mõrsjale ja peigmeelle."* The small gathering of guests and well-wishers raised their glasses of ginger ale in response. *"Morsialle ja sulhaselle . . .* To the bride and groom.*"* Everyone laughed in unison at the humor of having Canada Dry in their glasses instead of champagne, made necessary by the church's lack of liquor license.

A couple from the congregation offered the use of their summer cottage on Lake Willcocks north of the city for a weekend honeymoon, and the husband even offered to chauffeur them to the cottage in his automobile.

Meanwhile, some 4,600 air miles away, there were the first indications that Mauri Hyytiäinen may have been right about the impossibility of the Germans' winning the war. The siege on Moscow stalled just miles outside the city line. After encircling the city of Stalingrad for nearly a year, the German armies were pushed back by Russians at the end of January. The Germans began to retreat towards Poland and then their fatherland.

Mannerheim and the Finnish leadership knew then that in time, the Germans would lose. There was no way they could succeed in a war on two fronts, eastern and western. Mannerheim began looking for a way to make peace with the Allies.

Surprisingly, the United States offered to act as an intervening agent between Finland and the Soviet Union in preparing for a peace.

Molotov presented to the well-meaning American delegation the list of Russian demands. The Russian-Finnish border was to return to the one established after the Winter War in 1940. Heavy reparation payments were added to the list.

The Americans argued that the terms were too harsh for a people that had fought so valiantly gaainst a numerically superior force. The Russians reminded the Americans of the Finnish association with the Germans. The talks were cut off, and hostilities in Karelia resumed.

Onni was distressed at the news. But he was glad he and Helina didn't wait for the war to be over before they married.

Chapter Thirty-Nine:
Niagara Falls, ON
June 17, 1944

The first year of Onni's and Helina's married life was, all things considered, blissfully uneventful. Life around them in Canadian society was changing at a rapid pace, and not always in directions they would have considered favorable. The marriage was an island of security and happiness.

A shroud of sadness and fear fell over their quiet household, however, when word reached Toronto that in February 1944, the Russians had started a large-scale bombing campaign over Helsinki again. Civilians were killed. The campaign was expanded to include Turku and Tampere as well.

Onni and Helina were no better able to articulate out loud the implications of the successful Russian bombing tactics than were any of the other Finnish immigrants. The usual response was, "We've found a way to rebound from such setbacks before in this war, and surely we'll recover from this one, too."

Their wishful thinking seemed to be reinforced the next month when the Finnish government rejected the terms for peace that the Russians had announced publicly for all the world to hear. The Finns would continue to fight.

Canadian soldiers were fighting in Europe alongside the United States and Britain. It seemed that every third or fourth house on Kendal Avenue had at least a husband, father or adult son doing battle in Europe. Unbeknownst to the general population of Canada and many other lands, for at least two years starting in early 1942, President Roosevelt of the United States and Prime Minister Churchill of Great Britain had been laying secret plans for the single largest military campaign in the history of the world on the coast of France. Canadian Prime Minister William Lyon Mackenzie King hadn't been privy to the plans. He was simply informed by Roosevelt and Churchill that Canadian boys would play a role in this campaign.

Canada was beginning to face a shortage of men and women who volunteered for service. Talk was rampant about introducing the forced conscription of healthy young men between the ages of eighteen and twenty-five.

When Onni came home one evening from his day at the *Evening Telegram* and told Helina over dinner that it looked inevitable that conscription would be a fact of Canadian life as soon as the following year, 1943, Helina grew as silent as stone wall for the rest of the evening.

Helina did this from time to time. She would clean the dinner table and wash the dishes in total silence. At first, Onni was confused, wondering what he had said or done that made her angry and made her withdraw from him. If he pushed the matter and asked what was wrong, she often denied that there as anything wrong, and then retreated into her private cocoon of silence.

At other times, she would say that she wasn't ready to talk about whatever it was that caused her to withdraw emotionally.

On this particular evening, she came out of her cocoon as bedtime approached.

"Onni, if there is conscription, will it mean that you could be called up into service?"

"Not likely. The first preference will be for those who are citizens."

"Then don't apply for citizenship when you become eligible in October. Please don't. Please."

"You sound so very fearful."

"I *am* fearful. This whole war thing scares me. It's gone on so long. Almost five years now. Enough is enough. When will this damned fighting and killing finally end?"

"But the war is helping provide you with employment. You don't think, do you, that Canadian Engineering would hire all those women if the men were back home?"

Helina gave him a look in which her blue eyes had turned the color of anger.

"We're far away from the conflict here in Canada," Onni continued. "Just imagine our Finnish brothers and sisters where the fighting has come close to home."

"I *am* thinking about them, damnit Onni!. I lived through it for part of year, remember? You didn't."

Helina's remark hit a nerve in Onni. Anger wasn't the first emotion he felt at the time, however. Rather, it was his old companion, shame.

Why did she feel the need to add that last sentence? Doesn't she know that a part of me deep down is ashamed that I left my native country just a couple of months before its greatest need?

From that night on, Onni was more careful about bringing up news he'd heard that day down at the paper about the progress of the war. But Onni enjoyed the conversations with colleagues in the staff coffee break room. It felt so good to be able to participate using his growing facility in the English language.

A fellow single copy manager at the paper invited Onni and Helina to join him and his wife on a drive one Saturday to Niagara Falls. Because Onni and Helina didn't have a car, they hadn't actually been to the Falls before. Their outings had been limited to the places they could reach with the conveyance of the Toronto Transit Commission.

At first, Helina resisted saying yes to the invitation. Because she worked beside Helvi and several other Finnish women at Canadian Engineering, she could get by practically the whole day without having to speak more than a few words of English. She was made anxious by the thought of a whole day with a couple who didn't speak Finnish.

But Onni tried to reassure her that if Mrs. Linton is as thoughtful and nice as Richard, they would have nothing to worry about.

"Besides, this is an opportunity to see one of the seven wonders of the world close up."

On the Saturday morning, Richard and Eleanor Linton pulled up in front of 92 Kendal Avenue in their black Austin 12. People often said Richard was one of the "lucky ones" who were able to get extra gasoline ration cards because his work as a manager supplying piles of single copies of the *Evening Telegram* to stores and merchants in Toronto's suburbs like Scarborough beyond the range of TTC buses and street cars.

Richard's 1939 Austin 12 was one of the last models manufactured before automobile plants were converted to manufacturing munitions and artillery for the war effort.

Thanks to a public works project in the previous decade, the couples could take the new freeway to the Falls, the Queen Elizabeth Way, instead of poking along slowly on Lakeshore Drive through the center of shore communities.

Richard was proud of his wheels, and spent the first half-hour of the trip talking about all the new features of his Austin that cars didn't have before 1939. Onni acknowledged to himself a slight bit of jealousy that while Richard was driving to the stores he supplied with newspapers, he was transferring from one street car line to another, or waiting for a bus, rain or shine, to take him and his heavy load of newspapers to his dealers.

While Richard bragged about his car to Onni in the front seat, Eleanor tried to get to know Helina.

"How have you liked life in Canada since you came, Helina?"

"Oh, I like. It is far away from the war."

"Yes, we can be thankful. But the war affects life here in Canada, too. Our neighbor's son was killed in Sicily last year. His parents are heartbroken. I feel so sorry for them."

Helina tried to look attentive and polite. But the news of their neighbor's son's death in the war pulled a pall over the morning for Helina. Though the boy was a total stranger, it was as if he had been a close friend or a neighbor of Helina's.

Onni looked back at Helina and noticed her in the early stages of one of her emotional retreats. He tried to think of some other topic to bring up.

Before he could think of one, however, Richard shouted, in a voice loud enough for all three passengers to hear him, "Boy, that was some kind of operation over in Normandy a few weeks ago, wasn't it? All those ships and boats and planes and paratroopers landing all at once. I don't think the Krauts expected anything like that, do you?"

Richard was expecting some kind of verbal response from Onni. But being aware of Helina's probable reaction in the back seat, he said barely above the level of a whisper,

"Yes, that was amazing."

"This could just be the beginning of the end for Hitler," Richard continued, oblivious to Helina's silence in the back seat, and unable to catch on to the meaning of Onni's very tepid and subdued response.

Onni latched on to the idea that perhaps talk of the possible *end* of the war might pull Helina back from her retreat.

"All those Allied forces in France now is a lot for the Germans to fight," Onni said. "Maybe too much."

"And don't forget that some setbacks notwithstanding, like our neighbor's boy's death, Hitler has to plan for a defense of Germany from the soft belly of Europe in Italy."

Onni wasn't certain if Richard was cognizant of the Finns' mutual pact with the Germans. Certainly the gregarious Richard had never asked Onni about it, or mentioned it in any way. But it was a potential hornet's nest to avoid on a pleasant outing to Niagara Falls.

"I so hope that Normandy invasion leads to a quick invasion of Germany and an end to the war," Onni said.

He looked back at Helina to see if his mentioning such a hope might be cheering her up. She was displaying some subtle signs of coming back.

Eleanor had noticed Helina sitting quietly, and said, "Guys, let's talk about something else other than the war. We get enough news about it on the radio and in your paper. These fine folks have come to be far away from war, Richard."

"How do you feel about that, buddy?" Richard asked as he turned his head towards Onni beside him.

"It's funny, you know," Onni said, craning his neck and looking back one more time at Helina. "We immigrants came to a new land to think about a new future in a new country. But in these recent years, we've been spending more time thinking about the present situation in the old country we left."

Helina surprised everyone by speaking up. "I think a part of an immigrant's heart always stays back in the old country."

~~~~~~~~~~~~~~~~~~~~~~~~~~

Helina tossed and turned in their bed that night. The visit to Niagara Falls was pleasant in its own way. She'd seen photographs on postcards of the falls before. But she wasn't prepared for their breathtaking grandeur. As she stood by the railing overlooking them with Onni and the Lintons, she felt their awesome power.

But the conversation during the drive had unsettled her. The Lintons seemed so settled and rooted in Canada, and

284

their use of the English language so natural and lacking all self-consciousness. By comparison, she felt so unrooted in her Canadian surroundings even though it was now over three years that she'd been in Toronto. Speaking English was still so difficult.

It wasn't the trip to Niagara, however, that was keeping her awake. Earlier that week, she had opened a picture book about Finland in the church library and admired the artful professional photographs.

They were in black and white and depicted places and buildings in Finland she had never seen herself in person. They were typical enough of many scenes in her homeland. But in Helina's stirred imagination, the photos were transfigured into panoramas with brilliant color: the bright red of the sauna built on the shore an inviting blue lake; the luminous sunshine gleaming on the gentle waves; the dazzling white of the trunks of the pleasing birches contrasting with the fresh green of its leaves.

Oh, how Helina ached to insert herself magically into the scene in the photo. She longed to feel the crisp Finnish summer breeze against her skin, to breathe the clean air devoid of humidity into her lungs, to take in the familiar aroma of the liverworts on the edge of the woods.

She and Onni had been to a few saunas owned by Finns on the shores of various southern Ontario lakes like Lake Willcocks, but to her their setting lacked the beauty and inspiration of that scene in the photo. The photograph took her back to her grandmother's place at Kuosto on the shores of Oulujärvi. As she was trying to catch sleep that was eluding her, Helina played over and over in her mind the times she and her grandmother had picked blueberries in the woods behind her lake house, the heavenly taste of them fresh ff the bush, and the currants later in the summer just before she had to return to her parents in Vaala to begin school once again.

What is the matter with me? I know that there's nothing for me back home. You can't raise Aulis from the dead.

285

She whimpered quietly as she reminisced and tried to stifle it so as not awaken Onni.

But in a few minutes, Onni asked while still turned on his side on the bed towards the other side of the room, "Helina, what's wrong?"

Helina was annoyed at herself that she hadn't been as quiet as she thought she'd been.

"Nothing, dear one. Go back to sleep."

"I can tell that you aren't able to fall asleep. Did I do something or say something to upset you?"

"No, I assure you that you didn't."

"What is it, then? Did the Lintons say something."

"No, they were very nice."

"Was it the talk about the war, then?"

"No . . . it's not that."

Finally, she came out and said it. "I'm terribly home-sick."

It had been almost a year since she had run out suddenly from the common room at the church when the topic of conversation had been whether or not people were regretting the fact that hey had emigrated. Onni hadn't mentioned it to her afterwards or since. But now the incident came to the fore.

"I sensed something like that in you when you ran out of the fellowship room at the church when Revonlahti asked the group if they had any regrets about emigrating. Do you remember that?"

"Yes, I do. I think I realized at that moment that I did have some regrets. But I couldn't say anything because everyone else seemed to be so content with their life in Canada. I was sitting there feeling homesick."

"Homesickness usually goes away after a time."

"I'm not even sure if homesickness is the right word. I don't know. I'm being silly. There's nobody longing for me in Finland. I've got everything I need right here. I've got you. What more do I want?"

Onni turned over onto his back on the bed but remained silent.

Helina wondered if he was disappointed in her. But she chose to interpret his silence as an invitation to go on.

"I don't think it's homesickness I feel for a home I don't have in Finland any more. I lost that home when Aulis died. . . What it is, I guess, is that I don't feel I've really made a home *here*."

Helina regretted saying that. She hoped that Onni didn't think she was unhappy with their house on Kendal Avenue, or worse, that she was unhappy with him. She fell into an anxious silence.

Finally, Onni responded, "I guess that's a kind of homesickness, too."

"Do you ever feel that way, Onni?"

Helina could hear Onni taking a deep breath, which she recognized was what he did when he was considering something.

"Oh, sure, I miss mother and father and my sisters and grandparents, of course. And you know how I feel about the loss of Väinö. I feel sad sometimes, and a day doesn't go by when I don't wonder how the family is doing, and how Finland will fare in the rest of the war. . . But no, I guess I feel

Canada is my home now. At least I'm trying to make it my home."

Helina tried not to take Onni's remark as an indirect accusation that she *wasn't* trying.

"Oh, I'm trying to my make Canada my home, too, Onni. Really, I am. . . But maybe you're not home until it really *feels* like home. I'm trying my best, but I can't *make* my heart feel that this is home . . . at least not yet."

Chapter Forty:
Peurajoki
October 13, 1944

Dear Onni and Helina,

I write to you at a terribly chaotic and dangerous moment. I don't know how much the Canadian newspapers and radio have covered the events in distant Finland. We are, after all just a tiny, insignificant country caught up in the movements of large powers like Germany and Russia.

Forgive me If I am repeating things you already know.

It looked like the end of this war would come early last month with the signing of the ceasefire between us and Russia. As the day approached, father and I were saddened that brave little Finland had to admit defeat a second time. Was Väinö's life been sacrificed for naught? But on the other hand, we also felt relief that this very sad season of tragic events was apparently coming to a close.

But you may have already heard over there that it wasn't really the end at all. One of Stalin's demands in the ceasefire was that if the Germans did not retreat from the north of Finland at the Finns' request by the middle of last month, the Finns would have to drive them out by force. Stalin must have known that September 15 was a totally impossible deadline, and that we Finns would, therefore, have to go to war against the Germans. He was dooming us all to more bloodshed.

There have been German soldiers near Peurajoki through much of the Continuation War. I hadn't written you about that because I didn't want to alarm you. Do not be alarmed. Thankfully, it appears that the soldiers had been ordered to treat us locals with respect since we're on their side in the war against the Russians. They've left us alone for the most part. Occasionally, father catches a disobedient private trying to pull a carrot or two out of the ground for himself and chases him off the farm. Once father went out into the barn to get a shovel and who should he find in there but a German private involved in a crude and disgusting act with the young Anja Pulkkinen. The embarrassed soldier ran off, leaving the horrified Anja standing half-dressed in front of father. Father stepped aside, turned to look the other way, and allowed the poor misguided girl to run back home. We haven't mentioned a word of it to Anja's poor parents. I just hope the soldier didn't get her pregnant. It's shameful to even write about it.

The Finnish authorities ordered our evacuation from Peurajoki across the border to Sweden on September 7. We had only a few days to make preparations: close down our farm and *Mummu's* and *Pappa's,* slaughter the precious little livestock we have left and burn the carcasses, and load a few necessities onto the wagon.

It's one of those miracles of God that even in the middle of a war, the Germans didn't lift a finger to prevent the evacuation. Not one. In fact, some soldiers helped the frail, elder Paavolas pack their wagon and saw to it that Unto and Eila were safely on their way to Sweden.

We stayed at the farm of a really kind family a few kilometers west of Haparanda for almost two weeks. Then we were given the word to return to Peurajoki. We were very anxious about that, of course, because we hadn't heard a word of what had been going on there while we were gone.

We saw many Finnish soldiers on the road to Kemi, and evidence of destruction of buildings. The road to Peurajoki looked untouched by comparison, thank God. The Germans in the Peurajoki region are sufficiently off the beaten track that they could hide in the woods nearby and not be detected.

Our farm was unmolested and in good shape. But with the animals killed before we left, and the hay crop left unfinished, we had to start all over again from nothing. You'd think we would be used to it by now.

It does feel rather scary, however, knowing that there are German soldiers in the surrounding woods. We see smoke from their fires in the thick pine grove near the Honkanens' place. They treated us well when we were allies. But now Stalin has turned the Finns and Germans into enemies again. How will the Germans treat us now that we are on the opposing side trying to chase them back to Norway? War sure has a befuddling logic of its own, doesn't it?

Father thinks they called us back from the evacuation too soon. It's only a matter of time before Siilasvuo send troops up here, once they're finished elsewhere, to flush the Germans soldiers out of the woods and either shoot them or force them north to cross into Norway.

Aino Saarijärvi came back from her sister's in Pudasjärvi and told us of the unbelievable destruction there. As the Germans were forced to retreat from that area (not really far away from Peurajoki, is it?), they destroyed the food, confiscated the shotguns of the farmers, burned down the barns, and finally destroyed the bridge over the river on the Rovaniemi and Kuusamo roads so that if the Russians were to occupy the area or annex all of Finland the way they did Estonia and the others, they'd have to rebuild everything.

Father figures the Germans will probably let Peurajoki be, but in war, you can never be sure. We're just pawns in a bigger game.

All this is to say that for the time being, we and *Mummu* and *Pappa* are safe. We are so grateful that you made the decision to leave and go to Canada where you and Helina can be immune from the danger.

Write when you can. The mail was suspended during the evacuation, but it is slowly getting back to normal, at least here in Peurajoki.

All our love. May you be in God's hands.

Mother

Onni was very agitated as he read his mother's letter. Several times he had to put the letter down on the table and get up and walk around the room. With each paragraph, his eyes grew wider and his chest tighter.

Onni realized that the ocean separating Canada from Finland really had served as a buffer, in spite of his denial that it did. Because he hadn't had a source of daily updates from Finnish radio since he moved out of 31 Beverley Street, the developments in his home country were less on his mind. He felt ashamed that he had allowed complacency to creep in unnoticed. He and Helina had talked about purchasing a radio for precisely that purpose. But Onni knew Helina wanted to hear as little about the war back home as possible, so he didn't push the matter.

Letters from his mother had grown rare. Now he understood why. The life of his parents and grandparents had been in chaos, and he hadn't known. He had assumed that being in the far north, they were safely removed from active conflict. On the rare occasions that the Russo-Finnish conflict was in the news, the news organs in Canada focused entirely on the warfare in Karelia. That gave Onni the false impression that the rest of Finland was in a blissful state of serenity, that life went on as it usually did, uninterrupted by the war.

As he read further in the letter, he was ashamed that his thoughts were focused on himself, and how he was feeling. What about what mother and father were feeling? So, he tried to push his regretful musings about his own failure aside and try to focus on his mother's words in the letter, and the feelings of fear expressed there.

Again, he couldn't concentrate enough to finish the letter in ne reading. He had to get up again from his chair.

Onni felt as though he were drowning in his own shame. He felt dirty all over. If the Germans were to harm his parents or grandparents in any way, how could he live with himself? Wasn't it his responsibility, as the son, now the only surviving son, to help his parents in some way?

Helina hadn't come home from work yet. He knew he couldn't show his mother's letter to her, or speak of its contents with her. He felt so bereft and alone.

He put the letter away in a drawer in his bedroom dresser and left the house. He headed the four blocks east to Huron Street, and then turned south towards the church house. He hoped desperately that Hepola was there. Hepola was the only person other than Helina in whom he could confide.

He spilled out his raw reactions to the news in his mother's letter. He told Hepola that he felt he needed to *do* something, anything, that might ameliorate his parent's situation.

"I understand your anxiety, Onni," Hepola said when Onni mentioned the need to act somehow. "Please know that I do. But dear friend: you must ask yourself: is it your parents' situation you want to ameliorate? Or is it your *own* anxiety, your sense of helplessness because your parents are so far away?"

"I don't know what you mean," Onni said.

"Well, your feeling of being helpless now so far away here in Canada is a terrible feeling. I know, because I have felt it, too. So I preach the gospel even more fervently here than before, thinking that at least preaching about God's grace will make up for what I am not producing back in Finland."

He paused to see if Onni was catching the drift.

"I am wondering," Hepola went on, "if your urgent need to do something is the same thing. That if you do *something*, you will feel better about yourself?"

Onni thought about it a long time, and then spoke.

"I'm thinking seriously about finding a way back to Finland and volunteering for one of Siilasvuo's battalions that are serving in the north."

"Tell me more about that."

"I mean, if I can be there, maybe I can rout the Germans and make sure they leave my family and their farms alone."

"You seem to think you have a lot of power, don't you, Onni? Do you think that you can single-handedly protect your family? Isn't that rather heroic thinking?"

Onni looked offended. He came expecting support and encouragement from his pastor. What he was getting instead seemed more like criticism.

"I abandoned them once. I'd like to make it up to them now that perhaps I have a second chance."

"I understand, Onni. Believe me, I do. But I urge you to ask yourself if it's for your family and country you'd be going back, or to ease your own guilt and shame."

Those words penetrated and touched a nerve in Onni. He got up from his chair abruptly, said thank you very curtly, which amounted to a no thank you at all, and left the church house.

The Finnish consulate was still suspended by the Canadian government, so he couldn't go there to inquire about volunteering. He walked down to Esther's Café on Queen Street, hoping he'd see somebody there who knew the procedure.

Since it was getting past the hour for the afternoon coffee and *pulla* break, but not yet supper time, Esther's was almost empty. Disappointed, and more distressed than ever, Onni left and without thinking about it, turned up Beverley Street off Queen and stopped at the stairs leading to the door of 31 Beverley Street.

Just as on the very occasion Onni approached the boarding house for the first time in 1939, so now, Pellonpää was coming out the front door. He was startled by Onni's being in front of the door and impeding his egress.

"Mr. Pellonpää, I'm sure you've heard about the Germans in the north. Can I talk to you for a few minutes?"

"Well, I was just going down the street to buy some cigarettes since I still have a ration card for them. Come along, and when we get back to the house, you can talk."

When they got back from Pellonpää's errand, Onni couldn't wait to pour out his plan.

"I want to go back to Finland and volunteer for the Finnish army."

"Do you now?" Pellonpää asked. Onni was disappointed in Pellonpää's apparent indifference.

"Yes, it's not too late for me to make a contribution to the freedom of my homeland."

"No, I don't suppose it is," Pellonpää said with the same disinterest as before.

"No, I really mean it. My family may be in the direct path of the German retreat into Norway. I am afraid for them. I want in the worst way to go back and help."

"But you've received no training. I don't suppose they will want untrained volunteers."

Why is everyone opposing me on this?

"I've used a gun before. I can learn things in a hurry."

"Do you know about a thing called the Canadian Foreign Enlistment Act?"

Onni looked confused. He had a "No-I-don't- know-a-fucking-thing-about-it" look on his face.

"It's the law passed in 1937 outlawing Canadians from volunteer ingfor foreign wars. But, of course, you're not Canadian yet. But how it applies to you is this: the law forbids citizens of an enemy combatant from serving as a volunteer from Canada. You recall, don't you, that Finland and Canada are on opposite sides?"

"Yes," Onni chimed in immediately, "they *were* enemy combatants. But the ceasefire between Finland and Russia stipulates that the Finns work with the Russians *against* the Germans. Russia is an ally of Canada. That makes Finland an ally now, too, doesn't it?"

"I don't think Mr. Mackenzie King will be interested in assisting a citizen of a country that goes back and forth in its allegiances to go to war. I'm sorry, Onni."

Onni was obvious with his disappointment and anger at Pellonpää, who he assumed would be rejoicing at Onni's rising to the defense of their homeland.

"I can't stop you, boy," Pellonpää said when he noticed Onni's quite undisguised frustration. "But I can tell you this: If you can make your way to New York, or even Buffalo or Detroit, the American Legion over there might be able to help you."

Onni left Beverley Street and headed west on Queen Street as a man on a mission. He turned south on Spadina and hurried to the *Evening Telegram* building on Front Street. It was 5:20 pm., and he hoped that there was still someone lingering in the news department.

He asked one of the secretaries that he knew to find a phone number for the American Legion in Buffalo. With a piece of paper in his hand with the phone number, Onni went down the hall to his own office and hoped for some privacy there. Unless a manager was putting in extra time, he figured that the office would be empty.

Thankfully, it was. He knew it was against company policy to use the office telephone for personal long-distance calls. But he was so desperate for information from the American Legion that he was willing to risk getting caught by the department head when he examined the office telephone bill. Better to ask for forgiveness afterward than get turned down when asking for permission ahead of time.

He was actually surprised that at 5:30 pm, someone picked up the phone at the American Legion post in Buffalo. The woman answering said she didn't have the information Onni wanted, but that she would bring a Mr. Newman on the phone who did. Mr. Newman welcomed Onni's query about volunteering for the forces in Finland since the Legion wanted to be supportive now that the Finns had seen the light and come back over to the Allies' side. He provided all the information Onni needed.

Onni waited for the streetcar at Spadina and Queen to go home. His head was rushing with plans for the next steps. He knew that time was of the essence. The Germans were in the Peurajoki woods on the day his mother wrote the letter. He had to hurry to get back to Peurajoki as soon as possible.

Only when he took his seat on the streetcar did Onni begin to think of how to broach the subject with Helina.

Helina was already irritable when he came through the door. She said she was surprised to come home and find him gone without a note or any indication of where he was on his day off.

"I've been on a mission," he said, as if that were a satisfactory answer.

"A mission? What? Are you a missionary now?"

"No, a mission for information."

"Information about what?"

Onni knew that this was the moment of crisis. Either she agreed with his plan, or he had better be prepared to defend it and convince her that he had made up his mind, whether she likes it or not.

"I have to go back to Finland to volunteer in the army in northern Oulu province."

Helina wasn't sure she heard him correctly.

"What? What are you talking about?"

"I mean what I say. My family is in danger from both the Germans and the Russians. I *have* to go back and help."

"Help? How can you help?"

"By volunteering in the Finnish army that is tasked with driving out the Germans into Norway and then defending Finnish households from the Russians if they annex our country."

"This is foolish talk."

But when she saw that Onni was determined of the rightness of his notion, she began to lose the color of her face. It became the color of the white tablecloth on their table.

"Onni, I can't let you do this."

"I've made up my mind."

"But we never make a big decision without talking about it with each other first. You've made this decision without me."

"A letter arrived today from my mother. I hadn't known that they have had to evacuate to Sweden to avoid danger. They're back in Peurajoki now, but there are Germans all around."

"And you think that by going back, you can save them?"

298

"I think it's a son's responsibility to be there to help them. Väinö can't be there, so I have to."

"You're choosing your family over your wife? What am I supposed to do? Come with you? Stay here and be alone?"

"I won't be gone forever. Once the Germans have been chased over the border to Norway, I'm sure this part of the war will be over."

Helina turned away. She seemed too angry, too overcome by fear, to speak further.

Onni became frustrated at her retreating.

"I don't understand why you are so against my intention to go back and volunteer."

She had been walking towards the bedroom to escape the conflict. But at Onni's words, she stopped in her tracks. She turned around to face him. There were wet tears running down her cheeks.

"Because Onni, I have already lost one husband in this war. I can't bear the thought of being left alone again after the death of my second." Then she burst into uncontrolled crying. Her body was trembling mightily

Onni was silenced by her answer. A voice from within him, his conscience perhaps, told him to put his urgency about is plan aside for the time being, and to focus on his wife's feelings. He didn't know how it would be received, but he reached out and put his arms around her. She didn't pull her body back completely. But she held her head back from his and with her fists clenched in rage, she commenced hitting him repeatedly on his chest, emitting a cry with every blow.

Onni received the pounding silently and without retaliation. She grew exhausted from the effort, and then collapsed completely in his arms.

"You're a bastard, Onni."

"I didn't know how Aulis died. You never told me how. I didn't ask because I knew it was painful for you to talk about it."

She had calmed down. The trembling stopped, although she was still weeping. Onni went over to the counter in the kitchen and fetched a paper tissue and handed it to her. She began to wipe the corner of her eye.

"He was found shot just outside . . . Suomussalmi."

"Outside *Suomussalmi*? Why, that's where Väinö was shot, too." Onni shook his head in disbelief.

"Aulis was found the same day they found your brother. January 10, 1940."

"My God."

"That's why I became so silent, you remember, when you told me about Väinö. I couldn't believe that the world was so small that I would be talking face-to-face over a cup of coffee far away in Canada with a Finnish man whose brother had been killed with my husband."

Onni was staring down at the kitchen table. He shook his head back and forth, still trying to absorb this new piece of information.

"Oh, Onni. I'm so scared that if you do go back and fight as a volunteer, you'll never come back alive. Can't you see?"

All his desire to push his plan evaporated. For the moment at least, his excitement, his urgency, his rush to pack his bags and catch the train to Buffalo, dissolved. The day, especially this revelatory conversation with Helina had drained his energy. He stood and continued embracing Helina, open to hearing more about Aulis' death if she wanted to say more.

"I told you my surname was Mäki when we met. But that's only half true. It's really Riihimäki. I thought if I changed it, I might be able to forget the devastation of losing him so violently. I didn't want some nosy immigrant here to research the name and discover that my husband was a war casualty. It's not that I am ashamed of that. It's just that if people knew, I'd have to retell the story to everyone, and re-live his death a thousand times."

"I'm sorry. I didn't know."

"You didn't know because I didn't tell you. I appreci-ate that when we met, you didn't ask a lot of questions about Aulis or my past."

"But it wouldn't have changed how I feel about you. Because we have the death of Aulis and Väinö in common, I might even have felt closer to you, as I do now that I know."

"I regret that I haven't told you before. I'm sorry. I hadn't wanted to deceive you. I had my reasons that I thought were good. I wanted to leave it all behind, especially my ter-rible grief. I think that's why I finally made the decision to come to Canada. But I had to tell you now because you seemed so set on going back and taking up a rifle yourself."

"Let's talk about that some other time. I'm too tired and confused to think about it right now."

Helina was exhausted, too. But Onni's remark made her slightly uneasy. It sounded as though the subject wasn't quite closed.

The subject was closed, however. Perhaps not com-pletely in Onni's mind and heart, but between him and He-lina, it became a closed matter. For the next month or so, it wasn't a subject of conversation.

He wasn't resentful, exactly, that Helina had such strong, practically irresistible opposition to his volunteering in Finland. Her almost irrational disapproval was, after all,

301

based on a totally understandable foundation of grief over Aulis and fear that the same lethal fate would await Onni in the line forests of northern Oulu province. Onni could muster no rational argument that would have the power to alleviate such deeply felt emotions. Better to let go of the notion of returning quickly to Finland altogether for the sake of the marriage.

He went and talked about the matter again with Hepola. The questions Hepola had raised in their first conversation about Onni's plans had been bouncing around in his mind almost incessantly since the afternoon he had stopped in at the church house. Hearing himself talk about his plan with Pellonpää and later Helina, the plan did sound a little boyishly heroic. He had absented himself from all the fighting from 1939 to the middle of 1944. And now he was going to fly in like some *deus ex machina* and rescue his family in distress single-handedly?

Hepola affirmed Onni's positive impulse to protect his parents and fight for his homeland, but he said that the problem with the plan was just that: it was impulsive.

Onni didn't divulge to Hepola that right after their last meeting, he had felt an irresistible urge to get on a train for Buffalo and enlist in the American Legion, and do so the very next morning, if not that same evening. But Onni had pondered Hepola's words that afternoon as well. Though he had ruled Hepola's interpretation out of hand at the time, a few days later it made eminently good sense, he had to admit. He allowed that downright dread for his parents' possible fate, and his own lingering guilt for having left them on the eve of the Winter War, did, indeed, play a big part in his feverish half-considered preparations to make his way back to Finland.

It was a misguided attempt at atonement.

He thanked Pastor Hepola for encouraging him to use his brain at a time when his heart was overruling everything.

Helina refrained, wisely so, from asking Onni if he had abandoned his plan since she hadn't heard him say another word about it. Onni had gone to work at the *Evening Telegram* as usual, and he had enrolled in an English composition class that was offered at Harbord Collegiate two evenings a week. Helina figured that making such a commitment was not the kind of thing a man planning to go fight in Finland would be likely to make.

By mid-November, in fact, it became, in fact, a moot point. The conflict in northern Finland was not in reality what it seemed on paper. Onni had found it strange when he had read in his mother's letter that the Germans were most accommodating to the Peurajoki villagers in their retreat to Sweden. It turns out that the Germans and Finns were in effect playing one last trick on their mutual enemy, Stalin. The Finns were resistant to the Russians' insistence that the Finnish forces were to drive the Germans beyond its borders. That provision might keep Russian soldiers off Finnish soil. But the Finnish soldiers and population were exhausted by five years of warfare against an enemy superior in weaponry and manpower. Finnish boys were eager to get back to their farms and saunas and their women.

The collective thought was that for all the atrocities attributed to them elsewhere in Europe, the Germans had treated the Finns with surprising respect, if not consideration, so unexpected in wartime. Their incursion into Finland had, in effect, helped save Finland from becoming another Soviet Socialist Republic. The Finnish generals were extremely reluctant to fight against their brothers-in-arms so that the Russians would be free to focus all their energy on the push westward towards Berlin through eastern Europe.

The Finnish and German generals met secretly in Rovaniemi to coordinate a smooth, hopefully bloodless German retreat. The Finns went through the motions of advancing northward into Lapland. The Germans destroyed a few bridges and burned some barns to give to the Russians the impression that there had actually been armed conflict, being careful all the while to spare the homes of local farmers and villagers. It was all a ruse.

Stalin caught on to the joint deception, however, and pressured Mannerheim to get more serious about the advance. He even sent Russian troops to Oulu and Tornio to fortify the Finnish effort and, truth be told, to make sure the Finnish bastards were doing their job and not just looking busy.

By the middle of October, the last German tank and lorry carrying infantrymen rolled over the border into Norway. Peace was nor declared yet, however. That would have to wait until the next April when Hitler had swallowed the poison capsule in his bunker. Stalin couldn't trust the shifty Finns, and the Finns, for their part, were suspicious that with the Germans gone from Finnish soil, Stalin might move in and claim it for Mother Russia.

Onni ran into Pellonpää at Esther's Café one afternoon in late October. If Pellonpää was at all surprised to see Onni still in Canada, he didn't show it. He just said dismissively, "Decided to keep warm in bed with the little woman, eh, rather than freeze your ass in a trench in Lapland?"

Onni blushed and merely nodded. He didn't want to say more.

"Good thing, too," Pellonpää said with a chuckle. "Turns out you would have just gotten off the boat in Hanko, and then been told to walk right back up the gangplank into the ship."

Onni looked at the man with a question mark written on his face.

"I guess, then, that you haven't heard. By October 8, the Finnish military finished the job of pushing the Krauts out of the country in typically fine Finnish fashion, in other words, by themselves. My boy, you're off the hook. They haven't been accepting any new volunteers for over a month."

Now Onni could tell Helina with all finality, the subject truly was closed.

Onni and Helina made love later that night for the first time in many weeks. Even though in his mind Onni had for all practical purposes surrendered his plan to volunteer in Finland, his heart had remained so unsettled by his family's plight far away that he hadn't had the energy nor even the desire for making love. For her part, Helina had still been still unconvinced in her heart that the door to the matter was indeed closed until Onni came home with the news Pellonpää had shared.

They fell asleep immediately afterwards, the deep, restful, soothing sleep of two immigrants finally rooted and at home in a new land.

THE END

EPILOGUE
Toronto
December 24, 1954

The front door of the house at 355 Brookdale Avenue opened and Helina and her eight-year-old daughter Tyyne entered the foyer. From the family room in the rear of the house came the high pitched and excited voice of six-year-old Toivo.

"Mommy! You're home!"

Tyyne had come home, too, but in his excitement he overlooked his sister. Mommy was the one he had been waiting for.

Helina and Tyyne took off their boots and winter coats and hung them on the wooden coat rack by the front door. They made their way to the family room. Helina handed a copy of the newspaper, now called just simply *The Telegram*, to Onni, who had been named a reporter there in 1950.

"Did you check the ham?" she asked her husband.

"Just as ordered," Onni replied in mock military fashion.

Helina had placed the Christmas Eve ham in the oven before she and Tyyne had left for the cemetery. She took the baking pan out of the oven and added the potatoes Onni had peeled while she was gone and the carrots, and then put the filled pan back into the heat.

Toivo was excited at his mother's return from the cemetery because his father had said that once Mommy and Tyyne came back, they'd have their Christmas Eve dinner soon, and then finally open the gifts under the tree. Even though he had been warned not to, Toivo had snuck over to the Christmas tree when Onni was in the bathroom and made a count of the wrapped packages that had his name on the affixed tags.

His mother had taught him how to count two twenty-five in both English and Finnish, and to write and read his own name. He once asked Onni what the name Toivo meant, and was told, "Hope".

"Why did you name me Hope?"

"Because we have many hopes for you. We hope that you won't have to go through some of the tough times that your mother and I did. Most of all, we hope you and all the children born in 1948 like you can live your whole lives without war."

Helina and Tyyne had maintained the traditional Finnish custom of lighting a candle on the grave of a loved one on Christmas Eve. Onni's parents Martti and Tyyne were buried in Peurajoki, Finland, so they had to rely on Onni's older sisters Hilja and Alma to light candles on those graves.

When Onni and Helina had started to practice the custom on their first Christmas Eve as a married couple in 1944, Onni had suggested that they light a candle on the grave in Mount Pleasant Cemetery of Reino Hutari. They continued to do so every year. When Mrs. Pyykkönen died in 1951, they performed the same ritual faithfully at her grave as well.

The calm, self-assured Tyyne helped her mother set the table for the Christmas feast.

Toivo, however, was ever on the move. Sitting through the Christmas dinner was most difficult for him, knowing as he did that the presents were waiting under the Christmas tree to be opened. He finished his small portion of ham, mashed potatoes, turnip casserole and *rosoli* well before the others, hoping that he could be excused to the living room and wait for the others near the tree. No such luck, however. Onni told the disappointed dynamo to sit quietly and wait at the table while the rest of the family finished their meal.

To the boy, the waiting seemed to last forever. But finally, the others put down their knives and forks on their plates.

"*No niin*, Toivo. I suppose this is what you've been waiting for. Let's see what's under the tree."

The boy ran as though released from a prison and was sitting cross-legged by the tree as the latecomers came and took a seat on the sofa or easy chair. In recent years past, Tyyne had been the one designated to distribute the presents to their recipients because she could read the names of the tags. Months before Christmas, however, Toivo had lobbied hard with his parents to assume the responsibility that year. Tyyne, in fact, was happy to surrender the task which she now considered too childish.

Toivo seemed to find all the presents for himself first, and placed them in a cluster near where he had been sitting. Then he distributed the rest. He hadn't taken into consideration that when you are the one handing out the gifts, you have to wait until the space under the tree is empty before you can begin tearing the wrapping paper off your own gifts.

Tyyne opened her gifts and folded each piece of wrapping paper into a neat pile beside her. Toivo worked much faster and less meticulously, however. He received about three or four gifts. He couldn't focus very long on any one gift before he picked up and quickly examined one of the others.

"Don't you think there are a couple of presents missing?" Onni asked Tyyne.

Before Tyyne could answer, Toivo shouted, "The present from *Joulupukki!*"

"I wonder where *Joulupukki* left those presents? Onni asked. "Maybe this year he didn't leave any. . ."

"Father, yes he did. He always does."

"Oh, I remember now. I think I know where he left them."

Onni rose from his easy chair and left the room. Tyyne wasn't going to allow herself to be taken in by this hoax. She and a couple of her friends had figured out the "Santa Thing" on a walk home together from school one day.

Toivo, however, looked anxiously at Helina for reassurance.

Onni came back into the room carrying two wrapped packages. He handed one to Taina.

"Toivo, there's one for you here, too. But we have to wait until Tyyne has opened her gift from *Joulupukki* so that we can all see what he made for her this year."

Toivo was about to protest.

"Toivo," Helina said. "You have to learn to wait. You heard father say that there's one for you, too, didn't you?"

Tyyne unwrapped the box with her usual care. Through the cellophane front of the box, she could see what was in it.

"Chatty Cathy! I got a Chatty Cathy doll!"

Then Onni handed the exasperated Toivo an irregularly shaped present. Under its Christmas paper wrapping, it had the shape roughly of an oval a little over foot tall from its top to its bottom. Toivo was beginning to deduce what was under the wrapping from the feel of the object in his hands.

"A globe!" he shouted. "*Joulupukki* made me a globe!"

Onni looked on with pride and happy remembrance.

"Can you find the dot on the globe that shows where we live?" Helina asked.

Toivo stood up holding the globe. He walked over to where his mother was seated and placed his finger on a spot very near Toronto. Toivo couldn't read the name of the city. But he knew from studying a map in the family's atlas on the shelf in the living room the narrow blue shape of the lake which he had visited many times with his family.

Taking the globe over to his father, Toivo said, "Show me where you came from, father, and where Mummu and Pappa lived."

Onni took Toivo's index finger and placed it over a spot northeast of Oulu.

"Now, Toivo, show us where you think you might want to go when you grow up."

The boy closed his eyes tightly. He spun the globe around a few times. He stopped the whirling globe with his hand and waved his index finger back and forth above the surface of the sphere, as though looking for a place to land. Then he opened his eyes to see where his finger had landed.

His finger alighted firmly on a spot east of the Ural Mountains in Russia.

Wide-eyed with surprise, Onni and Helina looked at each other and laughed together at their son's fertile imagination, and the delicious irony of it.